Oliver Wendell Holmes

Our Hundred Days in Europe

Oliver Wendell Holmes

Our Hundred Days in Europe

ISBN/EAN: 9783743388512

Manufactured in Europe, USA, Canada, Australia, Japa

Cover: Foto ©Raphael Reischuk / pixelio.de

Manufactured and distributed by brebook publishing software (www.brebook.com)

Oliver Wendell Holmes

Our Hundred Days in Europe

OUR HUNDRED DAYS
IN EUROPE

BY

OLIVER WENDELL HOLMES

BOSTON AND NEW YORK
HOUGHTON, MIFFLIN AND COMPANY
The Riverside Press, Cambridge
1887

CONTENTS.

VII.

VIII.

INTRODUCTORY.

A PROSPECTIVE VISIT.

———◆———

AFTER an interval of more than fifty years I propose taking a second look at some parts of Europe. It is a Rip Van Winkle experiment which I am promising myself. The changes wrought by half a century in the countries I visited amount almost to a transformation. I left the England of William the Fourth, of the Duke of Wellington, of Sir Robert Peel; the France of Louis Philippe, of Marshal Soult, of Thiers, of Guizot. I went from Manchester to Liverpool by the new railroad, the only one I saw in Europe. I looked upon England from the box of a stage-coach, upon France from the coupé of a diligence, upon Italy from the cushion of a carrozza. The broken windows of Apsley House were still boarded up when I was in London. The asphalt pavement was not laid in Paris. The Obelisk of Luxor was lying in its great boat in the Seine, as I remember it. I did not see it erected; it must have been an exciting scene to witness, the engineer standing underneath, so as to be crushed by the great stone if it disgraced him by falling in the process. As for the dynasties which have overlaid each other like Dr. Schliemann's Trojan cities, there is no need of moralizing over a history which instead of Finis is constantly ending with What next?

With regard to the changes in the general conditions of society and the advance in human knowledge, think for one moment what fifty years have done! I have often imagined myself escorting some wise man of the past to our Saturday Club, where we often have distinguished strangers as our guests. Suppose there sat by me, I will not say Sir Isaac Newton, for he has been too long away from us, but that other great man, whom Professor Tyndall names as next to him in intellectual stature, as he passes along the line of master minds of his country, from the days of Newton to our own, — Dr. Thomas Young, who died in 1829. Would he or I be the listener, if we were side by side? However humble I might feel in such a presence, I should be so clad in the grandeur of the new discoveries, inventions, ideas, I had to impart to him that I should seem to myself like the ambassador of an Emperor. I should tell him of the ocean steamers, the railroads that spread themselves like cobwebs over the civilized and half-civilized portions of the earth, the telegraph and the telephone, the photograph and the spectroscope. I should hand him a paper with the morning news from London to read by the electric light, I should startle him with a friction match, I should amaze him with the incredible truths about anæsthesia, I should astonish him with the later conclusions of geology, I should dazzle him by the fully developed law of the correlation of forces, I should delight him with the cell-doctrine, I should confound him with the revolutionary apocalypse of Darwinism. All this change in the aspects, position, beliefs, of humanity since the time of Dr. Young's death, the date of my own graduation from college!

I ought to consider myself highly favored to

have lived through such a half century. But it seems to me that in walking the streets of London and Paris I shall revert to my student days, and appear to myself like a relic of a former generation. Those who have been born into the inheritance of the new civilization feel very differently about it from those who have lived their way into it. To the young and those approaching middle age all these innovations in life and thought are as natural, as much a matter of course, as the air they breathe; they form a part of the inner framework of their intelligence, about which their mental life is organized. To men and women of more than threescore and ten they are external accretions, like the shell of a mollusk, the jointed plates of an articulate. This must be remembered in reading anything written by those who knew the century in its teens; it is not likely to be forgotten, for the fact betrays itself in all the writer's thoughts and expressions.

The story of my first visit to Europe is briefly this: my object was to study the medical profession, chiefly in Paris, and I was in Europe about two years and a half, from April, 1833, to

October, 1835. I sailed in the packet ship Phil-
adelphia from New York for Portsmouth, where
we arrived after a passage of twenty-four days.
A week was spent in visiting Southampton,
Salisbury, Stonehenge, Wilton, and the Isle of
Wight. I then crossed the Channel to Havre,
from which I went to Paris. In the spring and
summer of 1834 I made my principal visit to
England and Scotland. There were other excursions to the Rhine and to Holland, to Switzerland and to Italy, but of these I need say
nothing here. I returned in the packet ship
Utica, sailing from Havre, and reaching New
York after a passage of forty-two days.

A few notes from my recollections will serve
to recall the period of my first visit to Europe,
and form a natural introduction to the experiences of my second. I take those circumstances
which happen to suggest themselves.

After a short excursion to Strasbourg, down
the Rhine, and through Holland, a small steamer
took us from Rotterdam across the Channel, and
we found ourselves in the British capital.

The great sight in London is — London. No
man understands himself as an infinitesimal

until he has been a drop in that ocean, a grain of sand on that sea-margin, a mote in its sunbeam, or the fog or smoke which stands for it; in plainer phrase, a unit among its millions.

I had two letters to persons in England: one to kind and worthy Mr. Petty Vaughan, who asked me to dinner; one to pleasant Mr. William Clift, conservator of the Hunterian Museum, who asked me to tea.

To Westminster Abbey. What a pity it could not borrow from Paris the towers of Notre Dame! But the glory of its interior made up for this shortcoming. Among the monuments, one to Rear Admiral Charles Holmes, a handsome young man, standing by a cannon. He accompanied Wolfe in his expedition which resulted in the capture of Quebec. Dryden has immortalized him, in the " Annus Mirabilis," as

"the Achates of the general's fight."

My relative, I will take it for granted, as I find him in Westminster Abbey. Blood is thicker than water, — and warmer than marble, I said to myself, as I laid my hand on the cold stone image of the once famous Admiral.

To the Tower, to see the lions, — of all sorts.

There I found a " poor relation," who made my acquaintance without introduction. A large baboon, or ape, — some creature of that family, — was sitting at the open door of his cage, when I gave him offence by approaching too near and inspecting him too narrowly. He made a spring at me, and if the keeper had not pulled me back would have treated me unhandsomely, like a quadrumanous rough, as he was. He succeeded in stripping my waistcoat of its buttons, as one would strip a pea-pod of its peas.

To Vauxhall Gardens. All Americans went there in those days, as they go to Madame Tussaud's in these times. There were fireworks and an exhibition of polar scenery. "Mr. Collins, the English PAGANINI," treated us to music on his violin. A comic singer gave us a song, of which I remember the line,

"You'll find it all in the agony bill."

This referred to a bill proposed by Sir Andrew Agnew, a noted Scotch Sabbatarian agitator.

To the opera to hear Grisi. The king, William the Fourth, was in his box; also the Princess Victoria, with the Duchess of Kent. The king tapped with his white-gloved hand on the ledge of the box when he was pleased with the singing. — To a morning concert and heard the real Paganini. To one of the lesser theatres and heard a monologue by the elder Mathews, who died a year or two after this time. To another theatre, where I saw Liston in Paul Pry. Is it not a relief that I am abstaining from description of what everybody has heard described?

To Windsor. Machinery to the left of the road. Recognized it instantly, by recollection of the plate in "Rees's Cyclopedia," as Herschel's great telescope. — Oxford. Saw only its outside. I knew no one there, and no one knew me. — Blenheim, — the Titians best remembered of its objects on exhibition. The great Derby day of the Epsom races. Went to the race with a coach-load of friends and acquaintances. Plenipotentiary, the winner, "rode by P. Connelly." So says Herring's picture of him, now before me. Chestnut, a great "bullock" of a horse, who easily beat the twenty-two that started. Every New England deacon ought to see one Derby day to learn what sort of a world this is he lives in. Man is a sporting as well as a praying animal.

Stratford-on-Avon. Emotions, but no scribbling of name on walls. — Warwick. The castle. A village festival, " The Opening of the Meadows," a true exhibition of the semi-barbarism which had come down from Saxon times. — Yorkshire. " The Hangman's Stone." Story told in my book called the " Autocrat," etc. York Cathedral. — Northumberland. Alnwick Castle. The figures on the walls which so frightened my man John when he ran away from Scotland in his boyhood.

Berwick-on-Tweed. A regatta going on; a very pretty show. Scotland. Most to be remembered, the incomparable loveliness of Edinburgh. — Sterling. The view of the Links of Forth from the castle. The whole country full of the romance of history and poetry. Made one acquaintance in Scotland, Dr. Robert Knox, who asked my companion and myself to breakfast. I was treated to five entertainments in Great Britain: the breakfast just mentioned; lunch with Mrs. Macadam, — the good old lady gave me bread, and not a stone; dinner with Mr. Vaughan; one with Mr. Stanley, the surgeon; tea with Mr. Clift, — for all which attentions I was then and am still grateful, for they were more than I had any claim to expect. Fascinated with Edinburgh. Strolls by Salisbury Crag; climb to the top of Arthur's Seat; delight of looking up at the grand old castle, of looking down on Holyrood Palace, of watching the groups on Calton Hill, wandering in the quaint old streets and sauntering on the sidewalks of the noble avenues, even at that time adding beauty to the new city. The weeks I spent in Edinburgh are among the most memorable of my European experiences. To the Highlands, to the Lakes, in short excursions; to Glasgow, seen to disadvantage under gray skies and with slippery pavements. Through England rapidly to Dover and to Calais, where I found the name of M. Dessein still belonging to the hotel I sought, and where I read Sterne's "Preface Written in a Désobligeante," sitting in the vehicle most like one that I could find in the stable. From Calais back to Paris, where I began working again.

All my travelling experiences, including a visit to Switzerland and Italy in the summer and autumn of 1835, were merely interludes of my student life in Paris. On my return to America, after a few years of hospital and private practice, I became a Professor in Harvard University, teaching Anatomy and Physiology, afterwards Anatomy alone, for the period of thirty-five years, during part of which time I paid some attention to literature, and became somewhat known as the author of several works in prose and verse which have been well received. My prospective visit will not be a professional one, as I resigned my office in 1882, and am no longer known chiefly as a teacher or a practitioner.

Boston, *April*, 1886.

OUR HUNDRED DAYS IN EUROPE.

I.

I BEGIN this record with the columnar, self-reliant capital letter to signify that there is no disguise in its egoisms. If it were a chapter of autobiography, this is what the reader would look for as a matter of course. Let him consider it as being such a chapter, and its egoisms will require no apology.

I have called the record *our* hundred days, because I was accompanied by my daughter, without the aid of whose younger eyes and livelier memory, and especially of her faithful diary, which no fatigue or indisposition was allowed to interrupt, the whole experience would have remained in my memory as a photograph out of focus.

We left Boston on the 29th of April, 1886, and reached New York on the 29th of August, four months of absence in all, of which nearly three weeks were taken up by the two passages, one week was spent in Paris, and the rest of the time in England and Scotland.

No one was so much surprised as myself at my undertaking this visit. Mr. Gladstone, a strong man for his years, is reported as saying that he is too old to travel, at least to cross the ocean, and he is younger than I am, — just four months, to a day, younger. It is true that Sir Henry Holland came to this country, and travelled freely about the world, after he was eighty years old; but his pitcher went to the well once too often, and met the usual doom of fragile articles. When my friends asked me why I did not go to Europe, I reminded them of the fate of Thomas Parr. He was only twice my age, and was getting on finely towards his two hundredth year, when the Earl of Arundel carried him up to London, and, being feasted and made a lion of, he found there a premature and early grave at the age of only one hundred and fifty-two years. He lies in Westminster Abbey, it is true, but he would probably have preferred the upper side of his own hearth-stone to the under side of the slab which covers him.

I should never have thought of such an expedition if it had not been suggested by a member of my family that I should accompany my daughter, who was meditating a trip to Europe. I remembered how many friends had told me I ought to go ; among the rest, Mr. Emerson, who had spoken to me repeatedly about it. I had not seen Europe for more than half a century, and I had a certain longing for one more sight of the places I remembered, and others it would be a delight to look upon. There were a few living persons whom I wished to meet. I was assured that I should be kindly received in England. All this was tempting enough, but there was an obstacle in the way which I feared, and, as it proved, not without good reason. I doubted whether I could possibly breathe in a narrow state-room. In certain localities I have found myself liable to attacks of asthma, and, although I had not had one for years, I felt sure that I could not escape it if I tried to sleep in a state-room. I did not escape it, and I am glad to tell my story about it, because it excuses some of my involuntary social shortcomings, and enables me to thank collectively all those kind members of the profession who trained all the artillery of the pharmacopœia upon my troublesome enemy, from bicarbonate of soda and Vichy water to arsenic and dynamite. One costly contrivance, sent me by the Reverend Mr. Haweis, whom I have never duly thanked for it, looked more like an angelic trump for me to blow in a better world than what I believe it is, an inhaling tube intended to prolong my mortal respiration. The best thing in my experience was recommended to me by an old friend in London. It was Himrod's asthma cure, one of the many powders, the smoke of which when burning is inhaled. It is made in Providence, Rhode Island, and I had to go to London to find it. It never failed to give at least temporary relief, but nothing enabled me to sleep in my state-room, though I had it all to myself, the upper berth being removed. After the first night and part of the second, I never lay down at all while at sea. The captain allowed me to have a candle and sit up in the saloon, where I worried through the night as I best might. How could I be in a fit condition to accept the attention of my friends in Liverpool, after sitting up every night

for more than a week ; and how could I be in a
mood for the catechizing of interviewers, without
having once lain down during the whole return
passage ?   I hope the reader will see why I mention these facts.   They explain and excuse many
things ; they have been alluded to, sometimes
with exaggeration, in the newspapers, and I
could not tell my story fairly without mentioning them.   I got along well enough as soon as I
landed, and have had no return of the trouble
since I have been back in my own home.   I will
not advertise an assortment of asthma remedies
for sale, but I assure my kind friends I have had
no use for any one of them since I have walked
the Boston pavements, drank, not the Cochitu-
ate, but the Belmont spring water, and breathed
the lusty air of my native northeasters.

My companion and I required an attendant,
and we found one of those useful androgynous
personages known as *courier-maids,* who had
travelled with friends of ours, and who was ready
to start with us at a moment's warning.   She
was of English birth, lively, short-gaited, serviceable, more especially in the first of her dual
capacities.   So far as my wants were concerned,

I found her zealous and active in providing for my comfort.

It was no sooner announced in the papers that I was going to England than I began to hear of preparations to welcome me.   An invitation to a club meeting was cabled across the Atlantic. One of my countrywomen who has a house in London made an engagement for me to meet friends at her residence.   A reverend friend, who thought I had certain projects in my head, wrote to me about lecturing: where I should appear, what fees I should obtain, and such business matters.   I replied that I was going to England to spend money, not to make it; to hear speeches, very possibly, but not to make them; to revisit scenes I had known in my younger days; to get a little change of my routine, which I certainly did; and to enjoy a little rest, which I as certainly did not, at least in London.   In a word, I wished a short vacation, and had no thought of doing anything more important than rubbing a little rust off and enjoying myself, while at the same time I could make my companion's visit somewhat pleasanter than it would be if she went without me.   The visit has answered most of its purposes for both of us, and if we have saved a few recollections which our friends can take any pleasure in reading, this slight record may be considered a work of super-erogation.

The Cephalonia was to sail at half past six in the morning, and at that early hour a company of well-wishers was gathered on the wharf at East Boston to bid us good-by. We took with us many tokens of their thoughtful kindness; flowers and fruits from Boston and Cambridge, and a basket of champagne from a Concord friend whose company is as exhilarating as the sparkling wine he sent us. With the other gifts came a small tin box, about as big as a common round wooden match box. I supposed it to hold some pretty gimcrack, sent as a pleasant part-ing token of remembrance. It proved to be a most valued daily companion, useful at all times, never more so than when the winds were blow-ing hard and the ship was struggling with the waves. There must have been some magic secret in it, for I am sure that I looked five years younger after closing that little box than

when I opened it.   Time will explain its mysterious power.

All the usual provisions for comfort made by
sea-going experts we had attended to.   Imper-
meable rugs and fleecy shawls, head-gear to
defy the rudest northeasters, sea-chairs of ample
dimensions, which we took care to place in as
sheltered situations as we could find, — all these
were a matter of course.   Everybody stays on
deck as much as possible, and lies wrapped up
and spread out at full length on his or her sea-
chair, so that the deck looks as if it had a row
of mummies on exhibition.   Nothing is more
comfortable, nothing, I should say, more indis-
pensable, than a hot-water bag, — or rather,
two hot-water bags; for they will burst sometimes, as I found out, and a passenger who has
become intimate with one of these warm bosom
friends feels its loss almost as if it were human.

Passengers carry all sorts of luxuries on board,
in the firm faith that they shall be able to profit
by them all.   Friends send them various indi-
gestibles.   To many all these well-meant preparations soon become a mockery, almost an insult.
It is a clear case of *Sic(k) vos non vobis.*   The

tougher neighbor is the gainer by these acts of kindness ; the generosity of a sea-sick sufferer in giving away the delicacies which seemed so desirable on starting is not ranked very high on the books of the recording angel. With us three things were best : grapes, oranges, and especially oysters, of which we had provided a half barrel in the shell. The " butcher " of the ship opened them fresh for us every day, and they were more acceptable than anything else.

Among our ship's company were a number of family relatives and acquaintances. We formed a natural group at one of the tables, where we met in more or less complete numbers. I myself never missed ; my companion, rarely. Others were sometimes absent, and sometimes came to time when they were in a very doubtful state, looking as if they were saying to themselves, with Lear, —

> " Down, thou climbing sorrow,
> Thy element 's below."

As for the intellectual condition of the passengers, I should say that faces were prevailingly vacuous, their owners half hypnotized, as it seemed, by the monotonous throb and tremor of the great sea-monster on whose back we were riding. I myself had few thoughts, fancies, emotions. One thing above all struck me as never before, — the terrible solitude of the ocean.

> " So lonely 't was that God himself
> Scarce seemed there to be."

Whole days passed without our seeing a single sail. The creatures of the deep which gather around sailing vessels are perhaps frightened off by the noise and stir of the steamship. At any rate, we saw nothing more than a few porpoises, so far as I remember.

No man can find himself over the abysses, the floor of which is paved with wrecks and white with the bones of the shrieking myriads of human beings whom the waves have swallowed up, without some thought of the dread possibilities hanging over his fate. There is only one way to get rid of them: that which an old sea-captain mentioned to me, namely, to keep one's self under opiates until he wakes up in the harbor where he is bound. I did not take this as serious advice, but its meaning is that one who has all his senses about him cannot help being anxious. My old friend, whose beard had been shaken in many a tempest, knew too well that there is cause enough for anxiety.

What does the reader suppose was the source of the most ominous thought which forced itself upon my mind, as I walked the decks of the mighty vessel? Not the sound of the rushing winds, nor the sight of the foam-crested billows; not the sense of the awful imprisoned force which was wrestling in the depths below me. The ship is made to struggle with the elements, and the giant has been tamed to obedience, and is manacled in bonds which an earthquake would hardly rend asunder. No! It was the sight of the *boats* hanging along at the sides of the deck, — the boats, always suggesting the fearful possibility that before another day dawns one may be tossing about in the watery Sahara, shelterless, fireless, almost foodless, with a fate before him he dares not contemplate. No doubt we should feel worse without the boats; still they are dreadful tell-tales. To all who remember Géricault's Wreck of the Medusa, — and those who have seen it do not forget it, — the picture the mind draws is one it shudders at.

To be sure, the poor wretches in the painting were on a raft, but to think of fifty people in one of these open boats! Let us go down into the cabin, where at least we shall not see them.

The first morning at sea revealed the mystery of the little round tin box. The process of *shaving*, never a delightful one, is a very unpleasant and awkward piece of business when the floor on which one stands, the glass in which he looks, and he himself are all describing those complex curves which make cycles and epicycles seem like simplicity itself. The little box contained a reaping machine, which gathered the capillary harvest of the past twenty-four hours with a thoroughness, a rapidity, a security, and a facility which were a surprise, almost a revelation. The idea of a guarded cutting edge is an old one; I remember the "Plantagenet" razor, so called, with the comb-like row of blunt teeth, leaving just enough of the edge free to do its work. But this little affair had a blade only an inch and a half long by three quarters of an inch wide. It had a long slender handle, which took apart for packing, and was put together with the greatest ease. It was, in short, a lawn-mower for the

masculine growth of which the proprietor wishes
to rid his countenance. The mowing operation
required no glass, could be performed with almost reckless boldness, as one cannot cut himself, and in fact had become a pleasant amusement instead of an irksome task. I have never
used any other means of shaving from that day
to this. I was so pleased with it that I exhib-
ited it to the distinguished tonsors of Burlington
Arcade, half afraid they would assassinate me
for bringing in an innovation which bid fair to
destroy their business. They probably took me
for an agent of the manufacturers; and so I
was, but not in their pay nor with their knowledge. I determined to let other persons know
what a convenience I had found the "Star
Razor" of Messrs. Kampf, of New York, without fear of reproach for so doing. I know my
danger, — does not Lord Byron say, " I have
even been accused of writing puffs for Warren's
blacking " ? I was once offered pay for a poem
in praise of a certain stove polish, but I declined. It is pure good-will to my race which
leads me to commend the Star Razor to all who
travel by land or by sea, as well as to all who
stay at home.

With the first sight of land many a passenger draws a long sigh of relief. Yet everybody knows that the worst dangers begin after we have got near enough to see the shore, for there are several ways of landing, not all of which are equally desirable. On Saturday, May 8th, we first caught a glimpse of the Irish coast, and at half past four in the afternoon we reached the harbor of Queenstown. A tug came off, bringing newspapers, letters, and so forth, among the rest some thirty letters and telegrams for me. This did not look much like rest, but this was only a slight prelude to what was to follow. I was in no condition to go on shore for sightseeing, as some of the passengers did.

We made our way through the fog towards Liverpool, and arrived at 1.30, on Sunday, May 9th. A special tug came to take us off: on it were the American consul, Mr. Russell, the vice-consul, Mr. Sewall, Dr. Nevins, and Mr. Rathbone, who came on behalf of our as yet unseen friend, Mr. Willett, of Brighton, England. Our Liverpool friends were meditating more hospitalities to us than, in our fatigued condition, we were equal to supporting. They very kindly, however, acquiesced in our wishes, which were for as much rest as we could possibly get before any attempt to busy ourselves with social engagements. So they conveyed us to the Grand Hotel for a short time, and then saw us safely off to the station to take the train for Chester, where we arrived in due season, and soon found ourselves comfortably established at the Grosvenor Arms Hotel. A large basket of Surrey primroses was brought by Mr. Rathbone to my companion. I had set before me at the hotel a very handsome floral harp, which my friend's friend had offered me as a tribute. It made melody in my ears as sweet as those hyacinths of Shelley's, the music of whose bells was so

> " delicate, soft, and intense,
> It was felt like an odor within the sense."

At Chester we had the blissful security of being unknown, and were left to ourselves. Americans know Chester better than most other old towns in England, because they so frequently stop there awhile on their way from Liverpool to London. It has a mouldy old cathedral, an old wall, partly Roman, strange old houses with overhanging upper floors, which make sheltered sidewalks and dark basements. When one sees an old house in New England with the second floor projecting a foot or two beyond the wall of the ground floor, the country boy will tell him that " them haouses was built so th't th' folks up-stairs could shoot the Injins when they was try-in' to git threew th' door or int' th' winder," There are plenty of such houses all over Eng-land, where there are no " Injins " to shoot. But the story adds interest to the somewhat lean traditions of our rather dreary past, and it is hardly worth while to disturb it. I always heard it in my boyhood. Perhaps it is true; certainly it was a very convenient arrange-ment for discouraging an untimely visit. The oval lookouts in porches, common in our Essex County, have been said to answer a similar pur-pose, that of warning against the intrusion of undesirable visitors. The walk round the old wall of Chester is wonderfully interesting and beautiful. At one part it overlooks a wide level field, over which the annual races are run. I noticed that here as elsewhere the short grass was starred with daisies. They are not consid-ered in place in a well-kept lawn. But remembering the cuckoo song in Love's Labour Lost, " When daisies pied . . . do paint the meadows with delight," it was hard to look at them as unwelcome intruders.

The old cathedral seemed to me particularly mouldy, and in fact too high-flavored with antiquity. I could not help comparing some of the ancient cathedrals and abbey churches to so many old cheeses. They have a tough gray rind and a rich interior, which find food and lodging for numerous tenants who live and die under their shelter or their shadow, — lowly servitors some of them, portly dignitaries others, humble holy ministers of religion many, I doubt not, — larvæ of angels, who will get their wings by and by. It is a shame to carry the comparison so far, but it is natural enough; for Cheshire cheeses are among the first things we think of as we enter that section of the country, and this venerable cathedral is the first that greets the eyes of great numbers of Americans.

We drove out to Eaton Hall, the seat of the Duke of Westminster, the many-millioned lord of a good part of London. It is a palace, high-roofed, marble - columned, vast, magnificent, everything but homelike, and perhaps homelike to persons born and bred in such edifices. A painter like Paul Veronese finds a palace like this not too grand for his banqueting scenes. But to those who live, as most of us do, in houses of moderate dimensions, snug, comfortable, which the owner's presence fills sufficiently, leaving room for a few visitors, a vast marble palace is disheartening and uninviting. I never get into a very large and lofty saloon without feeling as if I were a weak solution of myself, — my personality almost drowned out in the flood of space about me. The wigwam is more homelike than the cavern. Our wooden houses are a better kind of wigwam ; the marble palaces are artificial caverns, vast, resonant, chilling, good to visit, not desirable to live in, for most of us. One's individuality should betray itself in all that surrounds him ; he should *secrete* his shell, like a mollusk; if he can sprinkle a few pearls through it, so much the better. It is best, perhaps, that one should avoid being a duke and living in a palace, — that is, if he has his choice in the robing chamber where souls are fitted with their earthly garments.

One of the most interesting parts of my visit to Eaton Hall was my tour through the stables. The Duke is a famous breeder and lover of the turf. Mr. Rathbone and myself soon made the acquaintance of the chief of the stable department. Readers of Homer do not want to be reminded that *hippodamoio*, horse-subducr, is the genitive of an epithet applied as a chief honor to the most illustrious heroes. It is the last word of the last line of the Iliad, and fitly closes the account of the funeral pageant of Hector, the tamer of horses. We Americans are a little shy of confessing that any title or conventional grandeur makes an impression upon us. If at home we wince before any official with a sense of blighted inferiority, it is by general confession the clerk at the hotel office. There is an excuse for this, inasmuch as he holds our destinies in his hands, and decides whether, in case of accident, we shall have to jump from the third or sixth story window. Lesser grandeurs do not find us very impressible. There is, however, something about the man who deals in horses which takes down the spirit, however proud, of him who is unskilled in equestrian matters and unused to the horse-lover's vocabulary. We followed the master of the stables, meekly listening and once in a while questioning. I had to fall back on my reserves, and summoned up memories half a century old to gain the respect and win the confidence of the great horse-subduer. He showed us various fine animals, some in their stalls, some outside of them. Chief of all was the renowned Bend Or, a Derby winner, a noble and beautiful bay, destined in a few weeks to gain new honors on the same turf in the triumph of his offspring Ormonde, whose acquaintance we shall make by and by.

The next day, Tuesday, May 11th, at 4.25, we took the train for London. We had a saloon car, which had been thoughtfully secured for us through unseen, not unsuspected, agencies, which had also beautified the compartment with flowers.

Here are some of my first impressions of England as seen from the carriage and from the cars. — How very English! I recall Birket Foster's Pictures of English Landscape, — a beautiful, poetical series of views, but hardly more poetical than the reality. How thoroughly

England is *groomed !* Our New England out-
of-doors landscape often looks as if it had just
got out of bed, and had not finished its toilet.
The glowing green of everything strikes me :
green hedges in place of our rail-fences, always
ugly, and our rude stone-walls, which are not
wanting in a certain look of fitness approaching
to comeliness, and are really picturesque when
lichen-coated, but poor features of landscape as
compared to these universal hedges. I am disappointed in the trees, so far ; I have not seen
one large tree as yet. Most of those I see are of
very moderate dimensions, feathered all the way
up their long slender trunks, with a lop-sided
mop of leaves at the top, like a wig which has
slipped awry. I trust that I am not finding
everything *couleur de rose ;* but I certainly do
find the cheeks of children and young persons of
such brilliant rosy hue as I do not remember
that I have ever seen before. I am almost ready
to think this and that child's face has been colored from a pink saucer. If the Saxon youth
exposed for sale at Rome, in the days of Pope
Gregory the Great, had complexions like these
children, no wonder that the pontiff exclaimed,

Not *Angli*, but *angeli !* All this may sound a little extravagant, but I am giving my impressions without any intentional exaggeration. How far these first impressions may be modified by after-experiences there will be time enough to find out and to tell. It is better to set them down at once just as they are. A first impression is one never to be repeated; the second look will see much that was not noticed before, but it will not reproduce the sharp lines of the *first proof*, which is always interesting, no matter what the eye or the mind fixes upon. "I see men as trees walking." That first experience could not be mended. When Dickens landed in Boston, he was struck with the brightness of all the objects he saw, — buildings, signs, and so forth. When I landed in Liverpool, everything looked very dark, very dingy, very massive, in the streets I drove through. So in London, but in a week it all seemed natural enough.

We got to the hotel where we had engaged quarters, at eleven o'clock in the evening of Wednesday, the 12th of May. Everything was ready for us, — a bright fire blazing and supper waiting. When we came to look at the accom-

modations, we found they were not at all adapted
to our needs.   It was impossible to stay there
another night.   So early the next morning we
sent out our courier-maid, a dove from the ark,
to find us a place where we could rest the soles
of our feet.   London is a nation of something
like four millions of inhabitants, and one does
not feel easy without he has an assured place of
shelter.   The dove flew all over the habitable
districts of the city, — inquired at as many as
twenty houses.   No roosting-place for our little
flock of three.   At last the good angel who followed us everywhere, in one shape or another,
pointed the wanderer to a place which corresponded with all our requirements and wishes.
This was at No. 17 Dover Street, Mackellar's
Hotel, where we found ourselves comfortably
lodged and well cared for during the whole time
we were in London.   It was close to Piccadilly
and to Bond Street.   Near us, in the same range,
were Brown's Hotel and Batt's Hotel, both
widely known to the temporary residents of
London.

   We were but partially recovered from the
fatigues and trials of the voyage when our

arrival pulled the string of the social shower-bath, and the invitations began pouring down upon us so fast that we caught our breath, and felt as if we should be smothered. The first evening saw us at a great dinner-party at our well-remembered friend Lady Harcourt's. Twenty guests, celebrities and agreeable persons, with or without titles. The tables were radiant with silver, glistening with choice porcelain, blazing with a grand show of tulips. This was our "baptism of fire" in that long conflict which lasts through the London season. After dinner came a grand reception, most interesting, but fatiguing to persons hardly as yet in good condition for social service. We lived through it, however, and enjoyed meeting so many friends, known and unknown, who were very cordial and pleasant in their way of receiving us.

It was plain that we could not pretend to answer all the invitations which flooded our tables. If we had attempted it, we should have found no time for anything else. A secretary was evidently a matter of immediate necessity. Through the kindness of Mrs. Pollock, we found a young lady who was exactly fitted for the place. She was installed in the little room intended for her, and began the work of accepting with pleasure and regretting our inability, of acknowledging the receipt of books, flowers, and other objects, and being very sorry that we could not subscribe to this good object and attend that meeting in behalf of a deserving charity, — in short, writing almost everything for us except autographs, which I can warrant were always genuine. The poor young lady was almost tired out sometimes, having to stay at her table, on one occasion, so late as eleven in the evening, to get through her day's work. I simplified matters for her by giving her a set of formulæ as a base to start from, and she proved very apt at the task of modifying each particular letter to suit its purpose.

From this time forward continued a perpetual round of social engagements. Breakfasts, luncheons, dinners, teas, receptions with spread tables, two, three, and four deep of an evening, with receiving company at our own rooms, took up the day, so that we had very little time for common sight-seeing.

Of these kinds of entertainment, the breakfast, though pleasant enough when the company is agreeable, as I always found it, is the least convenient of all times and modes of visiting. You have already interviewed one breakfast, and are expecting soon to be coquetting with a tempting luncheon. If one had as many stomachs as a ruminant, he would not mind three or four serious meals a day, not counting the tea as one of them. The luncheon is a very convenient affair : it does not require special dress; it is informal; it is soon over, and may be made light or heavy, as one chooses. The afternoon tea is almost a necessity in London life. It is considered useful as " a pick me up," and it serves an admirable purpose in the social system. It costs the household hardly any trouble or expense. It brings people together in the easiest possible way, for ten minutes or an hour, just as their engagements or fancies may settle it. A cup of tea at the right moment does for the virtuous reveller all that Falstaff claims for a good sherris-sack, or at least the first half of its " twofold operation : " " It ascends me into the brain ; dries me there all the foolish and dull and crudy vapors which environ it; makes it apprehensive, quick, forgetive, full of nimble, fiery and delectable shapes, which delivered over to the voice, the tongue, which is the birth, becomes excellent wit."

But it must have the right brain to work upon, and I doubt if there is any brain to which it is so congenial and from which it brings so much as that of a first-rate London old lady. I came away from the great city with the feeling that this most complex product of civilization was nowhere else developed to such perfection. The octogenarian Londoness has been in society, — let us say the highest society, — all her days. She is as tough as an old macaw, or she would not have lasted so long. She has seen and talked with all the celebrities of three generations, all the beauties of at least half a dozen decades. Her wits have been kept bright by constant use, and as she is free of speech it requires some courage to face her. Yet nobody can be more agreeable, even to young persons, than one of these precious old dowagers. A great beauty is almost certainly thinking how she looks while one is talking with her; an authoress is waiting to have one praise her book;

but a grand old lady, who loves London society, who lives in it, who understands young people and all sorts of people, with her high-colored recollections of the past and her grand-maternal interests in the new generation, is the best of companions, especially over a cup of tea just strong enough to stir up her talking ganglions.

A breakfast, a lunch, a tea, is a circumstance, an occurrence, in social life, but a dinner is an event. It is the full-blown flower of that cultivated growth of which those lesser products are the buds. I will not try to enumerate, still less to describe, the various entertainments to which we were invited, and many of which we attended. Among the professional friends I found or made during this visit to London, none were more kindly attentive than Dr. Priestley, who, with his charming wife, the daughter of the late Robert Chambers, took more pains to carry out our wishes than we could have asked or hoped for. At his house I first met Sir James Paget and Sir William Gull, long well known to me, as to the medical profession everywhere, as preëminent in their several departments. If I were an interviewer or a newspaper reporter, I should be tempted to give the impression which the men and women of distinction I met made upon me; but where all were cordial, where all made me feel as nearly as they could that I belonged where I found myself, whether the ceiling were a low or a lofty one, I do not care to differentiate my hosts and my other friends. *Fortemque Gyan fortemque Cloanthum,* — I left my microscope and my test-papers at home.

Our friends, several of them, had a pleasant way of sending their carriages to give us a drive in the Park, where, except in certain permitted regions, the common numbered vehicles are not allowed to enter. Lady Harcourt sent her carriage for us to go to her sister's, Mrs. Mildmay's, where we had a pleasant little "tea," and met one of the most agreeable and remarkable of those London old ladies I have spoken of. For special occasions we hired an unnumbered carriage, with professionally equipped driver and footman.

Mrs. Bloomfield Moore sent her carriage for us to take us to a lunch at her house, where we met Mr. Browning, Sir Henry and Lady Layard, Oscar Wilde and his handsome wife, and other well-known guests. After lunch, recitations, songs, etc. House full of pretty things. Among other curiosities a portfolio of drawings illustrating Keeley's motor, which, up to this time, has manifested a remarkably powerful *vis inertiæ*, but which promises miracles. In the evening a grand reception at Lady Granville's, beginning (for us, at least) at eleven o'clock. The house a palace, and A—— thinks there were a thousand people there. We made the tour of the rooms, saw many great personages, had to wait for our carriage a long time, but got home at one o'clock.

English people have queer notions about iced-water and ice-cream. "You will surely die, eating such cold stuff," said a lady to my companion. "Oh, no," she answered, "but I should certainly die were I to drink your two cups of strong tea." I approved of this "counter" on the teacup, but I did not think either of them was in much danger.

The next day Rev. Mr. Haweis sent his carriage, and we drove in the Park. In the afternoon we went to our Minister's to see the American ladies who had been presented at the drawing-room. After this, both of us were glad to pass a day or two in comparative quiet, except that we had a room full of visitors. So many persons expressed a desire to make our acquaintance that we thought it would be acceptable to them if we would give a reception ourselves. We were thinking how we could manage it with our rooms at the hotel, which were not arranged so that they could be thrown together. Still, we were planning to make the best of them, when Dr. and Mrs. Priestley suggested that we should receive our company at their house. This was a surprise, and a most welcome one, and A—— and her kind friend busied themselves at once about the arrangements.

We went to a luncheon at Lansdowne House, Lord Rosebery's residence, not far from our hotel. My companion tells a little incident which may please an American six-year-old: "The eldest of the four children, Sibyl, a pretty, bright child of six, told me that she wrote a letter to the Queen. I said, ' Did you begin, Dear Queen ? ' 'No,' she answered, 'I began, Your Majesty, and signed myself, Your little humble servant, Sibyl." A very cordial and homelike reception at this great house, where a couple of hours were passed most agreeably.

On the following Sunday I went to Westminster Abbey to hear a sermon from Canon Harford on A Cheerful Life. A lively, wholesome, and encouraging discourse, such as it would do many a forlorn New England congregation good to hear. In the afternoon we both went together to the Abbey. Met our Beverly neighbor, Mrs. Vaughan, and adopted her as one of our party. The seats we were to have were full, and we had to be stowed where there was any place that would hold us. I was smuggled into a stall, going through long and narrow passages, between crowded rows of people, and found myself at last with a big book before me and a set of official personages around me, whose duties I did not clearly understand. I thought they might be mutes, or something of that sort, salaried to look grave and keep quiet. After service we took tea with Dean Bradley, and after tea we visited the Jerusalem Chamber. I had been twice invited to weddings in that famous room: once to the marriage of my friend Motley's daughter, then to that of Mr. Frederick Locker's daughter to Lionel Tennyson, whose recent death has been so deeply mourned. I never expected to see that Jerusalem in which Harry the Fourth died, but there I found myself in the large panelled chamber, with all its associations. The older memories came up but vaguely; an American finds it as hard to call back anything over two or three centuries old as a sucking-pump to draw up water from a depth of over thirty-three feet and a fraction. After this A—— went to a musical party, dined with the Vaughans, and had a good time among American friends.

The next evening we went to the Lyceum Theatre to see Mr. Irving. He had placed the Royal box at our disposal, so we invited our friends the Priestleys to go with us, and we all enjoyed the evening mightily. Between the scenes we went behind the curtain, and saw the very curious and admirable machinery of the dramatic spectacle. We made the acquaintance of several imps and demons, who were got up wonderfully well. Ellen Terry was as fascinating as ever. I remembered that once before I had met her and Mr. Irving behind the scenes. It was at the Boston Theatre, and while I was talking with them a very heavy piece of scenery came crashing down, and filled the whole place with dust. It was but a short distance from where we were standing, and I could not help thinking how near our several life-dramas came to a simultaneous *exeunt omnes*.

A long visit from a polite interviewer, shopping, driving, calling, arranging about the people to be invited to our reception, and an agreeable dinner at Chelsea with my American friend, Mrs. Merritt, filled up this day full enough, and left us in good condition for the next, which was to be a very busy one.

In the Introduction to these papers, I mentioned the fact that more than half a century ago I went to the famous Derby race at Epsom. I determined, if possible, to see the Derby of 1886, as I had seen that of 1834. I must have spoken of this intention to some interviewer, for I find the following paragraph in an English sporting newspaper, "The Field," for May 29th, 1886 : —

" The Derby has always been the one event

in the racing year which statesmen, philosophers, poets, essayists, and *littérateurs* desire to see once in their lives. A few years since Mr. Gladstone was induced by Lord Granville and Lord Wolverton to run down to Epsom on the Derby day. The impression produced upon the Prime Minister's sensitive and emotional mind was that the mirth and hilarity displayed by his compatriots upon Epsom race-course was Italian rather than English in its character. On the other hand, Gustave Doré, who also saw the Derby for the first and only time in his life, exclaimed, as he gazed with horror upon the faces below him, *Quelle scène brutale !* We wonder to which of these two impressions Dr. Oliver Wendell Holmes inclined, if he went last Wednesday to Epsom! Probably the well-known, etc., etc. — Of one thing Dr. Holmes may rest finally satisfied: the Derby of 1886 may possibly have seemed to him far less exciting than that of 1834; but neither in 1834 nor in any other year was the great race ever won by a better sportsman or more honorable man than the Duke of Westminster."

My desire to see the Derby of this year was

of the same origin and character as that which led me to revisit many scenes which I remembered. I cared quite as much about renewing old impressions as about getting new ones. I enjoyed everything which I had once seen all the more from the blending of my recollections with the present as it was before me.

The Derby day of 1834 was exceedingly windy and dusty. Our party, riding on the outside of the coach, was half smothered with the dust, and arrived in a very deteriorated condition, but recompensed for it by the extraordinary sights we had witnessed. There was no train in those days, and the whole road between London and Epsom was choked with vehicles of all kinds, from four-in-hands to donkey-carts and wheelbarrows. My friends and I mingled freely in the crowds, and saw all the "humours" of the occasion. The thimble-riggers were out in great force, with their light, movable tables, the cups or thimbles, and the "little jokers," and the coachman, the sham gentleman, the country greenhorn, all properly got up and gathered about the table. I think we had "Aunt Sally," too, — the figure with a pipe in her mouth, which one might shy a stick at for a penny or two and win something, I forget what. The clearing the course of stragglers, and the chasing about of the frightened little dog who had got in between the thick ranks of spectators, reminded me of what I used to see on old " artillery election " days.

It was no common race that I went to see in 1834. " It is asserted in the columns of a contemporary that Plenipotentiary was absolutely the best horse of the century." This was the winner of the race I saw so long ago. Herring's colored portrait, which I have always kept, shows him as a great, powerful chestnut horse, well deserving the name of "bullock," which one of the jockeys applied to him. " Rumor credits Dr. Holmes," so " The Field " says, " with desiring mentally to compare his two Derbies with each other." I was most fortunate in my objects of comparison. The horse I was about to see win was not unworthy of being named with the renowned champion of my earlier day. I quote from a writer in the " London Morning Post," whose words, it will be seen, carry authority with them : —

" Deep as has hitherto been my reverence for Plenipotentiary, Bay Middleton, and Queen of Trumps from hearsay, and for Don John, Crucifix, etc., etc., from my own personal knowledge, I am inclined to award the palm to Ormonde as the best three-year-old I have ever seen during close upon half a century's connection with the turf."

Ormonde, the Duke of Westminster's horse, was the son of that other winner of the Derby, Bend Or, whom I saw at Eaton Hall.

Perhaps some coeval of mine may think it was a rather youthful idea to go to the race. I cannot help that. I was off on my first long vacation for half a century, and had a right to my whims and fancies. But it was one thing to go in with a vast crowd at five and twenty, and another thing to run the risks of the excursion at more than thrice that age. I looked about me for means of going safely, and could think of nothing better than to ask one of the pleasantest and kindest of gentlemen, to whom I had a letter from Mr. Winthrop, at whose house I had had the pleasure of making his acquaintance. Lord Rosebery suggested that the best

way would be for me to go in the special train
which was to carry the Prince of Wales. First,
then, I was to be introduced to his Royal Highness, which office was kindly undertaken by our
very obliging and courteous Minister, Mr.
Phelps. After this all was easily arranged, and
I was cared for as well as if I had been Mr.
Phelps himself. On the grand stand I found
myself in the midst of the great people, who
were all very natural, and as much at their ease
as the rest of the world. The Prince is of a
lively temperament and a very cheerful aspect,
— a young girl would call him " jolly " as well
as " nice." I recall the story of " Mr. Pope "
and his Prince of Wales, as told by Horace
Walpole. " Mr. Pope, you don't love princes."
" Sir, I beg your pardon." " Well, you don't
love kings, then." " Sir, I own I love the lion
best before his claws are grown." Certainly,
nothing in Prince Albert Edward suggests any
aggressive weapons or tendencies. The lovely,
youthful - looking, gracious Alexandra, the always affable and amiable Princess Louise, the
tall youth who sees the crown and sceptre afar
off in his dreams, the slips of girls so like many

school misses we left behind us, — all these
grand personages, not being on exhibition, but
off enjoying themselves, just as I was and as
other people were, seemed very much like their
fellow - mortals. It is really easier to feel at
home with the highest people in the land than
with the awkward commoner who was knighted
yesterday. When "My Lord and Sir Paul"
came into the Club which Goldsmith tells us of,
the hilarity of the evening was instantly checked.
The entrance of a dignitary like the present
Prince of Wales would not have spoiled the fun
of the evening. If there is any one accomplish-
ment specially belonging to princes, it is that of
making the persons they meet feel at ease.

The grand stand to which I was admitted was
a little privileged republic. I remember Thackeray's story of his asking some simple question
of a royal or semi-royal personage whom he met
in the courtyard of an hotel, which question his
Highness did not answer, but called a subordi-
nate to answer for him. I had been talking
some time with a tall, good-looking gentleman,
whom I took for a nobleman to whom I had
been introduced. Something led me to think I

was mistaken in the identity of this gentleman. I asked him, at last, if he were not So and So. " No," he said, " I am Prince Christian." You are a Christian prince, anyhow, I said to my self, if I may judge by your manners.

I once made a similar mistake in addressing a young fellow-citizen of some social pretensions. I apologized for my error.

"No offence," he answered.

Offence indeed ! I should hope not. But he had not the "*manière de prince*," or he would never have used that word.

I must say something about the race I had taken so much pains to see. There was a preliminary race, which excited comparatively little interest. After this the horses were shown in the paddock, and many of our privileged party went down from the stand to look at them. Then they were brought out, smooth, shining, fine-drawn, frisky, spirit-stirring to look upon, — most beautiful of all the bay horse Ormonde, who could hardly be restrained, such was his eagerness for action. The horses disappear in the distance. — They are off, — not yet distinguishable, at least to me. A little waiting time, and they swim into our ken, but in what order of precedence it is as yet not easy to say. Here they come! Two horses have emerged from the ruck, and are sweeping, rushing, storming, towards us, almost side by side. One slides by the other, half a length, a length, a length and a half. Those are Archer's colors, and the beautiful bay Ormonde flashes by the line, winner of the Derby of 1886. "The Bard" has made a good fight for the first place, and comes in second. Poor Archer, the king of the jockeys! He will bestride no more Derby winners. A few weeks later he died by his own hand.

While the race was going on, the yells of the betting crowd beneath us were incessant. It must have been the frantic cries and movements of these people that caused Gustave Doré to characterize it as a brutal scene. The vast mob which thronged the wide space beyond the shouting circle just round us was much like that of any other fair, so far as I could see from my royal perch. The most conspicuous object was a man on an immensely tall pair of stilts, stalking about among the crowd. I think it probable that I had as much enjoyment in forming one of

the great mob in 1834 as I had among the grandeurs in 1886, but the last is pleasanter to remember and especially to tell of.

After the race we had a luncheon served us, a
comfortable and substantial one, which was very
far from unwelcome. I did not go to the Derby
to bet on the winner. But as I went in to
luncheon, I passed a gentleman standing in cus-
tody of a plate half covered with sovereigns.
He politely asked me if I would take a little
paper from a heap there was lying by the plate,
and add a sovereign to the collection already
there. I did so, and, unfolding my paper, found
it was a blank, and passed on. The pool, as I
afterwards learned, fell to the lot of the Turkish
Ambassador. I found it very windy and uncomfortable on the more exposed parts of the grand
stand, and was glad that I had taken a shawl
with me, in which I wrapped myself as if I had
been on shipboard. This, I told my English
friends, was the more civilized form of the
Indian's blanket. My report of the weather
does not say much for the English May, but it
is generally agreed upon that this is a backward
and unpleasant spring.

After my return from the race we went to a large dinner at Mr. Phelps's house, where we met Mr. Browning again, and the Lord Chancellor Herschel, among others. Then to Mrs. Cyril Flower's, one of the most sumptuous houses in London; and after that to Lady Rothschild's, another of the private palaces, with ceilings lofty as firmaments, and walls that might have been copied from the New Jerusalem. There was still another great and splendid reception at Lady Dalhousie's, and a party at Mrs. Smith's, but we were both tired enough to be willing to go home after what may be called a pretty good day's work at enjoying ourselves.

We had been a fortnight in London, and were now inextricably entangled in the meshes of the golden web of London social life.

II.

THE reader who glances over these papers, and, finding them too full of small details and the lesser personal matters which belong naturally to private correspondences, turns impatiently from them, has my entire sympathy and good-will. He is not one of those for whom these pages are meant. Having no particular interest in the writer or his affairs, he does not care for the history of " the migrations from the blue bed to the brown " and the many Mistress Quicklyisms of circumstantial narrative. Yet all this may be pleasant reading to relatives and friends.

But I must not forget that a new generation of readers has come into being since I have been writing for the public, and that a new generation of aspiring and brilliant authors has grown into general recognition. The dome of Boston State House, which is the centre of my little universe, was glittering in its fresh golden pellicle before I had reached the scriptural boundary of life. It has lost its lustre now, and the years which have dulled its surface have whitened the dome of that fragile structure in which my consciousness holds the session of its faculties. Time is not to be cheated. It is easy to talk of perennial youth, and to toy with the flattering fictions which every ancient personage accepts as true so far as he himself is concerned, and laughs at as foolish talk when he hears them applied to others. When, in my exulting immaturity, I wrote the lines not unknown to the reading public under the name of " The Last Leaf," I spoke of the possibility that I myself might linger on the old bough until the buds and blossoms of a new spring were opening and spreading all around me. I am not as yet the solitary survivor of my literary contemporaries, and, remembering who my few coevals are, it may well be hoped that I shall not be. But I feel lonely, very lonely, in the pages through which I wander. These are new names in the midst of which I find my own. In another sense I am very far from alone. I have daily assurances that I have a constituency of known and unknown personal friends, whose indulgence I have no need of asking. I know there are readers enough who will be pleased to follow me in my brief excursion, *because I am myself*, and will demand no better reason. If I choose to write for them, I do no injury to those for whom my personality is an object of indifference. They will find on every shelf some publications which are not intended for them, and which they prefer to let alone. No person is expected to help himself to everything set before him at a public table. I will not, therefore, hesitate to go on with the simple story of our Old World experiences.

Thanks to my Indian blanket, — my shawl, I mean, — I found myself nothing the worse for my manifold adventures of the 27th of May. The cold wind sweeping over Epsom downs reminded me of our own chilling easterly breezes; especially the northeasterly ones, which are to me less disagreeable than the southeasterly. But the poetical illusion about an English May,

> "Zephyr with Aurora playing,
> As he met her once a-Maying,"

and all that, received a shrewd thrust. Zephyr

ought to have come in an ulster, and offered Aurora a warm petticoat. However, in spite of all difficulties, I brought off my recollections of the Derby of 1886 in triumph, and am now waiting for the colored portrait of Ormonde with Archer on his back, — Archer, the winner of five Derby races, one of which was won by the American horse Iroquois. When that picture, which I am daily expecting, arrives, I shall have it framed and hung by the side of Herring's picture of Plenipotentiary, the horse I saw win the Derby in 1834. These two, with an old portrait of the great Eclipse, who, as my engraving of 1780 (Stubbs's) says, "was never beat, or ever had occation for Whip or Spur," will constitute my entire sporting gallery. I have not that vicious and demoralizing love of horse-flesh which makes it next to impossible to find a perfectly honest hippophile. But a racer is the realization of an ideal quadruped, —

"A pard-like spirit, beautiful and swift ; "

so ethereal, so bird-like, that it is no wonder that the horse about whom those old story-tellers lied so stoutly, — telling of his running a mile in a minute, — was called Flying Childers.

The roses in Mrs. Pfeiffer's garden were hardly out of flower when I lunched with her at her pretty villa at Putney. There I met Mr. Browning, Mr. Holman Hunt, Mrs. Ritchie, Miss Anna Swanwick, the translator of Æschylus, and other good company, besides that of my entertainer.

One of my very agreeable experiences was a call from a gentleman with whom I had corresponded, but whom I had never met. This was Mr. John Bellows, of Gloucester, publisher, printer, man of letters, or rather of words; for he is the author of that truly remarkable little manual, " The Bona Fide Pocket Dictionary of the French and English Languages." To the review of this little book, which is dedicated to Prince Lucien Bonaparte, the " London Times " devoted a full column. I never heard any one who had used it speak of it except with admiration. The modest Friend may be surprised to find himself at full length in my pages, but those who know the little miracle of typography, its conciseness, completeness, arrangement, will not wonder that I was gratified to see the author, who sent it to me, and who has written me most

interesting letters on the local antiquities of
Gloucester and its neighborhood.

We lunched that day at Lady Camperdown's,
where we were happy to meet Miss Frances
Power Cobbe.   In the afternoon we went by invitation to a "tea and talk" at the Reverend
Mr. Haweis's, at Chelsea.   We found the house
close packed, but managed to get through the
rooms, shaking innumerable hands of the reverend gentleman's parishioners and other visitors.
It was very well arranged, so as not to be too
fatiguing, and we left the cordial gathering in
good condition.   We drove home with Bishop
and Mrs. Ellicott.

After this Sir James Paget called, and took
me to a small and early dinner-party; and
A—— went with my secretary, the young lady
of whom I have spoken, to see "Human Nature," at Drury Lane Theatre.

On the following day, after dining with Lady
Holland (wife of Sir Henry, niece of Macaulay),
we went across the street to our neighbor's, Lady
Stanley's.   There was to be a great meeting of
schoolmistresses, in whose work her son, the
Honorable Lyulph Stanley, is deeply interested.

Alas! The schoolma'ams were just leaving as we entered the door, and all we saw of them was the trail of their descending robes. I was very sorry for this, for I have a good many friends among our own schoolmistresses, — friends whom I never saw, but know through the kind words they have addressed to me.

No place in London looks more reserved and exclusive than Devonshire House, standing back behind its high wall, extending along Piccadilly. There is certainly nothing in its exterior which invites intrusion. We had the pleasure of taking tea in the great house, accompanying our American friend, Lady Harcourt, and were graciously received and entertained by Lady Edward Cavendish. Like the other great houses, it is a museum of paintings, statues, objects of interest of all sorts. It must be confessed that it is pleasanter to go through the rooms with one of the ladies of the household than under the lead of a liveried servant. Lord Hartington came in while we were there. All the men who are distinguished in political life become so familiar to the readers of "Punch" in their caricatures, that we know them at sight. Even those who can claim no such public distinction are occasionally the subjects of the caricaturist, as some of us have found out for ourselves. A good caricature, which seizes the prominent features and gives them the character Nature hinted, but did not fully carry out, is a work of genius. Nature herself is a remorseless caricaturist, as our daily intercourse with our fellow men and women makes evident to us, and as is curiously illustrated in the figures of Charles Lebrun, showing the relations between certain human faces and those of various animals. Hardly an English statesman in bodily presence could be mistaken by any of " Punch's " readers.

On the same day that we made this quiet visit we attended a great and ceremonious assembly. There were two parts in the programme, in the first of which I was on the stage *solus*, — that is, without my companion ; in the second we were together. This day, Saturday, the 29th of May, was observed as the Queen's birthday, although she was born on the 24th. Sir William Harcourt gave a great dinner to the officials of his department, and later in the evening Lady Rosebery held a reception at the Foreign Office. On both these occasions everybody is expected to be in court dress, but my host told me I might present myself in ordinary evening dress. I thought that I might feel awkwardly among so many guests, all in the wedding garments, knee-breeches and the rest, without which I ventured among them. I never passed an easier evening in any company than among these official personages. Sir William took me under the shield of his ample presence, and answered all my questions about the various notable personages at his table in a way to have made my fortune if I had been a reporter. From the dinner I went to Mrs. Gladstone's, at 10 Downing Street, where A—— called for me. She had found a very small and distinguished company there, Prince Albert Victor among the rest. At half past eleven we walked over to the Foreign Office to Lady Rosebery's reception.

Here Mr. Gladstone was of course the centre of a group, to which I was glad to add myself. His features are almost as familiar to me as my own, for a photograph of him in his library has long stood on my revolving bookcase, with a large lens before it. He is one of a small circle of individuals in whom I have had and still have a special personal interest. The year 1809, which introduced me to atmospheric existence, was the birth-year of Gladstone, Tennyson, Lord Houghton, and Darwin. It seems like an honor to have come into the world in such company, but it is more likely to promote humility than vanity in a common mortal to find himself coeval with such illustrious personages. Men born in the same year watch each other, especially as the sands of life begin to run low, as we can imagine so many damaged hour-glasses to keep an eye on each other. Women, of course, never know who are their contemporaries.

Familiar to me as were the features of Mr. Gladstone, I looked upon him with astonishment. For he stood before me with epaulets on his shoulders and a rapier at his side, as military in his aspect as if he had been Lord Wolseley, to whom I was introduced a short time afterwards. I was fortunate enough to see and hear Mr. Gladstone on a still more memorable occasion, and can afford to leave saying what were my impressions of the very eminent statesman until I speak of that occasion.

A great number of invitations had been given out for the reception at Lady Rosebery's, — over two thousand, my companion heard it said. Whatever the number was, the crowd was very great, — so great that one might well feel alarmed for the safety of any delicate person who was in the *pack* which formed itself at one place in the course of the evening. Some obstruction must have existed *a fronte*, and the *vis a tergo* became fearful in its pressure on those who were caught in the jam. I began thinking of the crushes in which I had been caught, or which I had read and heard of : the terrible time at the execution of Holloway and Haggerty, where some forty persons were squeezed or trampled to death ; the Brooklyn Theatre and other similar tragedies ; the crowd I was in at the unveiling of the statue on the column of the Place Vendome, where I felt as one may suppose Giles Corey did when, in his misery, he called for " more weight " to finish him. But there was always a *deus ex machina* for us when we were in trouble. Looming up above the crowd was the smiling and encouraging countenance of the ever active, always present, always helpful

Mr. Smalley. He cleared a breathing space before us. For a short time it was really a formidable wedging together of people, and if a lady had fainted in the press, she might have run a serious risk before she could have been extricated. No more " marble halls " for us, if we had to undergo the *peine forte et dure* as the condition of our presence! We were both glad to escape from this threatened asphyxia, and move freely about the noble apartments. Lady Rosebery, who was kindness itself, would have had us stay and sit down in comfort at the supper-table, after the crowd had thinned, but we were tired with all we had been through, and ordered our carriage. *Ordered our carriage!*

> " I can call spirits from the vasty deep." . . .
> "*But will they come when you do call for them ?* "

The most formidable thing about a London party is getting away from it. " C'est le *dernier pas qui coute.*" A crowd of anxious persons in retreat is hanging about the windy door, and the breezy stairway, and the airy hall.

A stentorian voice, hard as that of Rhadamanthus, exclaims, —

" Lady Vere de Vere's carriage stops the way ! "

If my Lady Vere de Vere is not on hand, and that pretty quickly, off goes her carriage, and the stern voice bawls again, —

" Mrs. Smith's carriage stops the way ! "

Mrs. Smith's particular Smith may be worth his millions and live in his marble palace ; but if Mrs. Smith thinks her coachman is going to stand with his horses at that door until she appears, she is mistaken, for she is a minute late, and now the coach moves on, and Rhadamanthus calls aloud, —

" Mrs. Brown's carriage stops the way ! "

Half the lung fevers that carry off the great people are got waiting for their carriages.

I know full well that many readers would be disappointed if I did not mention some of the grand places and bring in some of the great names that lend their lustre to London society. We were to go to a fine musical party at Lady Rothschild's on the evening of the 30th of May. It happened that the day was Sunday, and if we had been as punctilious as some New England Sabbatarians, we might have felt compelled to decline the tempting invitation. But the party was given by a daughter of Abraham, and in every Hebrew household the true Sabbath was over. We were content for that evening to shelter ourselves under the old dispensation.

The party, or concert, was a very brilliant affair. Patti sang to us, and a tenor, and a violinist played for us. How we two Americans came to be in so favored a position I do not know; all I do know is that we were shown to our places, and found them very agreeable ones. In the same row of seats was the Prince of Wales, two chairs off from A——'s seat. Directly in front of A—— was the Princess of Wales, " in ruby velvet, with six rows of pearls encircling her throat, and two more strings falling quite low; " and next her, in front of me, the startling presence of Lady de Grey, formerly Lady Lonsdale, and before that Gladys Herbert. On the other side of the Princess sat the Grand Duke Michael of Russia.

As we are among the grandest of the grandees, I must enliven my sober account with an extract from my companion's diary: —

" There were several great beauties there, Lady Claude Hamilton, a queenly blonde, being one. Minnie Stevens Paget had with her the pretty Miss Langdon, of New York. Royalty had one room for supper, with its attendant lords and ladies. Lord Rothschild took me down to a long table for a sit-down supper, — there were some thirty of us. The most superb pink orchids were on the table. The [Thane] of —— sat next me, and how he stared before he was introduced! . . . This has been the finest party we have been to, sitting comfortably in such a beautiful ball-room, gazing at royalty in the flesh, and at the shades of departed beauties on the wall, by Sir Joshua and Gainsborough. It was a new experience to find that the royal lions fed up-stairs, and mixed animals below!"

A visit to Windsor had been planned, under the guidance of a friend whose kindness had already shown itself in various forms, and who, before we left England, did for us more than we could have thought of owing to any one person. This gentleman, Mr. Willett, of Brighton, called with Mrs. Willett to take us on the visit which had been arranged between us.

Windsor Castle, which everybody knows, or can easily learn, all about, is one of the largest of those huge caverns in which the descendants of the original cave men, when they have reached the height of human grandeur, delight to shelter themselves. It seems as if such a great hollow quarry of rock would strike a chill through every tenant, but modern improvements reach even the palaces of kings and queens, and the regulation temperature of the castle, or of its inhabited portions, is fixed at sixty-five degrees of Fahrenheit. The royal standard was not floating from the tower of the castle, and everything was quiet and lonely. We saw all we wanted to, — pictures, furniture, and the rest. My namesake, the Queen's librarian, was not there to greet us, or I should have had a pleasant half-hour in the library with that very polite gentleman, whom I had afterwards the pleasure of meeting in London.

After going through all the apartments in the castle that we cared to see, or our conductress cared to show us, we drove in the park, along the "three-mile walk," and in the by-roads leading from it. The beautiful avenue, the open spaces with scattered trees here and there, made this a most delightful excursion. I saw many fine oaks, one about sixteen feet of honest girth, but no one which was very remarkable. I wished I could have compared the handsomest of them with one in Beverly, which I never look at without taking my hat off. This is a young tree, with a future before it, if barbarians do not meddle with it, more conspicuous for its spread than its circumference, stretching not very far from a hundred feet from bough-end to bough-end. I do not think I saw a specimen of the British *Quercus robur* of such consummate beauty. But I know from Evelyn and Strutt what England has to boast of, and I will not challenge the British oak.

Two sensations I had in Windsor park, or forest, for I am not quite sure of the boundary which separates them. The first was the lovely sight of the *hawthorn* in full bloom. I had always thought of the hawthorn as a pretty shrub, growing in hedges; as big as a currant bush or a barberry bush, or some humble plant of that character. I was surprised to see it as a tree, standing by itself, and making the most delicious roof a pair of young lovers could imagine to sit under. It looked at a little distance like a young apple-tree covered with new-fallen snow.

I shall never see the word hawthorn in poetry again without the image of the snowy but far from chilling canopy rising before me.   It is the very bower of young love, and must have done more than any growth of the forest to soften the doom brought upon man by the fruit of the forbidden tree.   No wonder that

"In the spring a young man's fancy lightly turns to thoughts
    of love,"

with the object of his affections awaiting him in this boudoir of nature.   What a pity that Zekle, who courted Huldy over the apples she was peeling, could not have made love as the bucolic youth does, when

"Every shepherd tells his tale
Under the hawthorn in the dale" !

(I will have it *love*-tale, in spite of Warton's comment.)   But I suppose it does not make so much difference, for love transmutes the fruit in Huldy's lap into the apples of the Hesperides.

In this way it is that the associations with the poetry we remember come up when we find ourselves surrounded by English scenery.   The great poets build temples of song, and fill them with images and symbols which move us almost to adoration ; the lesser minstrels fill a panel or gild a cornice here and there, and make our hearts glad with glimpses of beauty. I felt all this as I looked around and saw the hawthorns in full bloom, in the openings among the oaks and other trees of the forest. Presently I heard a sound to which I had never listened before, and which I have never heard since : —

Coooo — coooo !

Nature had sent one cuckoo from her aviary to sing his double note for me, that I might not pass away from her pleasing show without once hearing the call so dear to the poets. It was the last day of spring. A few more days, and the solitary voice might have been often heard ; for the bird becomes so common as to furnish Shakespeare an image to fit "the skipping king : " —

> " He was but as the cuckoo is in June,
>   Heard, not regarded."

For the lyric poets the cuckoo is "companion of the spring," "darling of the spring ; " coming with the daisy, and the primrose, and the blossoming sweet-pea. Where the sound came from I could not tell ; it puzzled Wordsworth, with younger eyes than mine, to find whence issued

> " that cry
> Which made me look a thousand ways
> In bush, and tree, and sky."

Only one hint of the prosaic troubled my emotional delight: I could not help thinking how capitally the little rogue imitated the cuckoo clock, with the sound of which I was pretty well acquainted.

On our return from Windsor we had to get ready for another great dinner with our Minister, Mr. Phelps. As we are in the habit of considering our great officials as public property, and as some of my readers want as many glimpses of high life as a decent regard to republican sensibilities will permit, I will borrow a few words from the diary to which I have often referred: —

"The Princess Louise was there with the Marquis, and I had the best opportunity of seeing how they receive royalty at private houses. Mr. and Mrs. Phelps went down to the door to meet her the moment she came, and then Mr. Phelps entered the drawing-room with the Princess on his arm, and made the tour of the room with her, she bowing and speaking to each one of us. Mr. Goschen took me in to dinner, and Lord Lorne was on my other side. All of the flowers were of the royal color, red. It was a grand dinner. . . . The Austrian Ambassador, Count Karoli, took Mrs. Phelps in [to dinner], his position being higher than that of even the Duke [of Argyll], who sat upon her right."

It was a very rich experience for a single day: the stately abode of royalty, with all its manifold historical recollections, the magnificent avenue of forest trees, the old oaks, the hawthorn in full bloom, and the one cry of the cuckoo, calling me back to Nature in her spring-time freshness and glory; then, after that, a great London dinner-party at a house where the kind host and the gracious hostess made us feel at home, and where we could meet the highest people in the land, — the people whom we who live in a simpler way at home are naturally pleased to be with under such auspices. What of all this shall I remember longest? Let me not seem ungrateful to my friends who planned the excursion for us, or to those who asked us to the brilliant evening entertainment, but I feel as

Wordsworth felt about the cuckoo, — he will survive all the other memories.

> ' And I can listen to thee yet,
> Can lie upon the plain
> And listen, till I do beget
> That golden time again.''

Nothing is more hackneyed than an American's description of his feelings in the midst of the scenes and objects he has read of all his days, and is looking upon for the first time. To each of us it appears in some respects in the same way, but with a difference for every individual. We may smile at Irving's emotions at the first sight of a distinguished Englishman on his own soil, — the ingenious Mr. Roscoe, as an earlier generation would have called him. Our tourists, who are constantly going forward and back between England and America, lose all sense of the special distinctions between the two countries which do not bear on their personal convenience. Happy are those who go with unworn, unsatiated sensibilities from the New World to the Old ; as happy, it may be, those who come from the Old World to the New, but of that I cannot form a judgment.

On the first day of June we called by appointment upon Mr. Peel, the Speaker of the House of Commons, and went through the Houses of Parliament. We began with the train-bearer, then met the housekeeper, and presently were joined by Mr. Palgrave. The "Golden Treasury" stands on my drawing-room table at home, and the name on its title-page had a perfectly familiar sound. These accidental meetings with persons whom we know by their publications are very pleasant surprises.

Among other things to which Mr. Palgrave called our attention was the death-warrant of Charles the First. One name in the list of signers naturally fixed our eyes upon it. It was that of John Dixwell. A lineal descendant of the old regicide is very near to me by family connection, Colonel Dixwell having come to this country, married, and left a posterity, which has resumed the name, dropped for the sake of safety at the time when he, Goffe, and Whalley were in concealment in various parts of New England.

We lunched with the Speaker, and had the pleasure of the company of Archdeacon Farrar.

In the afternoon we went to a tea at a very grand house, where, as my companion says in her diary, " it took full six men in red satin knee-breeches to let us in." Another grand personage asked us to dine with her at her country place, but we were too full of engagements. In the evening we went to a large reception at Mr. Gosse's. It was pleasant to meet artists and scholars, — the kind of company to which we are much used in our æsthetic city. I found our host as agreeable at home as he was when in Boston, where he became a favorite, both as a lecturer and as a visitor.

Another day we visited Stafford House, where Lord Ronald Gower, himself an artist, did the honors of the house, showing us the pictures and sculptures, his own included, in a very obliging and agreeable way. I have often taken note of the resemblances of living persons to the portraits and statues of their remote ancestors. In showing us the portrait of one of his own farback progenitors, Lord Ronald placed a photograph of himself in the corner of the frame. The likeness was so close that the photograph might seem to have been copied from the painting, the dress only being changed. The Duke of Sutherland, who had just come back from America, complained that the dinners and lunches had used him up. I was fast learning how to sympathize with him.

Then to Grosvenor House to see the pictures. I best remember Gainsborough's beautiful Blue Boy, commonly so called, from the color of his dress, and Sir Joshua's Mrs. Siddons as the Tragic Muse, which everybody knows in engravings. We lunched in clerical company that day, at the Bishop of Gloucester and Bristol's, with the Archbishop of York, the Reverend Mr. Haweis, and others as guests. I told A—— that she was not sufficiently impressed with her position at the side of an archbishop; she was not *crumbling bread* in her nervous excitement. The company did not seem to remember Sydney Smith's remark to the young lady next him at a dinner-party: "My dear, I see you are nervous, by your crumbling your bread as you do. *I* always crumble bread when I sit by a bishop, and when I sit by an archbishop I crumble bread with both hands." That evening I had the pleasure of dining with the distinguished

Mr. Bryce, whose acquaintance I made in our own country, through my son, who has introduced me to many agreeable persons of his own generation, with whose companionship I am glad to mend the broken and merely fragmentary circle of old friendships.

The 3d of June was a memorable day for us, for on the evening of that day we were to hold our reception. If Dean Bradley had proposed our meeting our guests in the Jerusalem chamber, I should hardly have been more astonished. But these kind friends meant what they said, and put the offer in such a shape that it was impossible to resist it. So we sent out our cards to a few hundreds of persons, — those who we thought might like invitations. I was particularly desirous that many members of the medical profession whom I had not met, but who felt well disposed towards me, should be at this gathering. The meeting was in every respect a success. I wrote a prescription for as many baskets of champagne as would be consistent with the well-being of our guests, and such light accompaniments as a London company is wont to expect under similar circumstances.

My own recollections of the evening, unclouded
by its festivities, but confused by its multitudinous succession of introductions, are about as
definite as the Duke of Wellington's alleged
monosyllabic description of the battle of Waterloo. But A—— writes in her diary : " From
nine to twelve we stood, receiving over three
hundred people out of the four hundred and fifty
we invited." As I did not go to Europe to visit
hospitals or museums, I might have missed seeing
some of those professional brethren whose names
I hold in honor and whose writings are in my
library. If any such failed to receive our cards
of invitation, it was an accident which, if I had
known, I should have deeply regretted. So
far as we could judge by all we heard, our
unpretentious party gave general satisfaction.
Many different social circles were represented,
but it passed off easily and agreeably. I can
say this more freely, as the credit of it belongs
so largely to the care and self-sacrificing efforts
of Dr. Priestley and his charming wife.

I never refused to write in the birthday book
or the album of the humblest schoolgirl or
schoolboy, and I could not refuse to set my

name, with a verse from one of my poems, in
the album of the Princess of Wales, which was
sent me for that purpose. It was a nice new
book, with only two or three names in it, and
those of musical composers, — Rubinstein's, I
think, was one of them, — so that I felt honored
by the great lady's request. I ought to describe
the book, but I only remember that it was quite
large and sumptuously elegant, and that I copied
into it the last verse of a poem of mine called
" The Chambered Nautilus," as I have often
done for plain republican albums.

The day after our simple reception was notable for three social events in which we had our
part. The first was a lunch at the house of
Mrs. Cyril Flower, one of the finest in London,
— Surrey House, as it is called. Mr. Browning, who seems to go everywhere, and is one of
the vital elements of London society, was there
as a matter of course. Miss Cobbe, many of
whose essays I have read with great satisfaction,
though I cannot accept all her views, was a guest
whom I was very glad to meet a second time.

In the afternoon we went to a garden-party
given by the Princess Louise at Kensington

Palace, a gloomy-looking edifice, which might
be taken for a hospital or a poorhouse. Of all
the festive occasions which I attended, the gar-
den-parties were to me the most formidable.
They are all very well for young people, and for
those who do not mind the nipping and eager
air, with which, as I have said, the climate of
England, no less than that of America, falsifies
all the fine things the poets have said about
May, and, I may add, even June. We wandered about the grounds, spoke with the great
people, stared at the odd ones, and said to ourselves, — at least I said to myself, — with Hamlet,

"The air bites shrewdly, it is very cold."

The most curious personages were some East In-
dians, a chocolate-colored lady, her husband, and
children. The mother had a diamond on the
side of her nose, its setting riveted on the inside, one might suppose ; the effect was peculiar,
far from captivating. A—— said that she
should prefer the good old-fashioned nose-ring,
as we find it described and pictured by travellers. She saw a great deal more than I did, of
course. I quote from her diary: "The little

Eastern children made their native salaam to the Princess by prostrating themselves flat on their little stomachs in front of her, putting their hands between her feet, pushing them aside, and kissing the print of her feet!"

I really believe one or both of us would have run serious risks of catching our "death o' cold," if we had waited for our own carriage, which seemed forever in coming forward. The good Lady Holland, who was more than once our guardian angel, brought us home in hers. So we got warmed up at our own hearth, and were ready in due season for the large and fine dinner-party at Archdeacon Farrar's, where, among other guests, were Mrs. Phelps, our Minister's wife, who is a great favorite alike with Americans and English, Sir John Millais, Mr. Tyndall, and other interesting people.

I am sorry that we could not have visited Newstead Abbey. I had a letter from Mr. Thornton Lothrop to Colonel Webb, the present proprietor, with whom we lunched. I have spoken of the pleasure I had when I came accidentally upon persons with whose name and fame I had long been acquainted. A similar impression was that which I received when I found myself in the company of the bearer of an old, historic name. When my host at the lunch introduced a stately-looking gentleman as Sir Kenelm Digby, it gave me a start, as if a ghost had stood before me. I recovered myself immediately, however, for there was nothing of the impalpable or immaterial about the stalwart personage who bore the name. I wanted to ask him if he carried any of his ancestor's " powder of sympathy " about with him. Many, but not all, of my readers remember that famous man's famous preparation. When used to cure a wound, it was applied to the weapon that made it ; the part was bound up so as to bring the edges of the wound together, and by the wondrous influence of the sympathetic powder the healing process took place in the kindest possible manner. Sir Kenelm, the ancestor, was a gallant soldier, a grand gentleman, and the husband of a wonderfully beautiful wife, whose charms he tried to preserve from the ravages of time by various experiments. He was also the homœopathist of his day, the Elisha Perkins (metallic tractors) of his generation. The

" mind cure" people might adopt him as one of their precursors.

I heard a curious statement which was illustrated in the person of one of the gentlemen we met at this table. It is that English sporting men are often deaf on one side, in consequence of the noise of the frequent discharge of their guns affecting the right ear. This is a very convenient infirmity for gentlemen who indulge in slightly aggressive remarks, but when they are hit back never seem to be conscious at all of the *riposte*, — the return thrust of the fencer.

Dr. Allchin called and took me to a dinner, where I met many professional brothers, and enjoyed myself highly.

By this time every day was pledged for one or more engagements, so that many very attractive invitations had to be declined. I will not follow the days one by one, but content myself with mentioning some of the more memorable visits. I had been invited to the Rabelais Club, as I have before mentioned, by a cable message. This is a club of which the late Lord Houghton was president, and of which I am a member, as

are several other Americans. I was afraid that
the gentlemen who met,

    " To laugh and shake in Rabelais's easy-chair,"

might be more hilarious and demonstrative in
their mirth than I, a sober New Englander in
the superfluous decade, might find myself equal
to. But there was no uproarious jollity; on the
contrary, it was a pleasant gathering of literary
people and artists, who took their pleasure not
sadly, but serenely, and I do not remember a
single explosive guffaw.

Another day, after going all over Dudley
House, including Lady Dudley's boudoir, " in
light blue satin, the prettiest room we have
seen," A—— says, we went, by appointment, to
Westminster Abbey, where we spent two hours
under the guidance of Archdeacon Farrar. I
think no part of the Abbey is visited with so
much interest as Poets' Corner. We are all
familiarly acquainted with it beforehand. We
are all ready for " O rare Ben Jonson ! " as we
stand over the place where he was planted standing upright, as if he had been dropped into a
post-hole. We remember too well the foolish
and flippant mockery of Gay's " Life is a Jest."

If I were dean of the cathedral, I should be tempted to alter the *J* to a *G*. Then we could read it without contempt; for life *is* a gest, an achievement, — or always ought to be. Westminster Abbey is too crowded with monuments to the illustrious dead and those who have been considered so in their day to produce any other than a confused impression. When we visit the tomb of Napoleon at the Invalides, no sidelights interfere with the view before us in the field of mental vision. We see the Emperor; Marengo, Austerlitz, Waterloo, Saint Helena, come before us, with him as their central figure. So at Stratford, — the Cloptons and the John a Combes, with all their memorials, cannot make us lift our eyes from the stone which covers the dust that once breathed and walked the streets of Stratford as Shakespeare.

Ah, but here is one marble countenance that I know full well, and knew for many a year in the flesh! Is there an American who sees the bust of Longfellow among the effigies of the great authors of England without feeling a thrill of pleasure at recognizing the features of his native fellow-countryman in the Valhalla of his

ancestral fellow-countrymen? There are many
memorials in Poets' Corner and elsewhere in the
Abbey which could be better spared than that.
Too many that were placed there as luminaries
have become conspicuous by their obscurity in
the midst of that illustrious company. On the
whole, the Abbey produces a distinct sense of
being overcrowded. It appears too much like
a lapidary's store-room. Look up at the lofty
roof, which we willingly pardon for shutting out
the heaven above us, — at least in an average
London day; look down at the floor, and think
of what precious relics it covers; but do not
look around you with the hope of getting any
clear, concentrated, satisfying effect from this
great museum of gigantic funereal bricabrac.
Pardon me, shades of the mighty dead! I had
something of this feeling, but at another hour I
might perhaps be overcome by emotion, and
weep, as my fellow-countryman did at the grave
of the earliest of his ancestors. I should love
myself better in that aspect than I do in this
cold-blooded criticism; but it suggested itself,
and as no flattery can soothe, so no censure can
wound, "the dull, cold ear of death."

Of course we saw all the sights of the Abbey in a hurried way, yet with such a guide and expositor as Archdeacon Farrar our two hours' visit was worth a whole day with an undiscriminating verger, who recites his lesson by rote, and takes the life out of the little mob that follows him round by emphasizing the details of his lesson, until " Patience on a monument " seems to the sufferer, who knows what he wants and what he does not want, the nearest emblem of himself he can think of.   Amidst all the imposing recollections of the ancient edifice, one impressed me in the inverse ratio of its importance.   The Archdeacon pointed out the little holes in the stones, in one place, where the boys of the choir used to play marbles, before America was discovered, probably, — centuries before, it may be.   It is a strangely impressive glimpse of a living past, like the *graffiti* of Pompeii.   I find it is often the accident rather than the essential which fixes my attention and takes hold of my memory.   This is a tendency of which I suppose I ought to be ashamed, if we have any right to be ashamed of those idiosyncrasies which are ordered for us.   It is

the same tendency which often leads us to prefer
the picturesque to the beautiful. Mr. Gilpin
liked the donkey in a forest landscape better than
the horse. A touch of imperfection interferes
with the beauty of an object and lowers its level
to that of the picturesque. The accident of the
holes in the stone of the noble building, for the
boys to play marbles with, makes me a boy
again and at home with them, after looking with
awe upon the statue of Newton, and turning
with a shudder from the ghastly monument of
Mrs. Nightingale.

What a life must be that of one whose years
are passed chiefly in and about the great Abbey!
Nowhere does Macbeth's expression " dusty
death " seem so true to all around us. The dust
of those who have been lying century after century below the marbles piled over them, — the
dust on the monuments they lie beneath ; the
dust on the memories those monuments were
raised to keep living in the recollection of posterity, — dust, dust, dust, everywhere, and we
ourselves but shapes of breathing dust moving
amidst these objects and remembrances ! Come
away ! The good Archdeacon of the " Eternal

Hope " has asked us to take a cup of tea with him. The tea-cup will be a cheerful substitute for the funeral urn, and a freshly made infusion of the fragrant leaf is one of the best things in the world to lay the dust of sad reflections.

It is a somewhat fatiguing pleasure to go through the Abbey, in spite of the intense interest no one can help feeling. But my day had but just begun when the two hours we had devoted to the visit were over. At a quarter before eight, my friend Mr. Frederick Locker called for me to go to a dinner at the Literary Club. I was particularly pleased to dine with this association, as it reminded me of our own Saturday Club, which sometimes goes by the same name as the London one. They complimented me with a toast, and I made some kind of a reply. As I never went prepared with a speech for any such occasion, I take it for granted that I thanked the company in a way that showed my gratitude rather than my eloquence. And now, the dinner being over, my day was fairly begun.

This was to be a memorable date in the record of the year, one long to be remembered in the political history of Great Britain. For on

this day, the 7th of June, Mr. Gladstone was to
make his great speech on the Irish question, and
the division of the House on the Government
of Ireland Bill was to take place. The whole
country, to the corners of its remotest colony,
was looking forward to the results of this evening's meeting of Parliament. The kindness of
the Speaker had furnished me with a ticket, en-
titling me to a place among the " distinguished
guests," which I presented without modestly
questioning my right to the title.

The pressure for entrance that evening was
very great, and I, coming after my dinner with
the Literary Club, was late upon the ground.
The places for " distinguished guests " were already filled. But all England was in a conspi-
racy to do everything possible to make my visit
agreeable. I did not take up a great deal of
room, — I might be put into a seat with the am-
bassadors and foreign ministers. And among
them I was presently installed. It was now
between ten and eleven o'clock, as nearly as I
recollect. The House had been in session since
four o'clock. A gentleman was speaking, who
was, as my unknown next neighbor told me, Sir

Michael Hicks-Beach, a leading member, as we all know, of the opposition. When he sat down there was a hush of expectation, and presently Mr. Gladstone rose to his feet. A great burst of applause welcomed him, lasting more than a minute. His clean-cut features, his furrowed cheeks, his scanty and whitened hair, his well-shaped but not extraordinary head, all familiarized by innumerable portraits and emphasized in hundreds of caricatures, revealed him at once to every spectator. His great speech has been universally read, and I need only speak of the way in which it was delivered. His manner was forcible rather than impassioned or eloquent; his voice was clear enough, but must have troubled him somewhat, for he had a small bottle from which he poured something into a glass from time to time and swallowed a little, yet I heard him very well for the most part. In the last portion of his speech he became animated and inspiriting, and his closing words were uttered with an impressive solemnity: "Think, I beseech you, think well, think wisely, think not for a moment, but for the years that are to come, before you reject this bill."

After the burst of applause which followed the conclusion of Mr. Gladstone's speech, the House proceeded to the division on the question of passing the bill to a second reading. While the counting of the votes was going on there was the most intense excitement. A rumor ran round the House at one moment that the vote was going in favor of the second reading. It soon became evident that this was not the case, and presently the result was announced, giving a majority of thirty against the bill, and practically overthrowing the liberal administration. Then arose a tumult of applause from the conservatives and a wild confusion, in the midst of which an Irish member shouted, " Three cheers for the Grand Old Man ! " which were lustily given, with waving of hats and all but Donnybrook manifestations of enthusiasm.

I forgot to mention that I had a very advantageous seat among the diplomatic gentlemen, and was felicitating myself on occupying one of the best positions in the House, when an usher politely informed me that the Russian Ambassador, in whose place I was sitting, had arrived, and that I must submit to the fate of eviction.

Fortunately, there were some steps close by, on one of which I found a seat almost as good as the one I had just left.

It was now two o'clock in the morning, and I had to walk home, not a vehicle being attainable. I did not know my way to my headquarters, and I had no friend to go with me, but I fastened on a stray gentleman, who proved to be an ex-member of the House, and who accompanied me to 17 Dover Street, where I sought my bed with a satisfying sense of having done a good day's work and having been well paid for it.

III.

ON the 8th of June we visited the Record Office for a sight of the Domesday Book and other ancient objects of interest there preserved. As I looked at this too faithful memorial of an inexorable past, I thought of the battle of Hastings and all its consequences, and that reminded me of what I have long remembered as I read it in Dr. Robert Knox's " Races of Men." Dr. Knox was the monoculous Waterloo surgeon, with whom I remember breakfasting, on my first visit to England and Scotland. His celebrity is less owing to his book than to the unfortunate connection of his name with the unforgotten Burke and Hare horrors. This is his language in speaking of Hastings: " . . . that bloody field, surpassing far in its terrible results the unhappy day of Waterloo. From this the Celt has recovered, but not so the Saxon. To this day he feels, and feels deeply, the most disastrous day that ever befell his race; here he was trodden down by the Norman, whose iron heel is on him yet. . . . To this day the Saxon race in England have never recovered a tithe of their rights, and probably never will."

The Conqueror meant to have a thorough summing up of his stolen property. The Anglo-Saxon Chronicle says, — I quote it at second hand, — "So very straitly did he cause the survey to be made, that there was not a single hyde, nor a yardland of ground, nor — it is shameful to say what he thought no shame to do — was there an ox or a cow, or a pig passed by, and that was not down in the accounts, and then all these writings were brought to him." The "looting" of England by William and his "twenty thousand thieves," as Mr. Emerson calls his army, was a singularly methodical proceeding, and Domesday Book is a searching inventory of their booty, movable and immovable.

From this reminder of the past we turned to the remembrances of home; A——going to dine with a transplanted Boston friend and other ladies from that blessed centre of New England life, while I dined with a party of gentlemen at my friend Mr. James Russell Lowell's.

I had looked forward to this meeting with high expectations, and they were abundantly satisfied. I knew that Mr. Lowell must gather about him, wherever he might be, the choicest company, but what his selection would be I was curious to learn. I found with me at the table my own countrymen and his, Mr. Smalley and Mr. Henry James. Of the other guests, Mr. Leslie Stephen was my only old acquaintance in person; but Du Maurier and Tenniel I have met in my weekly " Punch " for many a year; Mr. Lang, Mr. Oliphant, Mr. Townsend, we all know through their writings; Mr. Burne Jones and Mr. Alma Tadema, through the frequent reproductions of their works in engravings, as well as by their paintings. If I could report a dinner-table conversation, I might be tempted to say something of my talk with Mr. Oliphant. I like well enough conversation which floats safely over the shallows, touching bottom at intervals with a commonplace incident or truism to push it along; I like better to find a few fathoms of depth under the surface; there is a still higher pleasure in the philosophical discourse which calls for the deep sea line to reach bottom ; but best of all, when one is in the right mood, is the contact of intelligences when they are off soundings in the ocean of thought. Mr. Oliphant is what many of us call a mystic, and I found a singular pleasure in listening to him. This dinner at Mr. Lowell's was a very remarkable one for the men it brought together, and I remember it with peculiar interest. My entertainer holds a master-key to London society, and he opened the gate for me into one of its choicest preserves on that evening.

I did not undertake to renew my old acquaintance with hospitals and museums. I regretted that I could not be with my companion, who went through the Natural History Museum with the accomplished director, Professor W. H. Flower. One old acquaintance I did resuscitate. For the second time I took the hand of Charles O'Byrne, the celebrated Irish giant of the last century. I met him, as in my first visit, at the Royal College of Surgeons, where I accompanied Mr. Jonathan Hutchinson. He was in the condition so longed for by Sydney Smith on a very hot day ; namely, with his flesh taken off, and sitting, or rather standing, in his bones.

The skeleton measures eight feet, and the living man's height is stated as having been eight feet two, or four inches, by different authorities. His hand was the only one I took, either in England or Scotland, which had not a warm grasp and a hearty welcome in it.

A—— went with Boston friends to see "Faust" a second time, Mr. Irving having offered her the Royal box, and the polite Mr. Bram Stoker serving the party with tea in the little drawing-room behind the box ; so that she had a good time while I was enjoying myself at a dinner at Sir Henry Thompson's, where I met Mr. Gladstone, Mr. Browning, and other distinguished gentlemen. These dinners of Sir Henry's are well known for the good company one meets at them, and I felt myself honored to be a guest on this occasion.

Among the pleasures I had promised myself was that of a visit to Tennyson, at the Isle of Wight. I feared, however, that this would be rendered impracticable by reason of the very recent death of his younger son, Lionel. But I learned from Mr. Locker-Lampson, whose daughter Mr. Lionel Tennyson had married, that the poet would be pleased to see me at his place, Farringford; and by the kind intervention of Mr. Locker-Lampson, better known to the literary world as Frederick Locker, arrangements were made for my daughter and myself to visit him. I considered it a very great favor, for Lord Tennyson has a poet's fondness for the tranquillity of seclusion, which many curious explorers of society fail to remember. Lady Tennyson is an invalid, and though nothing could be more gracious than her reception of us both, I fear it may have cost her an effort which she would not allow to betray itself. Mr. Hallam Tennyson and his wife, both of most pleasing presence and manners, did everything to make our stay agreeable. I saw the poet to the best advantage, under his own trees and walking over his own domain. He took delight in pointing out to me the finest and the rarest of his trees, — and there were many beauties among them. I recalled my morning's visit to Whittier at Oak Knoll, in Danvers, a little more than a year ago, when he led me to one of his favorites, an aspiring evergreen which shot up like a flame. I thought of the graceful American elms in front of

Longfellow's house and the sturdy English elms that stand in front of Lowell's. In this garden of England, the Isle of Wight, where everything grows with such a lavish extravagance of greenness that it seems as if it must bankrupt the soil before autumn, I felt as if weary eyes and overtasked brains might reach their happiest haven of rest. We all remember Shenstone's epigram on the pane of a tavern window. If we 'find our " warmest welcome at an inn," we find our most soothing companionship in the trees among which we have lived, some of which we may ourselves have planted. We lean against them, and they never betray our trust; they shield us from the sun and from the rain; their spring welcome is a new birth, which never loses its freshness; they lay their beautiful robes at our feet in autumn; in winter they " stand and wait," emblems of patience and of truth, for they hide nothing, not even the little leaf-buds which hint to us of hope, the last element in their triple symbolism.

This digression, suggested by the remembrance of the poet under his trees, breaks my narrative, but gives me the opportunity of pay-

ing a debt of gratitude. For I have owned
many beautiful trees, and loved many more outside of my own leafy harem. Those who write
verses have no special claim to be lovers of
trees, but so far as one is of the poetical temperament he is likely to be a tree-lover. Poets
have, as a rule, more than the average nervous
sensibility and irritability. Trees have no
nerves. They live and die without suffering,
without self-questioning or self-reproach. They
have the divine gift of silence. They cannot
obtrude upon the solitary moments when one is
to himself the most agreeable of companions.
The whole vegetable world, even " the meanest
flower that blows," is lovely to contemplate.
What if creation had paused there, and you or
I had been called upon to decide whether self-
conscious life should be added in the form of the
existing animal creation, and the hitherto peaceful universe should come under the rule of
Nature as we now know her,

" red in tooth and claw " ?

Are we not glad that the responsibility of the
decision did not rest on us ?

I am sorry that I did not ask Tennyson to

read or repeat to me some lines of his own.
Hardly any one perfectly understands a poem
but the poet himself. One naturally loves his
own poem as no one else can. It fits the mental
mould in which it was cast, and it will not
exactly fit any other. For this reason I had
rather listen to a poet reading his own verses
than hear the best elocutionist that ever spouted
recite them. He may not have a good voice or
enunciation, but he puts his heart and his inter-
penetrative intelligence into every line, word,
and syllable. I should have liked to hear Tennyson read such lines as

> "Laborious orient ivory, sphere in sphere;"

and in spite of my good friend Matthew Arnold's *in terrorem*, I should have liked to hear
Macaulay read,

> "And Aulus the Dictator
> Stroked Auster's raven mane,"

and other good mouthable lines, from the "Lays
of Ancient Rome." Not less should I like to
hear Mr. Arnold himself read the passage beginning, —

> "In his cool hall with haggard eyes
> The Roman noble lay."

The next day Mrs. Hallam Tennyson took A—— in her pony cart to see Alum Bay, The Needles, and other objects of interest, while I wandered over the grounds with Tennyson. After lunch his carriage called for us, and we were driven across the island, through beautiful scenery, to Ventnor, where we took the train to Ryde, and there the steamer to Portsmouth, from which two hours and a half of travel carried us to London.

My first visit to Cambridge was at the invitation of Mr. Gosse, who asked me to spend Sunday, the 13th of June, with him. The rooms in Neville Court, Trinity College, occupied by Sir William Vernon Harcourt when lecturing at Cambridge, were placed at my disposal. The room I slept in was imposing with the ensigns armorial of the Harcourts and others which ornamented its walls. I had great delight in walking through the quadrangles, along the banks of the Cam, and beneath the beautiful trees which border it. Mr. Gosse says that I stopped in the second court of Clare, and looked around and smiled as if I were bestowing my benediction. He was mistaken : I smiled as if I were receiving a benediction from my dear old grandmother; for Cambridge in New England is my mother town, and Harvard University in Cambridge is my Alma Mater. She is the daughter of Cambridge in Old England, and my relationship is thus made clear.

Mr. Gosse introduced me to many of the younger and some of the older men of the university. Among my visits was one never to be renewed and never to be forgotten. It was to the Master of Trinity, the Reverend William Hepworth Thompson. I hardly expected to have the privilege of meeting this very distinguished and greatly beloved personage, famous not alone for scholarship, or as the successor of Dr. Whewell in his high office, but also as having said some of the wittiest things which we have heard since Voltaire's *pour encourager les autres*. I saw him in his chamber, a feeble old man, but noble to look upon in all " the monumental pomp of age." He came very near belonging to the little group I have mentioned as my coevals, but was a year after us. Gentle, dignified, kindly in his address as if I had been

his schoolmate, he left a very charming impression. He gave me several mementoes of my
visit, among them a beautiful engraving of Sir
Isaac Newton, representing him as one of the
handsomest of men. Dr. Thompson looked as
if he could not be very long for this world, but
his death, a few weeks after my visit, was a
painful surprise to me. I had been just in time
to see "the last of the great men" at Cambridge, as my correspondent calls him, and I
was very grateful that I could store this memory
among the hoarded treasures I have been laying
by for such possible extra stretch of time as may
be allowed me.

My second visit to Cambridge will be spoken
of in due season.

While I was visiting Mr. Gosse at Cambridge,
A—— was not idle. On Saturday she went to
Lambeth, where she had the pleasure and honor
of shaking hands with the Archbishop of Canterbury in his study, and of looking about the
palace with Mrs. Benson. On Sunday she went
to the Abbey, and heard "a broad and liberal
sermon" from Archdeacon Farrar. Our young
lady-secretary stayed and dined with her, and

after dinner sang to her. "A peaceful, happy
Sunday," A—— says in her diary, — not less
peaceful, I suspect, for my being away, as my
callers must have got many a "not at 'ome"
from young Robert of the multitudinous buttons.

On Monday, the 14th of June, after getting
ready for our projected excursions, we had an
appointment which promised us a great deal
of pleasure. Mr. Augustus Harris, the enterprising and celebrated manager of Drury Lane
Theatre, had sent us an invitation to occupy a
box, having eight seats, at the representation of
" Carmen." We invited the Priestleys and
our Boston friends, the Shimminses, to take
seats with us. The chief singer in the opera was
Marie Roze, who looked well and sang well, and
the evening went off very happily. After the
performance we were invited by Mr. Harris to
a supper of some thirty persons, where we were
the special guests. The manager toasted me,
and I said something, — I trust appropriate;
but just what I said is as irrecoverable as the
orations of Demosthenes on the sea-shore, or the
sermons of St. Francis to the beasts and birds.

Of all the attentions I received in England,

this was, perhaps, the least to be anticipated or dreamed of. To be fêted and toasted and to make a speech in Drury Lane Theatre would not have entered into my flightiest conceptions, if I had made out a programme beforehand. It is a singularly gratifying recollection. Drury Lane Theatre is so full of associations with literature, with the great actors and actresses of the past, with the famous beauties who have stood behind the footlights and the splendid audiences that have sat before them, that it is an admirable nucleus for remembrances to cluster around. It was but a vague spot in memory before, but now it is a bright centre for other images of the past. That one evening seems to make me the possessor of all its traditions from the time when it rose from its ashes, when Byron's poem was written and recited, and when the brothers Smith gave us the "Address without a Phœnix," and all those exquisite parodies which make us feel towards their originals somewhat as our dearly remembered Tom Appleton did when he said, in praise of some real green turtle soup, that it was almost as good as mock.

With much regret we gave up an invitation

we had accepted to go to Durdans to dine with Lord Rosebery. We must have felt very tired indeed to make so great a sacrifice, but we had to be up until one o'clock getting ready for the next day's journey; writing, packing, and attending to what we left behind us as well as what was in prospect.

On the morning of Wednesday, June 16th, Dr. Donald Macalister called to attend us on our second visit to Cambridge, where we were to be the guests of his cousin, Alexander Macalister, Professor of Anatomy, who, with Mrs. Macalister, received us most cordially. There was a large luncheon-party at their house, to which we sat down in our travelling dresses. In the evening they had a dinner-party, at which were present, among others, Professor Stokes, President of the Royal Society, and Professor Wright. We had not heard much talk of political matters at the dinner-tables where we had been guests, but A—— sat near a lady who was very earnest in advocating the Irish side of the great impending question.

The 17th of June is memorable in the annals

of my country. On that day of the year 1775 the battle of Bunker's Hill was fought on the height I see from the window of my library, where I am now writing. The monument raised in memory of our defeat, which was in truth a victory, is almost as much a part of the furniture of the room as its chairs and tables; outside, as they are inside, furniture. But the 17th of June, 1886, is memorable to me above all the other anniversaries of that day I have known. For on that day I received from the ancient University of Cambridge, England, the degree of Doctor of Letters, " Doctor Litt.," in its abbreviated academic form. The honor was an unexpected one; that is, until a short time before it was conferred.

Invested with the academic gown and cap, I repaired in due form at the appointed hour to the Senate Chamber. Every seat was filled, and among the audience were youthful faces in large numbers, looking as if they were ready for any kind of outbreak of enthusiasm or hilarity.

The first degree conferred was that of LL. D., on Sir W. A. White, G. C. M., G. C. B., to whose long list of appended initials it seemed like throwing a perfume on the violet to add three more letters.

When I was called up to receive my honorary title, the young voices were true to the promise of the young faces. There was a great noise, not hostile nor unpleasant in its character, in answer to which I could hardly help smiling my acknowledgments. In presenting me for my degree the Public Orator made a Latin speech, from which I venture to give a short extract, which I would not do for the world if it were not disguised by being hidden in the mask of a dead language. But there will be here and there a Latin scholar who will be pleased with the way in which the speaker turned a compliment to the candidate before him, with a reference to one of his poems and to some of his prose works.

"*Juvat nuper audivisse eum cujus carmen prope primum 'Folium ultimum' nominatum est, folia adhuc plura e scriniis suis esse prolaturum. Novimus quanto lepore descripserit colloquia illa antemeridiana, symposia illa sobria et severa, sed eadem festiva et faceta, in quibus totiens mutata persona, modo poeta,*

*modo professor, modo princeps et arbiter, lo-
quendi, inter convivas suos regnat."*

I had no sooner got through listening to the
speech and receiving my formal sentence as
Doctor of Letters than the young voices broke
out in fresh clamor. There were cries of " A
speech! a speech! " mingled with the title of a
favorite poem by John Howard Payne, having
a certain amount of coincidence with the sound
of my name. The play upon the word was not
absolutely a novelty to my ear, but it was good-
natured, and I smiled again, and perhaps made
a faint inclination, as much as to say, " I hear
you, young gentlemen, but I do not forget that
I am standing on my dignity, especially now
since a new degree has added a moral cubit to
my stature." Still the cries went on, and at
last I saw nothing else to do than to edge back
among the silk gowns, and so lose myself and
be lost to the clamorous crowd in the mass of
dignitaries. It was not indifference to the
warmth of my welcome, but a feeling that I had
no claim to address the audience because some of
its younger members were too demonstrative. I
have not forgotten my very cordial reception,

which made me feel almost as much at home in the old Cambridge as in the new, where I was born and took my degrees, academic, professional, and honorary.

The university town left a very deep impression upon my mind, in which a few grand objects predominate over the rest, all being of a delightful character. I was fortunate enough to see the gathering of the boats, which was the last scene in their annual procession. The show was altogether lovely. The pretty river, about as wide as the Housatonic, I should judge, as that slender stream winds through " Canoe Meadow," my old Pittsfield residence, the gaily dressed people who crowded the banks, the flower-crowned boats, with the gallant young oarsmen who handled them so skilfully, made a picture not often equalled. The walks, the bridges, the quadrangles, the historic college buildings, all conspired to make the place a delight and a fascination. The library of Trinity College, with its rows of busts by Roubiliac and Woolner, is a truly noble hall. But beyond, above all the rest, the remembrance of King's College Chapel, with its audacious and richly wrought roof and its wide and lofty windows, glowing with old devices in colors which are ever fresh, as if just from the furnace, holds the first place in my gallery of Cambridge recollections.

I cannot do justice to the hospitalities which were bestowed upon us in Cambridge. Professor and Mrs. Macalister, aided by Dr. Donald Macalister, did all that thoughtful hosts could do to make us feel at home. In the afternoon the ladies took tea at Mr. Oscar Browning's. In the evening we went to a large dinner at the invitation of the Vice-Chancellor. Many little points which I should not have thought of are mentioned in A——'s diary. I take the following extract from it, toning down its vivacity more nearly to my own standard : —

"Twenty were there. The Master of St. John's took me in, and the Vice-Chancellor was on the other side. . . . The Vice-Chancellor rose and returned thanks after the meats and before the sweets, as usual. I have now got used to this proceeding, which strikes me as extraordinary. Everywhere here in Cambridge, and the same in Oxford, I believe, they say grace and give thanks. A gilded ewer and flat basin were passed, with water in the basin to wash with, and we all took our turn at the bath! Next to this came the course with the finger-bowls! . . . Why two baths?"

On Friday, the 18th, I went to a breakfast at the Combination Room, at which about fifty gentlemen were present, Dr. Sandys taking the chair. After the more serious business of the morning's repast was over, Dr. Macalister, at the call of the chairman, arose, and proposed my welfare in a very complimentary way. I of course had to respond, and I did so in the words which came of their own accord to my lips. After my unpremeditated answer, which was kindly received, a young gentleman of the university, Mr. Heitland, read a short poem, of which the following is the title: —

LINES OF GREETING TO DR. OLIVER WENDELL HOLMES.

AT BREAKFAST IN COMBINATION ROOM, ST. JOHN'S COLLEGE, CAMBRIDGE, ENGLAND.

I wish I dared quote more than the last two verses of these lines, which seemed to me, not unused to giving and receiving complimentary tributes, singularly happy, and were so considered by all who heard them. I think I may venture to give the two verses referred to : —

> " By all sweet memory of the saints and sages
>   Who wrought among us in the days of yore ;
> By youths who, turning now life's early pages,
>   Ripen to match the worthies gone before:
>
> " On us, O son of England's greatest daughter,
>   A kindly word from heart and tongue bestow ;
> Then chase the sunsets o'er the western water,
>   And bear our blessing with you as you go."

I need not say that I left the English Cambridge with a heart full of all grateful and kindly emotions.

I must not forget that I found at Cambridge, very pleasantly established and successfully practising his profession, a former student in the dental department of our Harvard Medical School, Dr. George Cunningham, who used to attend my lectures on anatomy. In the garden behind the quaint old house in which he lives is a large medlar-tree, — the first I remember seeing.

On this same day we bade good-by to Cambridge, and took the two o'clock train to Oxford,

where we arrived at half past five. At this first
visit we were to be the guests of Professor Max
Müller, at his fine residence in Norham Gardens. We met there, at dinner, Mr. Herkomer,
whom we have recently had with us in Boston,
and one or two others. In the evening we had
music; the professor playing on the piano, his
two daughters, Mrs. Conybeare and her unmar-
ried sister, singing, and a young lady playing the
violin. It was a very lovely family picture; a
pretty house, surrounded by attractive scenery;
scholarship, refinement, simple elegance, giving
distinction to a home which to us seemed a pattern of all we could wish to see beneath an English roof. It all comes back to me very sweetly,
but very tenderly and sadly, for the voice of the
elder of the two sisters who sang to us is heard
no more on earth, and a deep shadow has fallen
over the household we found so bright and
cheerful.

Everything was done to make me enjoy my
visit to Oxford, but I was suffering from a
severe cold, and was paying the penalty of too
much occupation and excitement. I missed a
great deal in consequence, and carried away a

less distinct recollection of this magnificent seat of learning than of the sister university.

If one wishes to know the magic of names, let him visit the places made memorable by the lives of the illustrious men of the past in the Old World. As a boy I used to read the poetry of Pope, of Goldsmith, and of Johnson. How could I look at the Bodleian Library, or wander beneath its roof, without recalling the lines from " The Vanity of Human Wishes " ?

> " When first the college rolls receive his name,
>   The young enthusiast quits his ease for fame ;
>   Resistless burns the fever of renown,
>   Caught from the strong contagion of the gown :
>   O'er Bodley's dome his future labors spread,
>   And Bacon's mansion trembles o'er his head."

The last line refers to Roger Bacon. " There is a tradition that the study of Friar Bacon, built on an arch over the bridge, will fall when a man greater than Bacon shall pass under it. To prevent so shocking an accident, it was pulled down many years since." We shall meet with a similar legend in another university city. Many persons have been shy of these localities, who were in no danger whatever of meeting the fate threatened by the prediction.

We passed through the Bodleian Library, only glancing at a few of its choicest treasures, among which the exquisitely illuminated missals were especially tempting objects of study. It was almost like a mockery to see them opened and closed, without having the time to study their wonderful miniature paintings. A walk through the grounds of Magdalen College, under the guidance of the president of that college, showed us some of the fine trees for which I was always looking. One of these, a wych-elm (Scotch elm of some books), was so large that I insisted on having it measured. A string was procured and carefully carried round the trunk, above the spread of the roots and below that of the branches, so as to give the smallest circumference. I was curious to know how the size of the trunk of this tree would compare with that of the trunks of some of our largest New England elms. I have measured a good many of these. About sixteen feet is the measurement of a large elm, like that on Boston Common, which all middle-aged people remember. From twenty-two to twenty-three feet is the ordinary maximum of the very largest trees.

I never found but one exceed it: that was the great Springfield elm, which looked as if it might have been formed by the coalescence from the earliest period of growth, of two young trees. When I measured this in 1837, it was twenty-four feet eight inches in circumference at five feet from the ground; growing larger above and below. I remembered this tree well, as we measured the string which was to tell the size of its English rival. As we came near the end of the string, I felt as I did when I was looking at the last dash of Ormonde and The Bard at Epsom. — Twenty feet, and a long piece of string left. — Twenty - one. — Twenty - two. — Twenty-three. — An extra heartbeat or two. — Twenty - four! — Twenty - five and six inches over!! — The Springfield elm may have grown a foot or more since I measured it, fifty years ago, but the tree at Magdalen stands ahead of all my old measurements. Many of the fine old trees, this in particular, may have been known in their younger days to Addison, whose favorite walk is still pointed out to the visitor.

I would not try to compare the two university towns, as one might who had to choose between them. They have a noble rivalry, each honoring the other, and it would take a great deal of weighing one point of superiority against another to call either of them the first, except in its claim to antiquity.

After a garden-party in the afternoon, a pleasant evening *at home*, when the professor played and his daughter Beatrice sang, and a garden-party the next day, I found myself in somewhat better condition, and ready for the next move.

At noon on the 23d of June we left for Edinburgh, stopping over night at York, where we found close by the station an excellent hotel, and where the next morning we got one of the best breakfasts we had in our whole travelling experience. At York we wandered to and through a flower-show, and *did* the cathedral, as people *do* all the sights they see under the lead of a paid exhibitor, who goes through his lesson like a sleepy old professor. I missed seeing the slab with the inscription *miserrimus*. There may be other stones bearing this sad superlative, but there is a story connected with this one, which sounds as if it might be true.

In the year 1834, I spent several weeks in

Edinburgh. I was fascinated by the singular beauties of that "romantic town," which Scott called his own, and which holds his memory, with that of Burns, as a most precious part of its inheritance. The castle with the precipitous rocky wall out of which it grows, the deep ravines with their bridges, pleasant Calton Hill and memorable Holyrood Palace, the new town and the old town with their strange contrasts, and Arthur's Seat overlooking all, — these varied and enchanting objects account for the fondness with which all who have once seen Edinburgh will always regard it.

We were the guests of Professor Alexander Crum Brown, a near relative of the late beloved and admired Dr. John Brown. Professor and Mrs. Crum Brown did everything to make our visit a pleasant one. We met at their house many of the best known and most distinguished people of Scotland. The son of Dr. John Brown dined with us on the day of our arrival, and also a friend of the family, Mr. Barclay, to whom we made a visit on the Sunday following. Among the visits I paid, none was more gratifying to me than one which I made to Dr. John

Brown's sister. No man could leave a sweeter memory than the author of " Rab and his Friends," of " Pet Marjorie," and other writings, all full of the same loving, human spirit. I have often exchanged letters with him, and I thought how much it would have added to the enjoyment of my visit if I could have taken his warm hand and listened to his friendly voice. I brought home with me a precious little manuscript, written expressly for me by one who had known Dr. John Brown from the days of her girlhood, in which his character appears in the same lovable and loving light as that which shines in every page he himself has written.

On Friday, the 25th, I went to the hall of the university, where I was to receive the degree of LL. D. The ceremony was not unlike that at Cambridge, but had one peculiar feature: the separate special investment of the candidate with the *hood*, which Johnson defines as " an ornamental fold which hangs down the back of a graduate." There were great numbers of students present, and they showed the same exuberance of spirits as that which had forced me to withdraw from the urgent calls at Cambridge.

The cries, if possible, were still louder and more persistent; they must have a speech and they would have a speech, and what could I do about it? I saw but one way of pacifying a crowd as noisy and long-breathed as that which for about the space of two hours cried out, "Great is Diana of the Ephesians!" So I stepped to the front and made a brief speech, in which, of course, I spoke of the "*perfervidum ingenium Scotorum.*" A speech without that would have been like that "Address without a Phœnix" before referred to. My few remarks were well received, and quieted the shouting Ephesians of the warm-brained and warm-hearted northern university. It gave me great pleasure to meet my friend Mr. Underwood, now American consul in Glasgow, where he has made himself highly esteemed and respected.

In my previous visit to Edinburgh in 1834, I was fond of rambling along under Salisbury Crags, and climbing the sides of Arthur's Seat. I had neither time nor impulse for such walks during this visit, but in driving out to dine at Nidrie, the fine old place now lived in by Mr. Barclay and his daughters, we passed under the crags and by the side of the great hill. I had never heard, or if I had I had forgotten, the name and the story of " Samson's Ribs." These are the columnar masses of rock which form the face of Salisbury Crags. There is a legend that one day one of these pillars will fall and crush the greatest man that ever passes under them. It is said that a certain professor was always very shy of "Samson's Ribs," for fear the prophecy might be fulfilled in his person. We were most hospitably received at Mr. Barclay's, and the presence of his accomplished and pleasing daughters made the visit memorable to both of us. There was one picture on their walls, that of a lady, by Sir Joshua, which both of us found very captivating. This is what is often happening in the visits we make. Some painting by a master looks down upon us from its old canvas, and leaves a lasting copy of itself, to be be stored in memory's picture gallery. These surprises are not so likely to happen in the New World as in the Old.

It seemed cruel to be forced to tear ourselves away from Edinburgh, where so much had been done to make us happy, where so much was left to see and enjoy, but we were due in Oxford, where I was to receive the last of the three degrees with which I was honored in Great Britain.

Our visit to Scotland gave us a mere glimpse of the land and its people, but I have a very vivid recollection of both as I saw them on my first visit, when I made an excursion into the Highlands to Stirling and to Glasgow, where I went to church, and wondered over the uncouth ancient psalmody, which I believe is still retained in use to this day. I was seasoned to that kind of poetry in my early days by the verses of Tate and Brady, which I used to hear " entuned in the nose ful swetely," accompanied by vigorous rasping of a huge bass-viol. No wonder that Scotland welcomed the song of Burns !

On our second visit to Oxford we were to be the guests of the Vice-Chancellor of the university, Dr. Jowett. This famous scholar and administrator lives in a very pleasant establishment, presided over by the Muses, but without the aid of a Vice-Chancelloress. The hospitality of this classic mansion is well known, and we added a second pleasant chapter to our previous experience under the roof of Professor Max Müller. There was a little company there before us, including the Lord Chancellor and Lady Herschel, Lady Camilla Wallop, Mr. Browning, and Mr. Lowell. We were too late, in consequence of the bad arrangement of the trains, and had to dine by ourselves, as the whole party had gone out to a dinner, to which we should have accompanied them had we not been delayed. We sat up long enough to see them on their return, and were glad to get to bed, after our day's journey from Edinburgh to Oxford.

At eleven o'clock on the following day we who were to receive degrees met at Balliol College, whence we proceeded in solemn procession to the Sheldonian Theatre. Among my companions on this occasion were Mr. John Bright, the Lord Chancellor Herschel, and Mr. Aldis Wright. I have an instantaneous photograph, which was sent me, of this procession. I can identify Mr. Bright and myself, but hardly any of the others, though many better acquainted with their faces would no doubt recognize them.

There is a certain sensation in finding one's self invested with the academic gown, conspicuous by its red facings, and the cap with its square top and depending tassel, which is not without its accompanying satisfaction. One can walk the streets of any of the university towns in his academic robes without being jeered at, as I am afraid he would be in some of our own thoroughfares. There is a noticeable complacency in the members of our Phi Beta Kappa society when they get the pink and blue ribbons in their buttonholes, on the day of annual meeting. How much more when the scholar is wrapped in those flowing folds, with their flaming borders, and feels the dignity of the distinction of which they are the symbol! I do not know how Mr. John Bright felt, but I cannot avoid the impression that some in the ranks which moved from Balliol to the Sheldonian felt as if Solomon in all his glory was not arrayed like the candidates for the degree of D. C. L.

After my experience at Cambridge and Edinburgh, I might have felt some apprehension about my reception at Oxford. I had always supposed the audience assembled there at the conferring of degrees was a more demonstrative one than that at any other of the universities, and I did not wish to be forced into a retreat by calls for a speech, as I was at Cambridge, nor to repeat my somewhat irregular proceeding of addressing the audience, as at Edinburgh. But when I found that Mr. John Bright was to be one of the recipients of the degree I felt safe, for if he made a speech I should be justified in saying a few words, if I thought it best ; and if he, one of the most eloquent men in England, remained silent, I surely need not make myself heard on the occasion. It was a great triumph for him, a liberal leader, to receive the testimonial of a degree from the old conservative university. To myself it was a graceful and pleasing compliment ; to him it was a grave and significant tribute. As we marched through the crowd on our way from Balliol, the people standing around recognized Mr. Bright, and cheered him vociferously.

The exercises in the Sheldonian Theatre were more complex and lasted longer than those at the other two universities. The candidate stepped forward and listened to one sentence, then made another move forward and listened to other words, and at last was welcomed to all the privileges conferred by the degree of Doctor of Common Law, which was announced as being bestowed upon him. Mr. Bright, of course, was received with immense enthusiasm. I had every reason to be gratified with my own reception. The only " chaffing " I heard was the question from one of the galleries, " Did he come in the One Hoss Shay ? " — at which there was a hearty laugh, joined in as heartily by myself. A part of the entertainment at this ceremony consisted in the listening to the reading of short extracts from the prize essays, some or all of them in the dead languages, which could not have been particularly intelligible to a large part of the audience. During these readings there were frequent *interpellations*, as the French call such interruptions, something like these : " That will do, sir ! " or " You had better stop, sir ! " — always, I noticed, with the *sir* at the end of the remark. With us it would have been " Dry up ! " or " Hold on ! " At last came forward the young poet of the occasion, who read an elaborate poem, " Savonarola," which was listened to in most respectful silence, and loudly applauded at its close, as I thought, deservedly. Prince and Princess Christian were among the audience. They were staying with Professor and Mrs. Max Müller, whose hospitalities I hope they enjoyed as much as we did. One or two short extracts from A——'s diary will enliven my record : " The Princess had a huge bouquet, and going down the aisle had to bow both ways at once, it seemed to me : but then she has the Guelph spine and neck! Of course it is necessary that royalty should have more elasticity in the frame than we poor ordinary mortals. After all this we started for a luncheon at All Souls, but had to wait (impatiently) for H. R. H. to rest herself, while our resting was done standing."

It is a long while since I read Madame d'Arblay's Recollections, but if I remember right, *standing* while royalty rests its bones is one of the drawbacks to a maid of honor's felicity.

" Finally, at near three, we went into a great luncheon of some fifty. There were different tables, and I sat at the one with royalty. The Provost of Oriel took me in, and Mr. Browning was on my other side. Finally, we went home to rest, but the others started out again to go to a garden-party, but that was beyond us." After all this came a dinner-party of twenty at the Vice-Chancellor's, and after that a reception, where among others we met Lord and Lady Coleridge, the lady resplendent in jewels. Even after London, this could hardly be called a day of rest.

The Chinese have a punishment which consists simply in keeping the subject of it awake, by the constant teasing of a succession of individuals employed for the purpose. The best of our social pleasures, if carried beyond the natural power of physical and mental endurance, begin to approach the character of such a penance. After this we got a little rest; did some mild sight-seeing, heard some good music, called on the Max Müllers, and bade them good-by with the warmest feeling to all the members of a household which it was a privilege to enter. There only remained the parting from our kind entertainer, the Vice-Chancellor, who added another to the list of places which in England and Scotland were made dear to us by hospitality, and are remembered as true homes to us while we were under their roofs.

On the second day of July we left the Vice-Chancellor's, and went to the Randolph Hotel to meet our friends, Mr. and Mrs. Willett, from Brighton, with whom we had an appointment of long standing. With them we left Oxford, to enter on the next stage of our pilgrimage.

IV

IT had been the intention of Mr. Willett to go with us to visit Mr. Ruskin, with whom he is in the most friendly relations. But a letter from Mr. Ruskin's sister spoke of his illness as being too serious for him to see company, and we reluctantly gave up this part of our plan.

My first wish was to revisit Stratford-on-Avon, and as our travelling host was guided in everything by our inclinations, we took the cars for Stratford, where we arrived at five o'clock in the afternoon. It had been arranged before-hand that we should be the guests of Mr. Charles E. Flower, one of the chief citizens of Stratford, who welcomed us to his beautiful mansion in the most cordial way, and made us once more at home under an English roof.

I well remembered my visit to Stratford in 1834. The condition of the old house in which Shakespeare was born was very different from that in which we see it to-day. A series of pho-

tographs taken in different years shows its grad-
ual transformation since the time when the old
projecting angular sign-board told all who ap-
proached "The immortal Shakespeare was born
in this House." How near the old house came
to sharing the fortunes of Jumbo under the man-
agement of our enterprising countryman, Mr.
Barnum, I am not sure ; but that he would have
"traded" for it, if the proprietors had been willing, I do not doubt, any more than I doubt that
he would make an offer for the Tower of London, if that venerable structure were in the market. The house in which Shakespeare was born
is the Santa Casa of England. What with my
recollections and the photographs with which I
was familiarly acquainted, it had nothing very
new for me. Its outside had undergone great
changes, but its bare interior was little altered.

My previous visit was a hurried one, — I took
but a glimpse, and then went on my way. Now,
for nearly a week I was a resident of Stratford-
on-Avon. How shall I describe the perfectly
ideal beauty of the new home in which I found
myself! It is a fine house, surrounded by delightful grounds, which skirt the banks of the

Avon for a considerable distance, and come close up to the enclosure of the Church of the Holy Trinity, beneath the floor of which lie the mortal remains of Shakespeare. The Avon is one of those narrow English rivers in which half a dozen boats might lie side by side, but hardly wide enough for a race between two rowing abreast of each other. Just here the river is comparatively broad and quiet, there being a dam a little lower down the stream. The waters were a perfect mirror, as I saw them on one of the still days we had at Stratford. I do not remember ever before seeing cows walking with their legs in the air, as I saw them reflected in the Avon. Along the banks the young people were straying. I wondered if the youthful swains quoted Shakespeare to their lady-loves. Could they help recalling Romeo and Juliet? It is quite impossible to think of any human being growing up in this place which claims Shakespeare as its child, about the streets of which he ran as a boy, on the waters of which he must have often floated, without having his image ever present. Is it so? There are some boys, from eight to ten or a dozen years old, fish-

ing in the Avon, close by the grounds of " Avon-
bank," the place at which we are staying. I
call to the little group. I say, " Boys, who
was this man Shakespeare, people talk so much
about ? " Boys turn round and look up with a
plentiful lack of intelligence in their counte-
nances. " Don't you know who he was nor what
he was ? " Boys look at each other, but confess
ignorance. — Let us try the universal stimulant
of human faculties. " Here are some pennies
for the boy that will tell me what that Mr.
Shakespeare was." The biggest boy finds his
tongue at last. " He was a writer, — he wrote
plays." That was as much as I could get out of
the youngling. I remember meeting some boys
under the monument upon Bunker Hill, and
testing their knowledge as I did that of the
Stratford boys. " What is this great stone pillar here for ? " I asked. " Battle fought here, —
great battle." " Who fought ? " " Americans
and British." (I never hear the expression
British*ers.*) " Who was the general on the
American side ? " " Don' know, — General
Washington or somebody." — What is an old
battle, though it may have settled the destinies

of a nation, to the game of base-ball between the Boston and Chicago Nines which is to come off to-morrow, or to the game of marbles which Tom and Dick are just going to play together under the shadow of the great obelisk which commemorates the conflict?

The room more especially assigned to me looked out, at a distance of not more than a stone's-throw, on the northern aspect of the church where Shakespeare lies buried. Workmen were busy on the roof of the transept. I could not conveniently climb up to have a talk with the roofers, but I have my doubts whether they were thinking all the time of the dust over which they were working. How small a matter literature is to the great seething, toiling, struggling, love-making, bread-winning, child-rearing, death-awaiting men and women who fill this huge, palpitating world of ours! It would be worth while to pass a week or a month among the plain, average people of Stratford. What is the relative importance in human well-being of the emendations of the text of Hamlet and the patching of the old trousers and the darning of the old stockings which task the needles of the hard-working households that fight the battle of life in these narrow streets and alleys? I ask the question; the reader may answer it.

Our host, Mr. Flower, is more deeply interested, perhaps, than any other individual in the "Shakespeare Memorial" buildings which have been erected on the banks of the Avon, a short distance above the Church of the Holy Trinity. Under Mr. Flower's guidance we got into one of his boats, and were rowed up the stream to the Memorial edifice. There is a theatre, in a round tower which has borrowed some traits from the octagon "Globe" theatre of Shakespeare's day; a Shakespeare library and portrait gallery are forming; and in due time these buildings, of stately dimensions and built solidly of brick, will constitute a Shakespearean centre which will attract to itself many mementoes now scattered about in various parts of the country.

On the 4th of July we remembered our native land with all the affectionate pride of temporary exiles, and did not forget to drink at lunch to the prosperity and continued happiness of the United States of America. In the afternoon we took to the boat again, and were rowed up the river to the residence of Mr. Edgar Flower, where we found another characteristic English family, with its nine children, one of whom was the typical English boy, most pleasing and attractive in look, voice, and manner.

I attempt no description of the church, the birthplace, or the other constantly visited and often described localities. The noble bridge, built in the reign of Henry VII. by Sir Hugh Clopton, and afterwards widened, excited my admiration. It was a much finer piece of work than the one built long afterwards. I have hardly seen anything which gave me a more striking proof of the thoroughness of the old English workmen. They built not for an age, but for all time, and the New Zealander will have to wait a long while before he will find in any one of the older bridges that broken arch from which he is to survey the ruins of London.

It is very pleasant to pick up a new epithet to apply to the poet upon whose genius our language has nearly exhausted itself. It delights me to speak of him in the words which I have just found in a memoir not yet a century old, as " the Warwickshire bard," " the inestimable Shakespeare."

Ever since Miss Bacon made her insane attempt to unearth what is left of Shakespeare's bodily frame, the thought of doing reverently and openly what she would have done by stealth has been entertained by psychologists, artists, and others who would like to know what were his cranial developments, and to judge from the conformation of the skull and face which of the various portraits is probably the true one. There is little doubt that but for the curse invoked upon the person who should disturb his bones, in the well-known lines on the slab which covers him, he would rest, like Napoleon, like Washington, in a fitting receptacle of marble or porphyry. In the transfer of his remains the curiosity of men of science and, artists would have been gratified, if decay had spared the more durable portions of his material structure. It was probably not against such a transfer that the lines were written, — whoever was their author, — but in the fear that they would be carried to the charnel-house.

" In this charnel-house was contained a vast collection of human bones. How long they had been deposited there is not easily to be determined; but it is evident, from the immense quantity contained in the vault, it could have been used for no other purpose for many ages." "It is probable that from an early contemplation of this dreary spot Shakespeare imbibed that horror of a violation of sepulture which is observable in many parts of his writings."

The body of Raphael was disinterred in 1833 to settle a question of identity of the remains, and placed in a new coffin of lead, which was deposited in a marble sarcophagus presented by the Pope. The sarcophagus, with its contents, was replaced in the same spot from which the remains had been taken. But for the inscription such a transfer of the bones of Shakespeare would have been proposed, and possibly carried out. Kings and emperors have frequently been treated in this way after death, and the proposition is no more an indignity than was that of the exhumation of the remains of Napoleon, or of André, or of the author of "Home, Sweet Home." But sentiment, a tender regard for the supposed wishes of the dead poet, and a natural dread of the consequences of violating a dying wish, coupled with the execration of its contem-

ner, are too powerful for the arguments of science and the pleadings of art. If Shakespeare's
body had been embalmed, — which there is no
reason that I know of to suppose, — the desire
to compare his features with the bust and the
portraits would have been much more imperative.
When the body of Charles the First was examined, under the direction of Sir Henry Halford,
in the presence of the Regent, afterwards George
the Fourth, the face would have been recognized
at once by all who were acquainted with Vandyke's portrait of the monarch, if the lithograph
which comes attached to Sir Henry's memoir is
an accurate representation of what they found.
Even the bony framework of the face, as I have
had occasion to know, has sometimes a striking
likeness to what it was when clothed in its natural features. As between the first engraved
portrait and the bust in the church, the form of
the bones of the head and face would probably
be decisive. But the world can afford to live
without solving this doubt, and leave his perish-
ing vesture of decay to its repose.

After seeing the Shakespeare shrines, we
drove over to Shottery, and visited the Anne

Hathaway cottage. I am not sure whether I ever saw it before, but it was as familiar to me as if I had lived in it. The old lady who showed it was agreeably communicative, and in perfect keeping with the place.

A delightful excursion of ten or a dozen miles carried our party, consisting of Mr. and Mrs. Flower, Mr. and Mrs. Willett, with A—— and myself, to Compton Wynyate, a most interesting old mansion, belonging to the Marquis of Northampton, who, with his daughter-in-law, Lady William Compton, welcomed us and showed us all the wonders of the place. It was a fine morning, but hot enough for one of our American July days. The drive was through English rural scenery; that is to say, it was lovely. The old house is a great curiosity. It was built in the reign of Henry the Eighth, and has passed through many vicissitudes. The place, as well as the edifice, is a study for the antiquarian. Remains of the old moat which surrounded it are still distinguishable. The twisted and variously figured chimneys are of singular variety and exceptional forms. Compton *Wynyate* is thought to get its name from the

vineyards formerly under cultivation on the hill-
sides, which show the signs of having been laid
out in terraces. The great hall, with its gallery,
and its hangings, and the long table made from
the trunk of a single tree, carries one back into
the past centuries. There are strange nooks
and corners and passages in the old building,
and one place, a queer little " cubby-hole," has
the appearance of having been a Roman Catho-
lic chapel. I asked the master of the house,
who pointed out the curiosities of the place most
courteously, about the ghosts who of course were
tenants in common with the living proprietors.
I was surprised when he told me there were
none. It was incredible, for here was every ac-
commodation for a spiritual visitant. I should
have expected at least one haunted chamber, to
say nothing of blood-stains that could never be
got rid of; but there were no legends of the su-
pernatural or the terrible.

Refreshments were served us, among which
were some hot-house peaches, ethereally delicate
as if they had grown in the Elysian Fields and
been stolen from a banquet of angels. After
this we went out on the lawn, where, at Lady

William Compton's request, I recited one or two poems; the only time I did such a thing in England.

It seems as if Compton Wynyate must have been written about in some novel or romance, — perhaps in more than one of both. It is the place of all others to be the scene of a romantic story. It lies so hidden away among the hills that its vulgar name, according to old Camden, was "Compton in the Hole." I am not sure that it was the scene of any actual conflict, but it narrowly escaped demolition in the great civil war, and in 1646 it was garrisoned by the Parliament army.

On the afternoon of July 6th, our hosts had a large garden-party. If nothing is more trying than one of these out-of-door meetings on a cold, windy, damp day, nothing can be more delightful than such a social gathering if the place and the weather are just what we could wish them. The garden-party of this afternoon was as near perfection as such a meeting could well be. The day was bright and warm, but not uncomfortably hot, to me, at least. The company strolled about the grounds, or rested on the piazzas, or watched the birds in the aviary, or studied rudimentary humanity in the monkey, or, better still, in a charming baby, for the first time on exhibition since she made the acquaintance of sunshine. Every one could dispose of himself or herself as fancy might suggest. I broke away at one time, and wandered alone by the side of the Avon, under the shadow of the tall trees upon its bank. The whole scene was as poetical, as inspiring, as any that I remember. It would be easy to write verses about it, but unwritten poems are so much better!

One reminiscence of that afternoon claims precedence over all the rest. The reader must not forget that I have been a medical practitioner, and for thirty-five years a professor in a medical school. Among the guests whom I met in the grounds was a gentleman of the medical profession, whose name I had often heard, and whom I was very glad to see and talk with. This was Mr. Lawson Tait, F. R. C. S., M. D., of Birmingham. Mr., or more properly Dr., Tait has had the most extraordinary success in a class of cases long considered beyond the reach of surgery. If I refer to it as a scientific *hari kari*, not for the taking but for the saving of life, I shall come near enough to its description. This operation is said to have been first performed by an American surgeon in Danville, Kentucky, in the year 1809. So rash and dangerous did it seem to most of the profession that it was sometimes spoken of as if to attempt it were a crime. Gradually, however, by improved methods, and especially by the most assiduous care in nursing the patient after the operation, the mortality grew less and less, until it was recognized as a legitimate and indeed an invaluable addition to the resources of surgery. Mr. Lawson Tait has had, so far as I have been able to learn, the most wonderful series of successful cases on record: namely, one hundred and thirty-nine consecutive operations without a single death.

As I sat by the side of this great surgeon, a question suggested itself to my mind which I leave the reader to think over. Which would give the most satisfaction to a thoroughly humane and unselfish being, of cultivated intelligence and lively sensibilities: to have written all the plays which Shakespeare has left as an inheritance for mankind, or to have snatched from the jaws of death more than a hundred fellow-creatures, — almost seven scores of suffering women, — and restored them to sound and comfortable existence? It would be curious to get the answers of a hundred men and a hundred women, of a hundred young people and a hundred old ones, of a hundred scholars and a hundred operatives. My own specialty is asking questions, not answering them, and I trust I shall not receive a peck or two of letters inquiring of me how I should choose if such a question were asked me. It may prove as fertile a source of dispute as " The Lady or the Tiger."

It would have been a great thing to pass a single night close to the church where Shakespeare's dust lies buried. A single visit by daylight leaves a comparatively slight impression. But when, after a night's sleep, one wakes up and sees the spire and the old walls full before him, that impression is very greatly deepened, and the whole scene becomes far more a reality. Now I was nearly a whole week at Stratford-on-Avon. The church, its exterior, its interior, the birthplace, the river, had time to make themselves permanent images in my mind. To effect this requires a certain amount of exposure, as much as in the case of a photographic negative.

And so we bade good-by to Stratford-on-Avon and its hospitalities, with grateful remembrances of our kind entertainers and all they did for our comfort and enjoyment.

Where should we go next? Our travelling host proposed Great Malvern, a famous watering-place, where we should find peace, rest, and good accommodations. So there we went, and soon found ourselves installed at the "Foley Arms" hotel. The room I was shown to looked out upon an apothecary's shop, and from the window of that shop stared out upon me a plaster bust which I recognized as that of Samuel Hahnemann. I was glad to change to another apartment, but it may be a comfort to some of his American followers to know that traces of homœopathy, — or what still continues to call itself so, — survive in the Old World, which we have understood was pretty well tired of it.

We spent several days very pleasantly at Great Malvern. It lies at the foot of a range of hills, the loftiest of which is over a thousand feet in height. A—— and I thought we would go to the top of one of these, known as the Beacon. We hired a "four-wheeler," dragged by a much-enduring horse and in charge of a civil young man. We turned out of one of the streets not far from the hotel, and found ourselves facing an ascent which looked like what I should suppose would be a pretty steep toboggan slide. We both drew back. "Facilis *ascensus*," I said to myself, "sed revocare gradum." It is easy enough to get up if you are dragged up, but how will it be to come down such a declivity? When we reached it on our return, the semi-precipice had lost all its terrors. We had seen and travelled over so much worse places that this little bit of slanting road seemed as nothing. The road which wound up to the summit of the Beacon was narrow and uneven. It ran close to the edge of the steep hillside, — so close that there were times when every one of our forty digits curled up like a bird's claw. If we went over, it would not be a fall down a good honest precipice, — a swish through the air and a smash at the bottom, —

but a tumbling, and a rolling over and over, and a bouncing and bumping, ever accelerating, until we bounded into the level below, all ready for the coroner. At one sudden turn of the road the horse's body projected so far over its edge that A—— declared if the beast had been an inch longer he would have toppled over. When we got close to the summit we found the wind blowing almost a gale. A—— says in her diary that I (meaning her honored parent) "nearly blew off from the top of the mountain." It is true that the force of the wind was something fearful, and seeing that two young men near me were exposed to its fury, I offered an arm to each of them, which they were not too proud to accept; A—— was equally attentive to another young person; and having seen as much of the prospect as we cared to, we were glad to get back to our four-wheeler and our hotel, after a perilous journey almost comparable to Mark Twain's ascent of the Riffelberg.

At Great Malvern we were deliciously idle. We walked about the place, rested quietly, drove into the neighboring country, and made a single excursion, — to Tewkesbury. There are few places better worth seeing than this fine old

town, full of historical associations and monumental relics. The magnificent old abbey church
is the central object of interest. The noble
Norman tower, one hundred and thirty-two feet
in height, was once surmounted by a spire,
which fell during divine service on Easter Day
of the year 1559. The arch of the west entrance
is sixteen feet high and thirty-four feet wide.
The fourteen columns of the nave are each six
feet and three inches in diameter and thirty feet
in height. I did not take these measurements
from the fabric itself, but from the guide-book,
and I give them here instead of saying that the
columns were huge, enormous, colossal, as they
did most assuredly seem to me. The old houses
of Tewkesbury compare well with the finest of
those in Chester. I have a photograph before
me of one of them, in which each of the three
upper floors overhangs the one beneath it, and
the windows in the pointed gable above project
over those of the fourth floor.

I ought to have visited the site of Holme
Castle, the name of which reminds me of my
own origin. " The meaning of the Saxon word
' Holme ' is a meadow surrounded with brooks,

and here not only did the castle bear the name, but the meadow is described as the ' Holme, — where the castle was.' " The final *s* in the name as we spell it is a frequent addition to old English names, as Camden mentions, giving the name Holmes among the examples. As there is no castle at the Holme now, I need not pursue my inquiries any further. It was by accident that I stumbled on this bit of archæology, and as I have a good many namesakes, it may perhaps please some of them to be told about it. Few of us hold any castles, I think, in these days, except those *châteaux en Espagne,* of which I doubt not, many of us are lords and masters.

In another of our excursions we visited a venerable church, where our attention was called to a particular monument. It was erected to the memory of one of the best of husbands by his " wretched widow," who records upon the marble that there never was such a man on the face of the earth before, and never will be again, and that there never was anybody so miserable as she, — no, never, never, never! These are not the exact words, but this is pretty nearly what she declares. The story is that she married again within a year.

From my window at the Foley Arms I can see the tower of the fine old abbey church of Malvern, which would be a centre of pilgrimages if it were in our country. But England is full of such monumental structures, into the history of which the local antiquarians burrow, and pass their peaceful lives in studying and writing about them with the same innocent enthusiasm that White of Selborne manifested in studying nature as his village showed it to him.

In our long drives we have seen everywhere the same picturesque old cottages, with the pretty gardens, and abundant flowers, and noble trees, more frequently elms than any other. One day — it was on the 10th of July — we found ourselves driving through what seemed to be a gentleman's estate, an ample domain, well wooded and well kept. On inquiring to whom this place belonged, I was told that the owner was Sir Edmund Lechmere. The name had a very familiar sound to my ears. Without rising from the table at which I am now writing, I have only to turn my head, and in full view, at the distance of a mile, just across the estuary of the Charles, shining in the morning sun, are the

roofs and spires and chimneys of East Cambridge, always known in my younger days as
Lechmere's Point. Judge Richard Lechmere
was one of our old Cambridge Tories, whose
property was confiscated at the time of the Revolution. An engraving of his handsome house,
which stands next to the Vassall house, long
known as Washington's headquarters, and since
not less celebrated as the residence of Longfellow, is before me, on one of the pages of the
pleasing little volume, " The Cambridge of
1776." I take it for granted that our Lechmeres were of the same stock as the owner of
this property. If so, he probably knows all
that I could tell him about his colonial relatives,
who were very grand people, belonging to a
little aristocratic circle of friends and relatives
who were faithful to their king and their church.
The Baroness Riedesel, wife of a Hessian officer
who had been captured, was for a while resident
in this house, and her name, scratched on a win-
dow-pane, was long shown as a sight for eyes
unused to titles other than governor, judge,
colonel, and the like. I was tempted to present
myself at Sir Edmund's door as one who knew

something about the Lechmeres in America, but I did not feel sure how cordially a descendant of the rebels who drove off Richard and Mary Lechmere would be received.

From Great Malvern we went to Bath, another place where we could rest and be comfortable. The Grand Pump-Room Hotel was a stately building, and the bath-rooms were far beyond anything I had ever seen of that kind. The remains of the old Roman baths, which appear to have been very extensive, are partially exposed. What surprises one all over the Old World is to see how deeply all the old civilizations contrive to get buried. Everybody seems to have lived in the cellar. It is hard to believe that the cellar floor was once the sunlit surface of the smiling earth.

I looked forward to seeing Bath with a curious kind of interest. I once knew one of those dear old English ladies whom one finds all the world over, with their prim little ways, and their gilt prayer-books, and lavender-scented handkerchiefs, and family recollections. She gave me the idea that Bath, a city where the great people often congregate, was more especially the paradise of decayed gentlewomen. There, she told me, persons with very narrow incomes — not *demi-fortunes*, but *demi-quart-de-fortunes* — could find everything arranged to accommodate their modest incomes. I saw the evidence of this everywhere. So great was the delight I had in looking in at the shop-windows of the long street which seemed to be one of the chief thoroughfares that, after exploring it in its full extent by myself, I went for A——, and led her down one side its whole length and up the other. In these shops the precious old dears could buy everything they wanted in the most minute quantities. Such tempting heaps of lumps of white sugar, only twopence! Such delectable cakes, two for a penny! Such seductive scraps of meat, which would make a breakfast nourishing as well as relishing, possibly even what called itself a dinner, blushing to see themselves labelled threepence or fourpence! We did not know whether to smile or to drop a tear, as we contemplated these baits hung out to tempt the coins from the exiguous purses of ancient maidens, forlorn widows, withered annuitants, stranded humanity in every stage of shipwrecked

penury. I am reminded of Thackeray's "Jack
Spiggot." "And what are your pursuits, Jack?
says I. 'Sold out when the governor died.
Mother lives at Bath. Go down there once a
year for a week. Dreadful slow. Shilling
whist.'" Mrs. Gaskell's picture of "Cranford"
is said to have been drawn from a village in
Cheshire, but Bath must have a great deal in
common with its "elegant economies." Do not
make the mistake, however, of supposing that
this splendid watering-place, sometimes spoken
of as "the handsomest city in Britain," is only
a city of refuge for people that have seen better
days. Lord Macaulay speaks of it as "that
beautiful city which charms even eyes familiar
with the masterpieces of Bramante and Palla-
dio." If it is not quite so conspicuous as a
fashionable resort as it was in the days of Beau
Nash or of Christopher Anstey, it has never lost
its popularity. Chesterfield writes in 1764,
"The number of people in this place is infinite,"
and at the present time the annual influx of visitors is said to vary from ten to fourteen thousand. Many of its public buildings are fine,
and the abbey church, dating from 1499, is an

object of much curiosity, especially on account of the sculptures on its western façade. These represent two ladders, with angels going up and down upon them, — suggested by a dream of the founder of the church, repeating that of Jacob.

On the 14th of July we left Bath for Salisbury. While passing Westbury, one of our fellow-passengers exclaimed, " Look out ! Look out ! " " What is it ? " " The horse ! the horse ! " All our heads turned to the window, and all our eyes fastened on the figure of a white horse, upon a hillside some miles distant. This was not the white horse which Mr. Thomas Hughes has made famous, but one of much less archaic aspect and more questionable history. A little book which we bought tells us all we care to know about it. " It is formed by excoriating the turf over the steep slope of the northern escarpment of Salisbury Plain." It was " remodelled " in 1778, and " restored " in 1873 at a cost of between sixty and seventy pounds. It is said that a smaller and ruder horse stood here from time immemorial, and was made to commemorate a victory of Alfred over the Danes. However that may be, the horse we now see on the hillside is a very modern-looking and well-shaped animal, and is of the following dimensions : length, 170 feet ; height from highest part of back, 128 feet ; thickness of body, 55 feet ; length of head, 50 feet ; eye, 6 by 8 feet. It is a very pretty little object as we see it in the distance.

Salisbury Cathedral was my first love among all the wonderful ecclesiastical buildings which I saw during my earlier journey. I looked forward to seeing it again with great anticipations of pleasure, which were more than realized.

Our travelling host had taken a whole house in the Close, — a privileged enclosure, containing the cathedral, the bishop's palace, houses of the clergy, and a limited number of private residences, one of the very best of which was given over entirely into the hands of our party during our visit. The house was about as near the cathedral as Mr. Flower's house, where we stayed at Stratford-on-Avon, was to the Church of the Holy Trinity. It was very completely furnished, and in the room assigned to me as my library I found books in various languages, showing that the residence was that of a scholarly person.

If one had to name the apple of the eye of England, I think he would be likely to say that Salisbury Cathedral was as near as he could come to it, and that the white of the eye was Salisbury Close. The cathedral is surrounded by a high wall, the gates of which, — its eyelids, — are closed every night at a seasonable hour, at which the virtuous inhabitants are expected to be in their safe and sacred quarters. Houses within this hallowed precinct naturally bring a higher rent than those of the unsanctified and unprotected region outside of its walls. It is a realm of peace, glorified by the divine edifice, which lifts the least imaginative soul upward to the heavens its spire seems trying to reach; beautified by rows of noble elms which stretch high aloft, as if in emulation of the spire; beatified by holy memories of the good and great men who have worn their lives out in the service of the church of which it is one of the noblest temples.

For a whole week we lived under the shadow of the spire of the great cathedral. *Our* house was opposite the north transept, only separated by the road in front of it from the cathedral grounds. Here, as at Stratford, I learned what it was to awake morning after morning and find that I was not dreaming, but there in the truth-telling daylight the object of my admiration, devotion, almost worship, stood before me. I need not here say anything more of the cathedral, except that its perfect exterior is hardly equalled in beauty by its interior, which looks somewhat bare and cold. It was my impression that there is more to study than to admire in the interior, but I saw the cathedral so much oftener on the outside than on the inside that I may not have done justice to the latter aspect of the noble building.

Nothing could be more restful than our week at Salisbury. There was enough in the old town besides the cathedral to interest us, — old buildings, a museum full of curious objects, and the old town itself. When I was there the first time, I remember that we picked up a guide-book in which we found a verse that has remained in my memory ever since. It is an epitaph on a native of Salisbury who died in Venice.

"Born in the English Venice, thou didst dye
    Dear Friend, in the Italian Salisbury."

This would be hard to understand except for the explanation which the local antiquarians give us of its significance. The Wiltshire Avon flows by or through the town, which is drained by brooks that run through its streets. These, which used to be open, are now covered over, and thus the epitaph becomes somewhat puzzling, as there is nothing to remind one of Venice in walking about the town.

While at Salisbury we made several excursions: to Old Sarum ; to Bemerton, where we saw the residence of holy George Herbert, and visited the little atom of a church in which he ministered; to Clarendon Park; to Wilton, the seat of the Earl of Pembroke, a most interesting place for itself and its recollections; and lastly to Stonehenge. My second visit to the great stones after so long an interval was a strange experience. But what is half a century to a place like Stonehenge? Nothing dwarfs an individual life like one of these massive, almost unchanging monuments of an antiquity which refuses to be measured. The " Shepherd of Salisbury Plain " was represented by an old man, who told all he knew and a good deal more about the great stones, and sheared a living, not from sheep, but from visitors, in the shape of shillings and sixpences. I saw nothing that wore unwoven wool on its back in the neighborhood of the monuments, but sheep are shown straggling among them in the photographs.

The broken circle of stones, some in their original position, some bending over like old men, some lying prostrate, suggested the thoughts which took form in the following verses. They were read at the annual meeting, in January, of the class which graduated at Harvard College in the year 1829. Eight of the fifty-nine men who graduated sat round the small table. There were several other classmates living, but infirmity, distance, and other peremptory reasons kept them from being with us. I have read forty poems at our successive annual meetings. I will introduce this last one by quoting a stanza from the poem I read in 1851 : —

> As one by one is falling
> Beneath the leaves or snows,

Each memory still recalling
　　The broken ring shall close,
Till the night winds softly pass
　　O'er the green and growing grass,
Where it waves on the graves
　　Of the "Boys of 'Twenty-nine."

THE BROKEN CIRCLE.

I stood on Sarum's treeless plain,
　　The waste that careless Nature owns;
Lone tenants of her bleak domain,
　　Loomed huge and gray the Druid stones.

Upheaved in many a billowy mound
　　The sea-like, naked turf arose,
Where wandering flocks went nibbling round
　　The mingled graves of friends and foes.

The Briton, Roman, Saxon, Dane,
　　This windy desert roamed in turn;
Unmoved these mighty blocks remain
　　Whose story none that lives may learn.

Erect, half buried, slant or prone,
　　These awful listeners, blind and dumb,
Hear the strange tongues of tribes unknown,
　　As wave on wave they go and come.

"Who are you, giants, whence and why?"
　　I stand and ask in blank amaze;

My soul accepts their mute reply :
    "A mystery, as are you that gaze.

"A silent Orpheus wrought the charm
    From riven rocks their spoils to bring;
A nameless Titan lent his arm
    To range us in our magic ring.

"But Time with still and stealthy stride,
    That climbs and treads and levels all,
That bids the loosening keystone slide,
    And topples down the crumbling wall, —

"Time, that unbuilds the quarried past,
    Leans on these wrecks that press the sod ;
They slant, they stoop, they fall at last,
    And strew the turf their priests have trod.

"No more our altar's wreath of smoke
    Floats up with morning's fragrant dew;
The fires are dead, the ring is broke,
    Where stood the many stand the few."

— My thoughts had wandered far away,
    Borne off on Memory's outspread wing,
To where in deepening twilight lay
    The wrecks of friendship's broken ring.

Ah me ! of all our goodly train
    How few will find our banquet hall !
Yet why with coward lips complain
    That this must lean and that must fall ?

Cold is the Druid's altar-stone,
　　Its vanished flame no more returns;
But ours no chilling damp has known, —
　　Unchanged, unchanging, still it burns.

So let our broken circle stand
　　A wreck, a remnant, yet the same,
While one last, loving, faithful hand
　　Still lives to feed its altar-flame!

My heart has gone back over the waters to my old friends and my own home. When this vision has faded, I will return to the silence of the lovely Close and the shadow of the great Cathedral.

V.

THE remembrance of home, with its early and precious and long-enduring friendships, has intruded itself among my recollections of what I saw and heard, of what I felt and thought, in the distant land I was visiting. I must return to the scene where I found myself when the suggestion of the broken circle ran away with my imagination.

The literature of Stonehenge is extensive, and illustrates the weakness of archæologists almost as well as the " Prætorium " of Scott's " Antiquary." " In 1823," says a local handbook, " H. Browne, of Amesbury, published ' An Illustration of Stonehenge and Abury,' in which he endeavored to show that both of these monuments were antediluvian, and that the latter was formed under the direction of Adam. He ascribes the present dilapidated condition of Stonehenge to the operation of the general deluge ; for, he adds, ' to suppose it to be the work of any people since the flood is entirely monstrous.'"

We know well enough how great stones,— pillars and obelisks, — are brought into place by means of our modern appliances. But if the great blocks were raised by a mob of naked Picts, or any tribe that knew none of the mechanical powers but the lever, how did they set them up and lay the cross-stones, the imposts, upon the uprights? It is pleasant, once in a while, to think how we should have managed any such matters as this if left to our natural resources. We are all interested in the make-shifts of Robinson Crusoe. Now the rudest tribes make cords of some kind, and the earliest, or almost the earliest, of artificial structures is an earth-mound. If a hundred, or hundreds, of men could drag the huge stones many leagues, as they must have done to bring them to their destined place, they could have drawn each of them up a long slanting mound ending in a sharp declivity, with a hole for the foot of the stone at its base. If the stone were now tipped over, it would slide into its place, and could be easily raised from its slanting position to the perpendicular. Then filling in the space between the mound and two contiguous stones, the impost could be dragged up to its position. I found a pleasure in working at this simple mechanical problem, as a change from the more imaginative thoughts suggested by the mysterious monuments.

One incident of our excursion to Stonehenge had a significance for me which renders it memorable in my personal experience. As we drove over the barren plain, one of the party suddenly exclaimed, "Look! Look! See the lark rising!" I looked up with the rest. There was the bright blue sky, but not a speck upon it which my eyes could distinguish. Again, one called out, "Hark! Hark! Hear him singing!" I listened, but not a sound reached my ear. Was it strange that I felt a momentary pang? *Those that look out at the windows are darkened, and all the daughters of music are brought low.* Was I never to see or hear the soaring songster at Heaven's gate, — unless, — unless, — if our mild humanized theology promises truly, I may perhaps hereafter listen to him singing far down beneath me? For in whatever world I may find myself, I hope I shall always love our poor little spheroid, so long my home, which some kind angel may point out to me as a gilded globule swimming in the sunlight far away. After walking the streets of pure gold in the New Jerusalem, might not one like a short vacation, to visit the well-remembered green fields and flowery meadows? I had a very sweet emotion of self-pity, which took the sting out of my painful discovery that the orchestra of my pleasing life-entertainment was unstringing its instruments, and the lights were being extinguished, — that the show was almost over. All this I kept to myself, of course, except so far as I whispered it to the unseen presence which we all feel is in sympathy with us, and which, as it seemed to my fancy, was looking into my eyes, and through them into my soul, with the tender, tearful smile of a mother who for the first time gently presses back the longing lips of her as yet unweaned infant.

On our way back from Stonehenge we stopped and took a cup of tea with a friend of our host, Mr. Nightingale. His house, a bachelor establishment, was very attractive to us by the beauty within and around it. His collection of "china," as Pope and old-fashioned people call all sorts of earthenware, excited the enthusiasm of our host, whose admiration of some rare pieces in the collection was so great that it would have run into envy in a less generous nature.

It is very delightful to find one's self in one of these English country residences. The house is commonly old, and has a history. It is oftentimes itself a record, like that old farmhouse my friend John Bellows wrote to me about, which chronicled half a dozen reigns by various architectural marks as exactly as if it had been an official register. "The stately homes of England," as we see them at Wilton and Longford Castle, are not more admirable in their splendors than "the blessed homes of England" in their modest beauty. Everywhere one may see here old parsonages by the side of ivy-mantled churches, and the comfortable mansions where generations of country squires have lived in peace, while their sons have gone forth to fight England's battles, and carry her flags of war and commerce all over the world. We in America can hardly be said to have such a possession as a family home. We encamp, — not under canvas, but in fabrics of wood or more lasting materials, which are pulled down after a brief occupancy by the builders, and possibly their children, or are modernized so that the former dwellers in them would never recognize their old habitations.

In my various excursions from Salisbury I was followed everywhere by the all-pervading presence of the towering spire. Just what it was in that earlier visit, when my eyes were undimmed and my sensibilities unworn, just such I found it now. As one drives away from the town, the roofs of the houses drop out of the landscape, the lesser spires disappear one by one, until the great shaft is left standing alone, — solitary as the broken statue of Ozymandias in the desert, as the mast of some mighty ship above the waves which have rolled over the foundering vessel. Most persons will, I think, own to a feeling of awe in looking up at it. Few can look down from a great height without creepings and crispations, if they do not get as far as vertigos and that aerial calenture which prompts them to jump from the pinnacle on which they are standing. It does not take much imagination to make one experience something of the same feeling in looking up at a very tall steeple or chimney. To one whose eyes are used to Park Street and the Old South steeples as standards of height, a spire which climbs four hundred feet towards the sky is a new sensation. Whether I am more " afraid of that which is high " than I was at my first visit, as I should be on the authority of Ecclesiastes, I cannot say, but it was quite enough for me to let my eyes climb the spire, and I had no desire whatever to stand upon that " bad eminence," as I am sure that I should have found it.

I soon noticed a slight deflection from the perpendicular at the upper part of the spire. This has long been observed. I could not say that I saw the spire quivering in the wind, as I felt that of Strasburg doing when I ascended it, — swaying like a blade of grass when a breath of air passes over it. But it has been, for at least two hundred years, nearly two feet out of the perpendicular. No increase in the deviation was found to exist when it was examined early in the present century. It is a wonder that this slight-looking structure can have survived the blasts, and thunderbolts, and earthquakes, and the weakening effects of time on its stones and timbers for five hundred years. Since the spire of Chichester Cathedral fell in 1861, sheathing itself in its tower like a sword dropping into its scabbard, one can hardly help looking with apprehension at all these lofty fabrics. I have before referred to the fall of the spire of Tewkesbury Abbey church, three centuries earlier. There has been a good deal of fear for the Salisbury spire, and great precautions have been taken to keep it firm, so that we may hope it will stand for another five hundred years. It ought to be a "joy forever," for it is a thing of beauty, if ever there were one.

I never felt inclined to play the part of the young enthusiast in "Excelsior," as I looked up at the weathercock which surmounts the spire. But the man who oils the weathercock-spindle has to get up to it in some way, and that way is by ladders which reach to within thirty feet of the top, where there is a small door, through which he emerges, to crawl up the remaining distance on the outside. "The situation and appearance," says one of the guide-books, "must be terrific, yet many persons have voluntarily and daringly clambered to the top, even in a state of intoxication." Such, I feel sure, was not the state of my most valued and exemplary clerical friend, who, with a cool head and steady nerves, found himself standing in safety at the top of the spire, with his hand upon the vane, which nothing terrestrial had ever looked down upon in its lofty position, except a bird, a bat, a sky-rocket, or a balloon.

In saying that the exterior of Salisbury Cathedral is more interesting than its interior, I was perhaps unfair to the latter, which only yields to the surpassing claims of the wonderful structure as seen from the outside. One may get a little tired of marble Crusaders, with their crossed legs and broken noses, especially if, as one sometimes finds them, they are covered with the pencilled autographs of cockney scribblers. But there are monuments in this cathedral which excite curiosity, and others which awaken the most striking associations. There is the "Boy Bishop," his marble effigy protected from vandalism by an iron cage. There is the skeleton figure representing Fox (who should have been called Goose), the poor creature who starved himself to death in trying to imitate the fast of forty days in the wilderness. Since this performance has been taken out of the list of miracles, it is not so likely to be repeated by fanatics. I confess to a strong suspicion that this is one of the ambulatory or movable stories, like the "hangman's stone" legend, which I have found in so many different parts of England. Skulls and crossbones, sometimes skeletons or skeleton-like figures, are not uncommon among the sepulchral embellishments of an earlier period. Where one of these figures is found, the forty-day-fast story is likely to grow out of it, as the mistletoe springs from the oak or apple tree.

With far different emotions we look upon the spot where lie buried many of the Herbert family, among the rest,

"Sidney's sister, Pembroke's mother,"

for whom Ben Jonson wrote the celebrated epitaph. I am almost afraid to say it, but I never could admire the line,

"Lies the subject of all verse,"

nor the idea of Time dropping his hour-glass and scythe to throw a dart at the fleshless figure of Death. This last image seems to me about the equivalent in mortuary poetry of Roubiliac's monument to Mrs. Nightingale in mortuary sculpture, — poor conceits both of them, without the suggestion of a tear in the verses or in the marble ; but the rhetorical exaggeration does not prevent us from feeling that we are standing by the resting-place of one who was

> "learn'd and fair and good"

enough to stir the soul of stalwart Ben Jonson, and the names of Sidney and Herbert make us forget the strange hyperboles.

History meets us everywhere, as we stray among these ancient monuments. Under that effigy lie the great bones of Sir John Cheyne, a mighty man of war, said to have been "over-thrown" by Richard the Third at the battle of Bosworth Field. What was left of him was un-earthed in 1789 in the demolition of the Beau-champ chapel, and his thigh-bone was found to be four inches longer than that of a man of common stature.

The reader may remember how my recollections started from their hiding-place when I came, in one of our excursions, upon the name of Lechmere, as belonging to the owner of a fine estate by or through which we were driving. I had a similar twinge of reminiscence at meeting with the name of Gorges, which is perpetuated by a stately monument at the end of the north aisle of the cathedral. Sir Thomas Gorges, Knight of Longford Castle, may or may not have been of the same family as the well-remembered grandiose personage of the New England Pilgrim period. The title this gentleman bore had a far more magnificent sound than those of his contemporaries, Governor Carver and Elder Brewster. No title ever borne among us has filled the mouth quite so full as that of " Sir Ferdinando Gorges, Lord Palatine of the Province of Maine," a province with " Gorgeana " (late the plantation of Agamenticus) as its capital. Everywhere in England a New Englander is constantly meeting with names of families and places which remind him that he comes of a graft from an old tree on a new stock. I could not keep down the associations called up by the name of Gorges. There is a

certain pleasure in now and then sprinkling our
prosaic colonial history with the holy water of a
high-sounding title; not that a "Sir" before a
man's name makes him any better, — for are
we not all equal, and more than equal, to each
other? — but it sounds pleasantly. Sir Harry
Vane and Sir Harry Frankland look prettily on
the printed page, as the illuminated capital at
the head of a chapter in an old folio pleases
the eye of the reader. Sir Thomas Gorges was
the builder of Longford Castle, now the seat of
the Earl of Radnor, whose family name is Bou-
verie. Whether our Sir Ferdinando was of the
Longford Castle stock or not I must leave to
my associates of the Massachusetts Historical
Society to determine.

We lived very quietly at our temporary home
in Salisbury Close. A pleasant dinner with the
Dean, a stroll through the grounds of the episcopal palace, with that perpetual feast of the
eyes which the cathedral offered us, made our
residence delightful at the time, and keeps it so
in remembrance. Besides the cathedral there
were the very lovely cloisters, the noble chapter-
house with its central pillar, — this structure

has been restored and rejuvenated since my earlier visit, — and there were the peaceful dwellings, where I insist on believing that only virtue and happiness are ever tenants. Even outside the sacred enclosure there is a great deal to enjoy, in the ancient town of Salisbury. One may rest under the Poultry Cross, where twenty or thirty generations have rested before him. One may purchase his china at the well-furnished establishment of the tenant of a spacious apartment of ancient date, — " the Halle of John Halle," a fine private edifice built in the year 1470, restored and beautified in 1834 ; the emblazonment of the royal arms having been executed by the celebrated architectural artist Pugin. The old houses are numerous, and some of them eminently picturesque.

Salisbury was formerly very unhealthy, on account of the low, swampy nature of its grounds. The Sanitary Reform, dating from about thirty years ago, had a great effect on the condition of the place. Before the drainage the annual mortality was twenty-seven in the thousand ; since the drainage twenty in the thousand, which is below that of Boston. In the Close, which is a little Garden of Eden, with no serpent in it that I could hear of, the deaths were only fourteen in a thousand. Happy little enclosure, where thieves cannot break through and steal, where Death himself hesitates to enter, and makes a visit only now and then at long intervals, lest the fortunate inhabitants should think they had already reached the Celestial City !

It must have been a pretty bitter quarrel that drove the tenants of the airy height of Old Sarum to remove to the marshy level of the present site of the cathedral and the town. I wish we could have given more time to the ancient fortress and cathedral town. This is one of the most interesting historic localities of Great Britain. We looked from different points of view at the mounds and trenches which marked it as a strongly fortified position. For many centuries it played an important part in the history of England. At length, however, the jealousies of the laity and the clergy, a squabble like that of "town and gown," but with graver underlying causes, broke up the harmony and practically ended the existence of the place except as a monument of the past. It

seems a pity that the headquarters of the Prince
of Peace could not have managed to maintain
tranquillity within its own borders. But so it
was; and the consequence followed that Old
Sarum, with all its grand recollections, is but a
collection of mounds and hollows, — as much a
tomb of its past as Birs Nimroud of that great
city, Nineveh. Old Sarum is now best remembered by its long-surviving privilege, as a bo-
rough, of sending two members to Parliament.
The farcical ceremony of electing two representatives who had no real constituency behind them
was put an end to by the Reform Act of 1832.

Wilton, the seat of the Earl of Pembroke,
within an easy drive's distance from Salisbury,
was the first nobleman's residence I saw in my
early visit. Not a great deal of what I then
saw had survived in my memory. I recall the
general effect of the stately mansion and its
grounds. A picture or two of Vandyke's had
not quite faded out of my recollection. I could
not forget the armor of Anne de Montmorenci,
— not another Maid of Orleans, but Constable
of France, — said to have been taken in battle
by an ancestor of the Herberts. It was one of

the first things that made me feel I was in the Old World. Miles Standish's sword was as far back as New England collections of armor carried us at that day. The remarkable gallery of ancient sculptures impressed me at the time, but no one bust or statue survived as a distinct image. Even the beautiful Palladian bridge had not pictured itself on my mental tablet as it should have done, and I could not have taken my oath that I had seen it. But the pretty English maidens whom we met on the day of our visit to Wilton, — daughters or granddaughters of a famous inventor and engineer, — still lingered as vague and pleasing visions, so lovely had they seemed among the daisies and primroses. The primroses and daisies were as fresh in the spring of 1886 as they were in the spring of 1833, but I hardly dared to ask after the blooming maidens of that early period.

One memory predominates over all others, in walking through the halls, or still more in wandering through the grounds, of Wilton House. Here Sir Philip Sidney wrote his " Arcadia," and the ever youthful presence of the man himself rather than the recollection of his writings takes possession of us. There are three young men in history whose names always present themselves to me in a special companionship: Pico della Mirandola, " the Phœnix of the Age " for his contemporaries; " the Admirable Crichton," accepting as true the accounts which have come down to us of his wonderful accomplishments; and Sidney, the Bayard of England, " that glorious star, that lively pattern of virtue and the lovely joy of all the learned sort, . . . born into the world to show unto our age a sample of ancient virtue." The English paragon of excellence was but thirty-two years old when he was slain at Zutphen, the Italian Phœnix but thirty-one when he was carried off by a fever, and the Scotch prodigy of gifts and attainments was only twenty-two when he was assassinated by his worthless pupil. Sir Philip Sidney is better remembered by the draught of water he gave the dying soldier than by all the waters he ever drew from the fountain of the Muses, considerable as are the merits of his prose and verse. But here, where he came to cool his fiery spirit after the bitter insult he had received from the Earl of Leicester; here, where he mused and wrote, and

shaped his lofty plans for a glorious future, he
lives once more in our imagination, as if his
spirit haunted the English Arcadia he loved so
dearly.

The name of Herbert, which we have met
with in the cathedral, and which belongs to the
Earls of Pembroke, presents itself to us once
more in a very different and very beautiful
aspect. Between Salisbury and Wilton, three
miles and a half distant, is the little village of
Bemerton, where "holy George Herbert" lived
and died, and where he lies buried. Many
Americans who know little else of him recall
the lines borrowed from him by Irving in the
"Sketch-Book" and by Emerson in "Nature."
The "Sketch-Book" gives the lines thus : —

> "Sweet day, so pure, so calm, so bright,
> The bridal of the earth and sky."

In other versions the fourth word is *cool* instead
of *pure*, and *cool* is, I believe, the correct reading. The day when we visited Bemerton was,
according to A——'s diary, "perfect." I was
struck with the calm beauty of the scene around
us, the fresh greenness of all growing things,
and the stillness of the river which mirrored the

heavens above it. It must have been this re-
flection which the poet was thinking of when he
spoke of the bridal of the earth and sky. The
river is the Wiltshire Avon; not Shakespeare's
Avon, but the southern stream of the same
name, which empties into the British Channel.

So much of George Herbert's intellectual and
moral character repeat themselves in Emerson
that if I believed in metempsychosis I should
think that the English saint had reappeared in
the American philosopher. Their features have
a certain resemblance, but the type, though an
exceptional and fine one, is not so very rare. I
found a portrait in the National Gallery which
was a good specimen of it; the bust of a near
friend of his, more intimate with him than almost any other person, is often taken for that of
Emerson. I see something of it in the portrait
of Sir Philip Sidney, and I doubt not that traces
of a similar mental resemblance ran through
the whole group, with individual characteristics
which were in some respects quite different. I
will take a single verse of Herbert's from Emerson's "Nature," — one of the five which he
quotes : —

> " Nothing hath got so far
> But man hath caught and kept it as his prey ;
>   His eyes dismount the highest star :
>   He is in little all the sphere.
> Herbs gladly cure our flesh because that they
>   Find their acquaintance there."

Emerson himself fully recognizes his obligations to " the beautiful psalmist of the seventeenth century," as he calls George Herbert. There are many passages in his writings which sound as if they were paraphrases from the elder poet. From him it is that Emerson gets a word he is fond of, and of which his imitators are too fond : —

> " Who sweeps a room as for thy laws
>   Makes that and the action *fine.*"

The little chapel in which Herbert officiated is perhaps half as long again as the room in which I am writing, but it is four or five feet narrower, — and I do not live in a palace. Here this humble servant of God preached and prayed, and here by his faithful and loving service he so endeared himself to all around him that he has been canonized by an epithet no other saint of the English Church has had bestowed upon him. His life as pictured by Izaak Walton is, to borrow one of his own lines,

" A box where sweets compacted lie ; "

and I felt, as I left his little chapel and the parsonage which he rebuilt as a free-will offering, as a pilgrim might feel who had just left the holy places at Jerusalem.

Among the places which I saw in my first visit was Longford Castle, the seat of the Earl of Radnor. I remembered the curious triangular building, constructed with reference to the doctrine of the Trinity, as churches are built in the form of the cross. I remembered how the omnipresent spire of the great cathedral, three miles away, looked down upon the grounds about the building as if it had been their next-door neighbor. I had not forgotten the two celebrated Claudes, Morning and Evening. My eyes were drawn to the first of these two pictures when I was here before ; now they turned naturally to the landscape with the setting sun. I have read my St. Ruskin with due reverence, but I have never given up my allegiance to Claude Lorraine. But of all the fine paintings at Longford Castle, no one so much impressed me at my recent visit as the portrait of Erasmus by Hans Holbein. This is one of those pictures which help to make the Old World worth a voyage across the Atlantic. Portraits of Erasmus are not uncommon; every scholar would know him if he met him in the other world with the look he wore on earth. All the etchings and their copies give a characteristic presentation of the spiritual precursor of Luther, who pricked the false image with his rapier which the sturdy monk slashed with his broadsword. What a face it is which Hans Holbein has handed down to us in this wonderful portrait at Longford Castle! How dry it is with scholastic labor, how keen with shrewd scepticism, how worldly-wise, how conscious of its owner's wide-awake sagacity! Erasmus and Rabelais, — Nature used up all her arrows for their quivers, and had to wait a hundred years and more before she could find shafts enough for the outfit of Voltaire, leaner and keener than Erasmus, and almost as free in his language as the audacious creator of Gargantua and Pantagruel.

I have not generally given descriptions of the curious objects which I saw in the great houses and museums which I visited. There is, however, a work of art at Longford Castle so remark-

able that I must speak of it. I was so much
struck by the enormous amount of skilful ingenuity and exquisite workmanship bestowed upon
it that I looked up its history, which I found in
the " Beauties of England and Wales." ' This
is what is there said of the wonderful steel chair:
" It was made by Thomas Rukers at the city of
Augsburgh, in the year 1575, and consists of
more than 130 compartments, all occupied by
groups of figures representing a succession of
events in the annals of the Roman Empire, from
the landing of Æneas to the reign of Rodolphus
the Second." It looks as if a life had gone into
the making of it, as a pair or two of eyes go to
the working of the bridal veil of an empress.

Fifty years ago and more, when I was at
Longford Castle with my two companions, who
are no more with us, we found there a pleasant,
motherly old housekeeper, or attendant of some
kind, who gave us a draught of home-made ale
and left a cheerful remembrance with us, as, I
need hardly say, we did with her, in a material-
ized expression of our good-will. It always
rubbed very hard on my feelings to offer money
to any persons who had served me well, as if they

were doing it for their own pleasure. It may
have been the granddaughter of the kindly old
matron of the year 1833 who showed us round,
and possibly, if I had sunk a shaft of inquiry,
I might have struck a well of sentiment. But

"Take, O boatman, thrice thy fee,"

carried into practical life, is certain in its finan-
cial result to the subject of the emotional impulse, but is less sure to call forth a tender
feeling in the recipient. One will hardly find it
worth while to go through the world weeping
over his old recollections, and paying gold instead of silver and silver instead of copper to
astonished boatmen and bewildered chamber-
maids.

On Sunday, the 18th of July, we attended
morning service at the cathedral. The congregation was not proportioned to the size of the
great edifice. These vast places of worship
were built for ages when faith was the rule and
questioning the exception. I will not say that
faith has grown cold, but it has cooled from
white heat to cherry red or a still less flaming
color. As to church attendance, I have heard
the saying attributed to a great statesman, that

"once a day is Orthodox, but twice a day is Puritan." No doubt many of the same class of people that used to fill the churches stay at home and read about evolution or telepathy, or whatever new gospel they may have got hold of. Still the English seem to me a religious people ; they have leisure enough to say grace and give thanks before and after meals, and their institutions tend to keep alive the feelings of reverence which cannot be said to be distinctive of our own people.

In coming out of the cathedral, on the Sunday I just mentioned, a gentleman addressed me as a fellow-countryman. There is something, — I will not stop now to try and define it, — but there is something by which we recognize an American among the English before he speaks and betrays his origin. Our new friend proved to be the president of one of our American colleges ; an intelligent and well-instructed gentleman, of course. By the invitation of our host he came in to visit us in the evening, and made himself very welcome by his agreeable conversation.

I took great delight in wandering about the

old town of Salisbury. There are no such surprises in our oldest places as one finds in Chester, or Tewkesbury, or Stratford, or Salisbury,
and I have no doubt in scores or hundreds of
similar places which I have never visited. The
best substitute for such rambles as one can take
through these mouldy boroughs (or burrows) is
to be found in such towns as Salem, Newbury-
port, Portsmouth. Without imagination, Shakespeare's birthplace is but a queer old house, and
Anne Hathaway's home a tumble-down cottage.
With it, one can see the witches of Salem Village sailing out of those little square windows,
which look as if they were made on purpose for
them, or stroll down to Derby's wharf and gaze
at "Cleopatra's Barge," precursor of the yachts
of the Astors and Goulds and Vanderbilts, as
she comes swimming into the harbor in all her
gilded glory. But it must make a difference
what the imagination has to work upon, and I
do not at all wonder that Mr. Ruskin would not
wish to live in a land where there are no old
ruins of castles and monasteries. Man will not
live on bread only; he wants a great deal more,
if he can get it, — frosted cake as well as corn-

bread ; and the New World keeps the imagination on plain and scanty diet, compared to
the rich traditional and historic food which fur-
nishes the banquets of the Old World.

What memories that week in Salisbury and
the excursions from it have left in my mind's
picture gallery ! The spire of the great cathedral had been with me as a frequent presence
during the last fifty years of my life, and this
second visit has deepened every line of the impression, as Old Mortality refreshed the inscrip-
tions on the tombstones of the Covenanters. I
find that all these pictures which I have brought
home with me to look at, with

> " that inward eye
> Which is the bliss of solitude,"

are becoming clearer and brighter as the excitement of overcrowded days and weeks gradually
calms down. I can *be* in those places where I
passed days and nights, and became habituated
to the sight of the cathedral, or of the Church
of the Holy Trinity, at morning, at noon, at
evening, whenever I turned my eyes in its direction. I often close my eyelids, and startle my
household by saying, " Now I am in Salisbury,"

or " Now I am in Stratford." It is a blessed thing to be able, in the twilight of years, to illuminate the soul with such visions. The Charles, which flows beneath my windows, which I look upon between the words of the sentence I am now writing, only turning my head as I sit at my table, — the Charles is hardly more real to me than Shakespeare's Avon, since I floated on its still waters, or strayed along its banks and saw the cows reflected in the smooth expanse, their legs upward, as if they were walking the skies as the flies walk the ceiling. Salisbury Cathedral stands as substantial in my thought as our own King's Chapel, since I slumbered by its side, and arose in the morning to find it still there, and not one of those unsubstantial fabrics built by the architect of dreams.

On Thursday, the 22d of July, we left Salisbury for Brighton, where we were to be guests at Arnold House, the residence of our kind host. Here we passed another delightful week, with everything around us to contribute to our quiet comfort and happiness. The most thoughtful of entertainers, a house filled with choice works of art, fine paintings, and wonderful pottery, pleasant walks and drives, a visitor now and then, Mr. and Mrs. Goldwin Smith among the number, rest and peace in a magnificent city built for enjoyment, — what more could we have asked to make our visit memorable? Many watering-places look forlorn and desolate in the intervals of "the season." This was not the time of Brighton's influx of visitors, but the city was far from dull. The houses are very large, and have the grand air, as if meant for princes; the shops are well supplied; the salt breeze comes in fresh and wholesome, and the noble esplanade is lively with promenaders and Bath chairs, some of them occupied by people evidently ill or presumably lame, some, I suspect, employed by healthy invalids who are too lazy to walk. I took one myself, drawn by an old man, to see how I liked it, and found it very convenient, but I was tempted to ask him to change places and let me drag him.

With the aid of the guide-book I could describe the wonders of the pavilion and the various changes which have come over the great watering-place. The grand walks, the two piers, the aquarium, and all the great sights which are shown to strangers deserve full attention from the tourist who writes for other travellers, but none of these things seem to me so interesting as what we saw and heard in a little hamlet which has never, so far as I know, been vulgarized by sight-seers. We drove in an open carriage, — Mr. and Mrs. Willett, A——, and myself, — into the country, which soon became bare, sparsely settled, a long succession of rounded hills and hollows. These are the South Downs, from which comes the famous mutton known all over England, not unknown at the table of our Saturday Club and other well-spread boards. After a drive of ten miles or more we arrived at a little "settlement," as we Americans should call it, and drove up to the door of a modest parsonage, where dwells the shepherd of the South Down flock of Christian worshippers. I hope that the good clergyman, if he ever happens to see what I am writing, will pardon me for making mention of his hidden retreat, which he himself speaks of as "one of the remoter nooks of the old country." Nothing I saw in England brought to my mind Goldsmith's picture of "the man to all the country dear," and his surroundings, like this visit. The church dates, if I remember right, from the thirteenth century. Some of its stones show marks, as it is thought, of having belonged to a Saxon edifice. The massive leaden font is of a very great antiquity. In the wall of the church is a narrow opening, at which the priest is supposed to have sat and listened to the confession of the sinner on the outside of the building. The dead lie all around the church, under stones bearing the dates of several centuries. One epitaph, which the unlettered Muse must have dictated, is worth recording. After giving the chief slumberer's name the epitaph adds, —

"Here lies on either side, the remains of each of his former wives."

Those of a third have found a resting-place close by, behind him.

It seemed to me that Mr. Bunner's young man in search of Arcady might look for it here with as good a chance of being satisfied as anywhere I can think of. But I suppose that men and women and especially boys, would prove to be a good deal like the rest of the world, if one lived here long enough to learn all about them. One thing I can safely say, — an English man or boy never goes anywhere without his fists. I saw a boy of ten or twelve years, whose pleasant face attracted my attention. I said to the rector, "That is a fine-looking little fellow, and I should think an intelligent and amiable kind of boy." "Yes," he said, "yes; he can strike from the shoulder pretty well, too. I had to stop him the other day, indulging in that exercise." Well, I said to myself, we have not yet reached the heaven on earth which I was fancying might be embosomed in this peaceful-looking hollow. Youthful angels can hardly be in the habit of striking from the shoulder. But the well-known phrase, belonging to the pugilist rather than to the priest, brought me back from the ideal world into which my imagination had wandered.

Our week at Brighton was passed in a very quiet but most enjoyable way. It could not be otherwise with such a host and hostess, always arranging everything with reference to our well-being and in accordance with our wishes. I became very fond of the esplanade, such a public walk as I never saw anything to compare with. In these tranquil days, and long, honest nights of sleep, the fatigues of what we had been through were forgotten, the scales showed that we were becoming less ethereal every day, and we were ready for another move.

We bade good-by to our hosts with the most grateful and the warmest feeling towards them, after a month of delightful companionship and the experience of a hospitality almost too generous to accept, but which they were pleased to look upon as if we were doing them a favor.

On the 29th of July we found ourselves once more in London.

VI

WE found our old quarters all ready and awaiting us. Mrs. Mackellar's motherly smile, Sam's civil bow, and the rosy cheeks of many-buttoned Robert made us feel at home as soon as we crossed the threshold.

The dissolution of Parliament had brought " the season " abruptly to an end. London was empty. There were three or four millions of people in it, but the great houses were for the most part left without occupants except their liveried guardians. We kept as quiet as possible, to avoid all engagements. For now we were in London for London itself, to do shopping, to see sights, to be our own master and mistress, and to live as independent a life as we possibly could.

The first thing we did on the day of our arrival was to take a hansom and drive over to Chelsea, to look at the place where Carlyle passed the larger part of his life. The whole

region about him must have been greatly
changed during his residence there, for the
Thames Embankment was constructed long after he removed to Chelsea. We had some little difficulty in finding the place we were in
search of. Cheyne (pronounced " Chainie ")
Walk is a somewhat extended range of buildings. Cheyne Row is a passage which reminded
me a little of my old habitat, Montgomery
Place, now Bosworth Street. Presently our attention was drawn to a marble medallion portrait on the corner building of an ordinary-look-
ing row of houses. This was the head of Carlyle, and an inscription informed us that he
lived for forty-seven years in the house No. 24
of this row of buildings. Since Carlyle's home
life has been made public, he has appeared to us
in a different aspect from the ideal one which
he had before occupied. He did not show to
as much advantage under the Boswellizing process as the dogmatist of the last century, dear
old Dr. Johnson. But he remains not the less
one of the really interesting men of his generation, — a man about whom we wish to know
all that we have a right to know.

The sight of an old nest over which two or three winters have passed is a rather saddening one. The dingy three-story brick house in which Carlyle lived, one in a block of similar houses, was far from attractive. It was untenanted, neglected; its windows were unwashed, a pane of glass was broken; its threshold appeared untrodden, its whole aspect forlorn and desolate. Yet there it stood before me, all covered with its associations as an ivy-clad tower with its foliage. I wanted to see its interior, but it looked as if it did not expect a tenant and would not welcome a visitor. Was there nothing but this forbidding house-front to make the place alive with some breathing memory? I saw crossing the street a middle-aged woman, — a decent body, who looked as if she might have come from the lower level of some not opulent but respectable household. She might have some recollection of an old man who was once her neighbor. I asked her if she remembered Mr. Carlyle. Indeed she did, she told us. She used to see him often, in front of his house, putting bits of bread on the railing for the birds. He did not like to see anything wasted, she said. The merest scrap of information, but genuine and pleasing; an instantaneous photograph only, but it makes a pretty vignette in the volume of my reminiscences. There are many considerable men in every generation of mankind, but not a great number who are personally interesting, — not a great many of whom we feel that we cannot know too much; whose foibles, even, we care to know about; whose shortcomings we try to excuse; who are not models, but whose special traits make them attractive. Carlyle is one of these few, and no revelations can prevent his interesting us. He was not quite finished in his prenatal existence. The bricklayer's mortar of his father's calling stuck to his fingers through life, but only as the soil he turned with his ploughshare clung to the fingers of Burns. We do not wish either to have been other than what he was. Their breeding brings them to the average level, carries them more nearly to the heart, makes them a simpler expression of our common humanity. As we rolled in the cars by Ecclefechan, I strained my eyes to take in every point of the landscape, every cottage, every spire, if by any chance I could find one in that lonely region. There was not a bridge nor a bit of masonry of any kind that I did not eagerly scrutinize, to see if it were solid and honest enough to have been built by Carlyle's father. Solitary enough the country looked. I admired Mr. Emerson's devotion in seeking his friend in his bare home among what he describes as the "desolate heathery hills" about Craigenputtock, which were, I suppose, much like the region through which we were passing.

It is one of the regrets of my life that I never saw or heard Carlyle. Nature, who seems to be fond of trios, has given us three dogmatists, all of whom greatly interested their own generation, and whose personality, especially in the case of the first and the last of the trio, still interests us, — Johnson, Coleridge, and Carlyle. Each was an oracle in his way, but unfortunately oracles are fallible to their descendants. The author of "Taxation no Tyranny" had wholesale opinions, and pretty harsh ones, about us Americans, and did not soften them in expression : "Sir, they are a race of convicts, and ought to be thankful for anything we allow

them short of hanging." We smile compla-
cently when we read this outburst, which Mr.
Croker calls in question, but which agrees with
his saying in the presence of Miss Seward, "I
am willing to love all mankind *except an American.*"

A generation or two later comes along Coleridge, with his circle of reverential listeners.
He says of Johnson that his fame rests princi-
pally upon Boswell, and that "his *bow-wow* manner must have had a good deal to do with the
effect produced." As to Coleridge himself, his
contemporaries hardly know how to set bounds
to their exaltation of his genius. Dibdin comes
pretty near going into rhetorical hysterics in
reporting a conversation of Coleridge's to which
he listened: "The auditors seemed to be wrapt
in wonder and delight, as one observation more
profound, or clothed in more forcible language,
than another fell from his tongue. . . . As I
retired homeward I thought a SECOND JOHNSON
had visited the earth to make wise the sons of
men." And De Quincey speaks of him as "the
largest and most spacious intellect, the subtlest
and most comprehensive, in my judgment, that

has yet existed amongst men. " One is sometimes tempted to wish that the superlative could
be abolished, or its use allowed only to old experts. What are men to do when they get to
heaven, after having exhausted their vocabulary
of admiration on earth ?

Now let us come down to Carlyle, and see
what he says of Coleridge. We need not take
those conversational utterances which called
down the wrath of Mr. Swinburne, and found
expression in an epigram which violates all the
proprieties of literary language. Look at the
full-length portrait in the Life of Sterling.
Each oracle denies his predecessor, each magi-
cian breaks the wand of the one who went before him. There were Americans enough ready
to swear by Carlyle until he broke his staff in
meddling with our anti-slavery conflict, and buried it so many fathoms deep that it could never
be fished out again. It is rather singular that
Johnson and Carlyle should each of them have
shipwrecked his sagacity and shown a terrible
leak in his moral sensibilities on coming in contact with American rocks and currents, with
which neither had any special occasion to con-

cern himself, and which both had a great deal better have steered clear of.

But here I stand once more before the home of the long-suffering, much-laboring, loud-complaining Heraclitus of his time, whose very smile had a grimness in it more ominous than his scowl. Poor man! Dyspeptic on a diet of oatmeal porridge; kept wide awake by crowing cocks; drummed out of his wits by long-continued piano-pounding; sharp of speech, I fear, to his high-strung wife, who gave him back as good as she got! I hope I am mistaken about their every-day relations, but again I say, poor man! — for all his complaining must have meant real discomfort, which a man of genius feels not less, certainly, than a common mortal.

I made a second visit to the place where he lived, but I saw nothing more than at the first. I wanted to cross the threshold over which he walked so often, to see the noise-proof room in which he used to write, to look at the chimney-place down which the soot came, to sit where he used to sit and smoke his pipe, and to conjure up his wraith to look in once more upon his old deserted dwelling. That vision was denied me.

After visiting Chelsea we drove round through Regent's Park. I suppose that if we use the superlative in speaking of Hyde Park, Regent's Park will be the comparative, and Battersea Park the positive, ranking them in the descending grades of their hierarchy. But this is my conjecture only, and the social geography of London is a subject which only one who has become familiarly acquainted with the place should speak of with any confidence. A stranger coming to our city might think it made little difference whether his travelling Boston acquaintance lived in Alpha Avenue or in Omega Square, but he would have to learn that it is farther from one of these places to the other, a great deal farther, than it is from Beacon Street, Boston, to Fifth Avenue, New York.

An American finds it a little galling to be told that he must not drive in his *numbered* hansom or four-wheeler except in certain portions of Hyde Park. If he is rich enough to keep his own carriage, or if he will pay the extra price of a vehicle not vulgarized by being on the numbered list, he may drive anywhere that his Grace or his Lordship does, and perhaps have a mean sense of satisfaction at finding him-self in the charmed circle of exclusive " gigman-ity." It is a pleasure to meet none but well-dressed and well-mannered people, in well-appointed equipages. In the highroad of our own country, one is liable to fall in with people and conveyances that it is far from a pleasure to meet. I was once driving in an open carriage, with members of my family, towards my own house in the country town where I was then living. A cart drawn by oxen was in the road in front of us. Whenever we tried to pass, the men in it turned obliquely across the road and prevented us, and this was repeated again and again. I could have wished I had been driving in Hyde Park, where clowns and boors, with their carts and oxen, do not find admittance. Exclusiveness has its conveniences.

The next day, as I was strolling through Burlington Arcade, I saw a figure just before me which I recognized as that of my townsman, Mr. Abbott Lawrence. He was accompanied by his son, who had just returned from a trip round the planet. There are three grades of recognition, entirely distinct from each other:

the meeting of two persons of different countries who speak the same language, — an American and an Englishman, for instance; the meeting of two Americans from different cities, as of a Bostonian and a New Yorker or a Chicagonian; and the meeting of two from the same city, as of two Bostonians.

The difference of these recognitions may be illustrated by supposing certain travelling philosophical instruments, endowed with intelligence and the power of speech, to come together in their wanderings, — let us say in a restaurant of the Palais Royal. "Very hot," says the talking Fahrenheit (Thermometer) from Boston, and calls for an ice, which he plunges his bulb into and cools down. In comes an intelligent and socially disposed English Barometer. The two travellers greet each other, not exactly as old acquaintances, but each has heard very frequently about the other, and their relatives have been often associated. "We have a good deal in common," says the Barometer. "Of the same blood, as we may say; quicksilver is thicker than water." "Yes," says the little Fahrenheit, "and we are both of the same mercurial temperament." While their columns are dancing up and down with laughter at this somewhat tepid and low-pressure pleasantry, there come in a New York Réaumur and a Centigrade from Chicago. The Fahrenheit, which has got warmed up to *temperate*, rises to *summer heat*, and even a little above it. They enjoy each other's company mightily. To be sure, their scales differ, but have they not the same freezing and the same boiling point? To be sure, each thinks his own scale is the true standard, and at home they might get into a contest about the matter, but here in a strange land they do not think of disputing. Now, while they are talking about America and their own local atmosphere and temperature, there comes in a second Boston Fahrenheit. The two of the same name look at each other for a moment, and rush together so eagerly that their bulbs are endangered. How well they understand each other! Thirty-two degrees marks the freezing point. Two hundred and twelve marks the boiling point. They have the same scale, the same fixed points, the same record: no wonder they prefer each other's company!

I hope that my reader has followed my illustration, and finished it off for himself. Let me give a few practical examples. An American and an Englishman meet in a foreign land. The Englishman has occasion to mention his weight, which he finds has gained in the course of his travels. "How much is it now?" asks the American. "Fourteen stone. How much do you weigh?" "Within four pounds of two hundred." Neither of them takes at once any clear idea of what the other weighs. The American has never thought of his own, or his friends', or anybody's weight in *stones* of fourteen pounds. The Englishman has never thought of any one's weight in *pounds*. They can calculate very easily with a slip of paper and a pencil, but not the less is their language but half intelligible as they speak and listen. The same thing is in a measure true of other matters they talk about. "It is about as large a space as the Common," says the Boston man. "It is as large as St. James's Park," says the Londoner. "As high as the State House," says the Bostonian, or "as tall as Bunker Hill Monument," or "about as big as the Frog Pond," where the Londoner would take St. Paul's, the Nelson Column, the Serpentine, as his standard of comparison. The difference of scale does not stop here; it runs through a great part of the objects of thought and conversation. An average American and an average Englishman are talking together, and one of them speaks of the beauty of a field of corn. They are thinking of two entirely different objects: one of a billowy level of soft waving wheat, or rye, or barley; the other of a rustling forest of tall, jointed stalks, tossing their plumes and showing their silken epaulettes, as if every stem in the ordered ranks were a soldier in full regimentals. An Englishman planted for the first time in the middle of a well-grown field of Indian corn would feel as much lost as the babes in the wood. Conversation between two Londoners, two New Yorkers, two Bostonians, requires no foot-notes, which is a great advantage in their intercourse.

To return from my digression and my illustration. I did not do a great deal of shopping myself while in London, being contented to have it done for me. But in the way of looking in at shop windows I did a very large business. Cer-

tain windows attracted me by a variety in unity
which surpassed anything I have been accustomed to. Thus one window showed every con-
ceivable convenience that could be shaped in
ivory, and nothing else. One shop had such a
display of magnificent dressing-cases that I
should have thought a whole royal family was
setting out on its travels. I see the cost of one
of them is two hundred and seventy guineas.
Thirteen hundred and fifty dollars seems a good
deal to pay for a dressing-case.

On the other hand, some of the first-class
tradesmen and workmen make no show whatever. The tailor to whom I had credentials,
and who proved highly satisfactory to me, as he
had proved to some of my countrymen and to
Englishmen of high estate, had only one small
sign, which was placed in one of his windows,
and received his customers in a small room that
would have made a closet for one of our stylish
merchant tailors. The bootmaker to whom I
went on good recommendation had hardly anything about his premises to remind one of his
calling. He came into his studio, took my
measure very carefully, and made me a pair of

what we call Congress boots, which fitted well when once on my feet, but which it cost more trouble to get into and to get out of than I could express my feelings about without dangerously enlarging my limited vocabulary.

Bond Street, Old and New, offered the most inviting windows, and I indulged almost to profligacy in the prolonged inspection of their contents. Stretching my walk along New Bond Street till I came to a great intersecting thoroughfare, I found myself in Oxford Street. Here the character of the shop windows changed at once. Utility and convenience took the place of show and splendor. Here I found various articles of use in a household, some of which were new to me. It is very likely that I could have found most of them in our own Boston Cornhill, but one often overlooks things at home which at once arrest his attention when he sees them in a strange place. I saw great numbers of illuminating contrivances, some of which pleased me by their arrangement of reflectors. Bryant and May's safety matches seemed to be used everywhere. I procured some in Boston with these names on the box, but the label said they were made in Sweden, and they diffused vapors that were enough to produce asphyxia. I greatly admired some of Dr. Dresser's water-cans and other contrivances, modelled more or less after the antique, but I found an abundant assortment of them here in Boston, and I have one I obtained here more original in design and more serviceable in daily use than any I saw in London. I should have regarded Wol-verhampton, as we glided through it, with more interest, if I had known at that time that the inventive Dr. Dresser had his headquarters in that busy-looking town.

One thing, at least, I learned from my London experience: better a small city where one knows all it has to offer, than a great city where one has no disinterested friend to direct him to the right places to find what he wants. But of course there are some grand magazines which are known all the world over, and which no one should leave London without entering as a looker-on, if not as a purchaser.

There was one place I determined to visit, and one man I meant to see, before returning. The place was a certain book-store or book-shop, and the person was its proprietor, Mr. Bernard Quaritch. I was getting very much pressed for time, and I allowed ten minutes only for my visit. I never had any dealings with Mr. Quaritch, but one of my near relatives had, and I had often received his catalogues, the scale of prices in which had given me an impression almost of sublimity. I found Mr. Bernard Quaritch at No. 15 Piccadilly, and introduced myself, not as one whose name he must know, but rather as a stranger, of whom he might have heard through my relative. The extensive literature of catalogues is probably little known to most of my readers. I do not pretend to claim a thorough acquaintance with it, but I know the luxury of reading good catalogues, and such are those of Mr. Quaritch. I should like to deal with him; for if he wants a handsome price for what he sells, he knows its value, and does not offer the refuse of old libraries, but, on the other hand, all that is most precious in them is pretty sure to pass through his hands, sooner or later.

"Now, Mr. Quaritch," I said, after introducing myself, "I have ten minutes to pass with you. You must not open a book; if you do I

am lost, for I shall have to look at every illuminated capital, from the first leaf to the colophon."
Mr. Quaritch did not open a single book, but let
me look round his establishment, and answered
my questions very courteously. It so happened
that while I was there a gentleman came in
whom I had previously met, — my namesake,
Mr. Holmes, the Queen's librarian at Windsor
Castle. My ten minutes passed very rapidly in
conversation with these two experts in books,
the bibliopole and the bibliothecary. No place
that I visited made me feel more thoroughly
that I was in London, the great central mart of
all that is most precious in the world.

*Leave at home all your guineas, ye who
enter here,* would be a good motto to put over
his door, unless you have them in plenty and
can spare them, in which case *Take all your
guineas with you* would be a better one. For
you can here get their equivalent, and more than
their equivalent, in the choicest products of the
press and the finest work of the illuminator, the
illustrator, and the binder. You will be sorely
tempted. But do not be surprised when you
ask the price of the volume you may happen to

fancy. You are not dealing with a *bouquiniste* of the Quais, in Paris. You are not foraging in an old book-shop of New York or Boston. Do not suppose that I undervalue these dealers in old and rare volumes. Many a much-prized rarity have I obtained from Drake and Burnham and others of my townsmen, and from Denham in New York; and in my student years many a choice volume, sometimes even an Aldus or an Elzevir, have I found among the trumpery spread out on the parapets of the quays. But there is a difference between going out on the Fourth of July with a militia musket to shoot any catbird or " chipmunk " that turns up in a piece of woods within a few miles of our own cities, and shooting partridges in a nobleman's preserves on the First of September. I confess to having felt a certain awe on entering the precincts made sacred by their precious contents. The lord and master of so many *Editiones Principes*, the guardian of this great nursery full of *incunabula*, did not seem to me like a simple tradesman. I felt that I was in the presence of the literary purveyor of royal and imperial libraries, the man before whom million-

aires tremble as they calculate, and billionaires
pause and consider. I have recently received
two of Mr. Quaritch's catalogues, from which I
will give my reader an extract or two, to show
him what kind of articles this prince of biblio-
poles deals in.

Perhaps you would like one of those romances
which turned the head of Don Quixote. Here
is a volume which will be sure to please you.
It is on one of his lesser lists, confined princi-
pally to Spanish and Portuguese works: —

" Amadis de Gaula . . . folio, gothic letter,
FIRST EDITION, unique . . . red morocco super
extra, *doublé* with olive morocco, richly gilt,
tooled to an elegant Grolier design, gilt edges
. . . in a neat case."

A pretty present for a scholarly friend. A
nice old book to carry home for one's own
library. Two hundred pounds — one thousand
dollars — will make you the happy owner of
this volume.

But if you would have also on your shelves
the first edition of the " Cronica del famoso ca-
baluero cid Ruy Diaz Campadero," not " richly
gilt," not even bound in leather, but in " cloth

boards," you will have to pay two hundred and ten pounds to become its proprietor. After this you will not be frightened by the thought of paying three hundred dollars for a little quarto giving an account of the Virginia Adventurers. You will not shrink from the idea of giving something more than a hundred guineas for a series of Hogarth's plates. But when it comes to Number 1001 in the May catalogue, and you see that if you would possess a first folio Shakespeare, "untouched by the hand of any modern renovator," you must be prepared to pay seven hundred and eighty-five pounds, almost four thousand dollars, for the volume, it would not be surprising if you changed color and your knees shook under you. No doubt some brave man will be found to carry off that prize, in spite of the golden battery which defends it, perhaps to Cincinnati, or Chicago, or San Francisco. But do not be frightened. These Alpine heights of extravagance climb up from the humble valley where shillings and sixpences are all that are required to make you a purchaser.

One beauty of the Old World shops is that

if a visitor comes back to the place where he left them fifty years before, he finds them, or has a great chance of finding them, just where they stood at his former visit. In driving down to the old city, to the place of business of the Barings, I found many streets little changed. Temple Bar was gone, and the much-abused griffin stood in its place. There was a shop close to Temple Bar, where, in 1834, I had bought some brushes. I had no difficulty in finding Prout's, and I could not do less than go in and buy some more brushes. I did not ask the young man who served me how the old shopkeeper who attended to my wants on the earlier occasion was at this time. But I thought what a different color the locks these brushes smooth show from those that knew their predecessors in the earlier decade!

I ought to have made a second visit to the Tower, so tenderly spoken of by Artemus Ward as "a sweet boon," so vividly remembered by me as the scene of a personal encounter with one of the animals then kept in the Tower menagerie. But the project added a stone to the floor of the underground thoroughfare which is paved with good intentions.

St. Paul's I must and did visit. The most striking addition since I was there is the massive monument to the Duke of Wellington. The great temple looked rather bare and unsympathetic. Poor Dr. Johnson, sitting in semi-nude exposure, looked to me as unhappy as our own half-naked Washington at the national capital. The Judas of Matthew Arnold's poem would have cast his cloak over those marble shoulders, if he had found himself in St. Paul's, and have earned another respite. We brought away little, I fear, except the grand effect of the dome as we looked up at it. It gives us a greater idea of height than the sky itself, which we have become used to looking upon.

A second visit to the National Gallery was made in company with A——. It was the repetition of an attempt at a draught from the Cup of Tantalus. I was glad of a sight of the Botticellis, of which I had heard so much, and others of the more recently acquired paintings of the great masters; of a sweeping glance at the Turners; of a look at the well-remembered Hogarths and the memorable portraits by Sir Joshua. I carried away a confused mass of im-

pressions, much as the soldiers that sack a city
go off with all the precious things they can
snatch up, huddled into clothes-bags and pillow-
cases. I am reminded, too, of Mr. Galton's
composite portraits ; a thousand glimpses, as one
passes through the long halls lined with paintings, all blending in one not unpleasing general
effect, out of which emerges from time to time
some single distinct image.

In the same way we passed through the exhibition of paintings at the Royal Academy. I
noticed that A—— paid special attention to the
portraits of young ladies by John Sargent and
by Collier, while I was more particularly struck
with the startling portrait of an ancient personage in a full suit of wrinkles, such as Rembrandt
used to bring out with wonderful effect. Hunt-
ing in couples is curious and instructive ; the
scent for this or that kind of game is sure to be
very different in the two individuals.

I made but two brief visits to the British
Museum, and I can easily instruct my reader so
that he will have no difficulty, if he will follow
my teaching, in learning how not to see it.
When he has a spare hour at his disposal, let

him drop in at the Museum, and wander among its books and its various collections. He will know as much about it as the fly that buzzes in at one window and out at another. If I were asked whether I brought away anything from my two visits, I should say, Certainly I did. The fly sees some things, not very intelligently, but he cannot help seeing them. The great round reading-room, with its silent students, impressed me very much. I looked at once for the Elgin Marbles, but casts and photographs and engravings had made me familiar with their chief features. I thought I knew something of the sculptures brought from Nineveh, but I was astonished, almost awe-struck, at the sight of those mighty images which mingled with the visions of the Hebrew prophets. I did not marvel more at the skill and labor expended upon them by the Assyrian artists than I did at the enterprise and audacity which had brought them safely from the mounds under which they were buried to the light of day and the heart of a great modern city. I never thought that I should live to see the Birs Nimroud laid open, and the tablets in which the history of Nebuchadnezzar was recorded spread before me. The Empire of the Spade in the world of history was founded at Nineveh by Layard, a great province added to it by Schliemann, and its boundary extended by numerous explorers, some of whom are diligently at work at the present day. I feel very grateful that many of its revelations have been made since I have been a tenant of the travelling residence which holds so many secrets in its recesses.

There is one lesson to be got from a visit of an hour or two to the British Museum, — namely, the fathomless abyss of our own ignorance. One is almost ashamed of his little paltry heartbeats in the presence of the rushing and roaring torrent of Niagara. So if he has published a little book or two, collected a few fossils, or coins, or vases, he is crushed by the vastness of the treasures in the library and the collections of this universe of knowledge.

I have shown how not to see the British Museum; I will tell how to see it.

Take lodgings next door to it, — in a garret, if you cannot afford anything better, — and pass all your days at the Museum during the whole period of your natural life. At threescore and ten you will have some faint conception of the contents, significance, and value of this great British institution, which is as nearly as any one spot the *nœud vital* of human civilization, a stab at which by the dagger of anarchy would fitly begin the reign of chaos.

On the 3d of August, a gentleman, Mr. Wedmore, who had promised to be my guide to certain interesting localities, called for me, and we took a hansom for the old city. The first place we visited was the Temple, a collection of buildings with intricate passages between them, some of the edifices reminding me of our college dormitories. One, however, was a most extraordinary exception, — the wonderful Temple church, or rather the ancient part of it which is left, the round temple. We had some trouble to get into it, but at last succeeded in finding a slip of a girl, the daughter of the janitor, who unlocked the door for us. It affected my imagination strangely to see this girl of a dozen years old, or thereabouts, moving round among the monuments which had kept their place there for some six or seven hundred years; for the church was built in the year 1185, and the most recent of the crusaders' monuments is said to date as far back as 1241. Their effigies have lain in this vast city, and passed unharmed through all its convulsions. The Great Fire must have crackled very loud in their stony ears, and they must have shaken day and night, as the bodies of the victims of the Plague were rattled over the pavements.

Near the Temple church, in a green spot among the buildings, a plain stone laid flat on the turf bears these words: " Here lies Oliver Goldsmith." I believe doubt has been thrown upon the statement that Goldsmith was buried in that place, but, as some poet ought to have written,

> Where doubt is disenchantment
> ' T is wisdom to believe.

We do not " drop a tear " so often as our Della Cruscan predecessors, but the memory of the author of the " Vicar of Wakefield " stirred my feelings more than a whole army of crusaders would have done. A pretty rough set of fili- busters they were, no doubt.

The whole group to which Goldsmith belonged

came up before me, and as the centre of that group the great Dr. Johnson ; not the Johnson of the " Rambler," or of " The Vanity of Human Wishes," or even of " Rasselas," but Boswell's Johnson, dear to all of us, the " Grand Old Man " of his time, whose foibles we care more for than for most great men's virtues. Fleet Street, which he loved so warmly, was close by. Bolt Court, entered from it, where he lived for many of his last years, and where he died, was the next place to visit. I found Fleet Street a good deal like Washington Street as I remember it in former years. When I came to the place pointed out as Bolt Court, I could hardly believe my eyes that so celebrated a place of residence should be entered by so humble a passageway. I was very sorry to find that No. 3, where he lived, was demolished, and a new building erected in its place. In one of the other houses in this court he is said to have labored on his dictionary. Near by was a building of mean aspect, in which Goldsmith is said to have at one time resided. But my kind conductor did not profess to be well acquainted with the local antiquities of this quarter of London.

If I had a long future before me, I should like above all things to study London with a dark lantern, so to speak, myself in deepest shadow and all I wanted to see in clearest light. Then I should want time, time, time. For it is a sad fact that sight-seeing as commonly done is one of the most wearying things in the world, and takes the life out of any but the sturdiest or the most elastic natures more efficiently than would a reasonable amount of daily exercise on a treadmill. In my younger days I used to find that a visit to the gallery of the Louvre was followed by more fatigue and exhaustion than the same amount of time spent in walking the wards of a hospital.

Another grand sight there was, not to be overlooked, namely, the Colonial Exhibition. The popularity of this immense show was very great, and we found ourselves, A —— and I, in the midst of a vast throng, made up of respectable and comfortable looking people. It was not strange that the multitude flocked to this exhibition. There was a jungle, with its (stuffed) monsters, — tigers, serpents, elephants; there were carvings which may well have cost a life

apiece, and stuffs which none but an empress
or a millionairess would dare to look at.   All
the arts of the East were there in their perfection, and some of the artificers were at their
work.   We had to content ourselves with a
mere look at all these wonders.   It was a pity;
instead of going to these fine shows tired, sleepy,
wanting repose more than anything else, we
should have come to them fresh, in good condition, and had many days at our disposal.   I
learned more in a visit to the Japanese exhibition in Boston than I should have learned in
half a dozen half-awake strolls through this multitudinous and most imposing collection of all

> " The gorgeous East with richest hand
>   Showers on her kings,"

and all the masterpieces of its wonder-working
artisans.

One of the last visits we paid before leaving
London for a week in Paris was to the South
Kensington Museum.   Think of the mockery of
giving one hour to such a collection of works of
art and wonders of all kinds !   Why should I
consider it worth while to say that we went there
at all ?   All manner of objects succeeded each

other in a long series of dissolving views, so to speak, nothing or next to nothing having a chance to leave its individual impress. In the battle for life which took place in my memory, as it always does among the multitude of claimants for a permanent hold, I find that two objects came out survivors of the contest. The first is the noble cast of the column of Trajan, vast in dimensions, crowded with history in its most striking and enduring form; a long array of figures representing in unquestioned realism the military aspect of a Roman army. The second case of survival is thus described in the catalogue: " An altar or shrine of a female saint, recently acquired from Padua, is also ascribed to the same sculptor [Donatello]. This very valuable work of art had for many years been used as a drinking-trough for horses. A hole has been roughly pierced in it." I thought the figure was the most nearly perfect image of heavenly womanhood that I had ever looked upon, and I could have gladly given my whole hour to sitting — I could almost say kneeling — before it in silent contemplation. I found the curator of the Museum, Mr. Soden Smith, shared

my feelings with reference to the celestial loveliness of this figure.   Which is best, to live in
a country where such a work of art is taken for
a horse-trough, or in a country where the products from the studio of a self-taught handi-
craftsman, equal to the shaping of a horse-trough
and not much more, are put forward as works
of art?

A little time before my visit to England, before I had even thought of it as a possibility, I
had the honor of having two books dedicated to
me by two English brother physicians.   One of
these two gentlemen was Dr. Walshe, of whom
I shall speak hereafter; the other was Dr. J.
Milner Fothergill.   The name Fothergill was
familiar to me from my boyhood.   My old townsman, Dr. Benjamin Waterhouse, who died in
1846 at the age of ninety-two, had a great deal
to say about his relative Dr. John Fothergill,
the famous Quaker physician of the last century,
of whom Benjamin Franklin said, " I can hardly
conceive that a better man ever existed."   Dr.
and Mrs. Fothergill sent us some beautiful flowers a little before we left, and when I visited
him he gave me a medallion of his celebrated
kinsman.

London is a place of mysteries. Looking out of one of the windows at the back of Dr. Fothergill's house, I saw an immense wooden blind, such as we have on our windows in summer, but reaching from the ground as high as the top of the neighboring houses. While admitting the air freely, it shut the property to which it belonged completely from sight. I asked the meaning of this extraordinary structure, and learned that it was put up by a great nobleman, of whose subterranean palace and strange seclusion I had before heard. Common report attributed his unwillingness to be seen to a disfiguring malady with which he was said to be afflicted. The story was that he was visible only to his valet. But a lady of quality, whom I met in this country, told me she had seen him, and observed nothing to justify it. These old countries are full of romances and legends and *diableries* of all sorts, in which truth and lies are so mixed that one does not know what to believe. What happens behind the high walls of the old cities is as much a secret as were the doings inside the prisons of the Inquisition.

Little mistakes sometimes cause us a deal

of trouble. This time it was the presence or absence of a single letter which led us to fear that an important package destined to America had miscarried. There were two gentlemen unwittingly involved in the confusion. On inquiring for the package at Messrs. Low, the publishers, Mr. Watts, to whom I thought it had been consigned, was summoned. He knew nothing about it, had never heard of it, was evidently utterly ignorant of us and our affairs. While we were in trouble and uncertainty, our Boston friend, Mr. James R. Osgood, came in. "Oh," said he, "it is Mr. Watt you want, the agent of a Boston firm," and gave us the gentleman's address. I had confounded Mr. Watt's name with Mr. Watts's name. "W'at's in a name?" A great deal sometimes. I wonder if I shall be pardoned for quoting six lines from one of my after-dinner poems of long ago : —

— One vague inflection spoils the whole with doubt,
One trivial letter ruins all, left out ;
A knot can change a felon into clay,
A not will save him, spelt without the k ;
The smallest word has some unguarded spot,
And danger lurks in i without a dot.

I should find it hard to account for myself during our two short stays in London in the month of August, separated by the week we passed in Paris. The ferment of continued over-excitement, calmed very much by our rest in the various places I have mentioned, had not yet wholly worked itself off. There was some of that everlasting shopping to be done. There were photographs to be taken, a call here and there to be made, a stray visitor now and then, a walk in the morning to get back the use of the limbs which had been too little exercised, and a drive every afternoon to one of the parks, or the Thames Embankment, or other locality. After all this, an honest night's sleep served to round out the day, in which little had been effected besides making a few purchases, writing a few letters, reading the papers, the Boston " Weekly Advertiser " among the rest, and making arrangements for our passage homeward.

The sights we saw were looked upon for so short a time, most of them so very superficially, that I am almost ashamed to say that I have been in the midst of them and brought home so little. I remind myself of my boyish amusement of *skipping stones*, — throwing a flat stone so that it shall only touch the water, but touch it in half a dozen places before it comes to rest beneath the smooth surface. The drives we took showed us a thousand objects which arrested our attention. Every street, every bridge, every building, every monument, every strange vehicle, every exceptional personage, was a show which stimulated our curiosity. For we had not as yet changed our Boston eyes for London ones, and very common sights were spectacular and dramatic to us. I remember that one of our New England country boys exclaimed, when he first saw a block of city dwellings, " Darn it all, who ever see anything like that 'are ? Sich a lot o' haousen all stuck together ! " I must explain that " haousen " used in my early days to be as common an expression in speaking of houses among our country-folk as its phonetic equivalent ever was in Saxony. I felt not unlike that country-boy.

In thinking of how much I missed seeing, I sometimes have said to myself, " Oh, if the carpet of the story in the Arabian Nights would only take me up and carry me to London for one week, — just one short week, — setting me down fresh from quiet, wholesome living, in my usual good condition, and bringing me back at the end of it, what a different account I could give of my experiences! But it is just as well as it is. Younger eyes have studied and will study, more instructed travellers have pictured and will picture, the great metropolis from a hundred different points of view. No person can be said to know London. The most that any one can claim is that he knows something of it. I am now just going to leave it for another great capital, but in my concluding pages I shall return to Great Britain, and give some of the general impressions left by what I saw and heard in our mother country.

VII.

STRAITENED as we were for time, it was impossible to return home without a glimpse, at least, of Paris. Two precious years of my early manhood were spent there under the reign of Louis Philippe, king of the French, *le Roi Citoyen*. I felt that I must look once more on the places I knew so well, — once more before shutting myself up in the world of recollections. It is hardly necessary to say that a lady can always find a little shopping, and generally a good deal of it, to do in Paris. So it was not difficult to persuade my daughter that a short visit to that city was the next step to be taken.

We left London on the 5th of August to go *via* Folkestone and Boulogne. The passage across the Channel was a very smooth one, and neither of us suffered any inconvenience. Boulogne as seen from the landing did not show to great advantage. I fell to thinking of Brummel, and what a satisfaction it would have been to treat him to a good dinner, and set him talking about the days of the Regency. Boulogne was all Brummel in my associations, just as Calais was all Sterne. I find everywhere that it is a distinctive personality which makes me want to linger round a spot, more than an important historical event. There is not much worth remembering about Brummel; but his audacity, his starched neckcloth, his assumptions and their success, make him a curious subject for the student of human nature.

Leaving London at twenty minutes before ten in the forenoon, we arrived in Paris at six in the afternoon. I could not say that the region of France through which we passed was peculiarly attractive. I saw no fine trees, no pretty cottages, like those so common in England. There was little which an artist would be tempted to sketch, or a traveller by the railroad would be likely to remember.

The place where we had engaged lodgings was Hôtel d'Orient, in the Rue Daunou. The situation was convenient, very near the Place Vendôme and the Rue de la Paix. But the house was undergoing renovations which made it as unpresentable as a moulting fowl. Scrubbing, painting of blinds, and other perturbing processes did all they could to make it uncomfortable. The courtyard was always sloppy, and the whole condition of things reminded me forcibly of the state of Mr. Briggs's household while the mason was carrying out the complex operations which began with the application of "a little compo." (I hope all my readers remember Mr. Briggs, whose adventures as told by the pencil of John Leech are not unworthy of comparison with those of Mr. Pickwick as related by Dickens.) Barring these unfortunate conditions, the hotel was commendable, and when in order would be a desirable place of temporary residence.

It was the dead season of Paris, and everything had the air of suspended animation. The solitude of the Place Vendôme was something oppressive ; I felt, as I trod its lonely sidewalk, as if I were wandering through Tadmor in the Desert. We were indeed as remote, as unfriended, — I will not say as melancholy or as slow, — as Goldsmith by the side of the lazy Scheldt or the wandering Po. Not a soul did

either of us know in that great city. Our most
intimate relations were with the people of the
hotel and with the drivers of the fiacres. These
last were a singular looking race of beings.
Many of them had a dull red complexion,
almost brick color, which must have some
general cause. I questioned whether the red
wine could have something to do with it. They
wore glazed hats, and drove shabby vehicles for
the most part; their horses would not compare
with those of the London hansom drivers, and
they themselves were not generally inviting in
aspect, though we met with no incivility from
any of them. One, I remember, was very
voluble, and over-explained everything, so that
we became afraid to ask him a question. They
were fellow-creatures with whom one did not
naturally enter into active sympathy, and the
principal point of interest about the fiacre and
its arrangements was whether the horse was
fondest of trotting or of walking. In one of
our drives we made it a point to call upon our
Minister, Mr. McLane, but he was out of town.
We did not bring a single letter, but set off exactly as if we were on a picnic.

While A—— and her attendant went about making their purchases, I devoted myself to the sacred and pleasing task of reviving old memories. One of the first places I visited was the house I lived in as a student, which in my English friend's French was designated as "Noomero sankont sank Roo Monshure ler Pranse." I had been told that the whole region thereabout had been transformed by the creation of a new boulevard. I did not find it so. There was the house, the lower part turned into a shop, but there were the windows out of which I used to look along the Rue Vaugirard, — *au troisième* the first year, *au second* the second year. Why should I go mousing about the place? What would the shopkeeper know about M. Bertrand, my landlord of half a century ago; or his first wife, to whose funeral 1 went; or his second, to whose bridal I was bidden?

I ought next to have gone to the hospital La Pitié, where I passed much of my time during those two years. But the people there would not know me, and my old master's name, Louis, is but a dim legend in the wards where he used to teach his faithful band of almost worshipping students. Besides, I have not been among hospital beds for many a year, and my sensibilities are almost as impressible as they were before daily habit had rendered them comparatively callous.

How strange it is to look down on one's venerated teachers, after climbing with the world's progress half a century above the level where we left them! The stethoscope was almost a novelty in those days. The microscope was never mentioned by any clinical instructor I listened to while a medical student. *Nous avons changé tout cela* is true of every generation in medicine, — changed oftentimes by improvement, sometimes by fashion or the pendulum-swing from one extreme to another.

On my way back from the hospital I used to stop at the beautiful little church St. Etienne du Mont, and that was one of the first places to which I drove after looking at my student-quarters. All was just as of old. The tapers were burning about the tomb of St. Genevieve. Samson, with the jawbone of the ass, still crouched and sweated, or looked as if he did, under the weight of the pulpit. One might question how well the preacher in the pulpit liked the suggestion of the figure beneath it. The sculptured screen and gallery, the exquisite spiral stairways, the carved figures about the organ, the tablets on the walls, — one in partic- ular relating the fall of two young girls from the gallery, and their miraculous protection from injury, — all these images found their counter- part in my memory. I did not remember how very beautiful is the stained glass in the *char- niers*, which must not be overlooked by vis- itors.

It is not far from St. Etienne du Mont to the Pantheon. I cannot say that there is any odor of sanctity about this great temple, which has been consecrated, if I remember correctly, and, I will not say desecrated, but secularized from time to time, according to the party which hap- pened to be uppermost. I confess that I did not think of it chiefly as a sacred edifice, or as the resting-place, more or less secure, of the "*grands hommes*" to whom it is dedicated. I was thinking much more of Foucault's grand experiment, one of the most sublime visible demonstrations of a great physical fact in the records of science. The reader may not happen to remember it, and will like, perhaps, to be reminded of it. Foucault took advantage of the height of the dome, nearly three hundred feet, and had a heavy weight suspended by a wire from its loftiest point, forming an immense pendulum, — the longest, I suppose, ever constructed. Now a moving body tends to keep its original plane of movement, and so the great pendulum, being set swinging north and south, tended to keep on in the same direction. But the earth was moving under it, and as it rolled from west to east the plane running through the north and south poles was every instant changing. Thus the pendulum appeared to change its direction, and its deviation was shown on a graduated arc, or by the marks it left in a little heap of sand which it touched as it swung. This experiment on the great scale has since been repeated on the small scale by the aid of other contrivances.

My thoughts wandered back, naturally enough, to Galileo in the Cathedral at Pisa. It was the swinging of the suspended lamp in that edifice which set his mind working on the laws which govern the action of the pendulum. While he was meditating on this physical problem, the priest may have been holding forth on the dangers of meddling with matters settled by Holy Church, who stood ready to enforce her edicts by the logic of the rack and the fagot. An inference from the above remarks is that what one brings from a church depends very much on what he carries into it.

The next place to visit could be no other than the Café Procope. This famous resort is the most ancient and the most celebrated of all the Parisian cafés. Voltaire, the poet J. B. Rousseau, Marmontel, Sainte Foix, Saurin, were among its frequenters in the eighteenth century. It stands in the Rue des Fossés-Saint-Germain, now Rue de l'Ancienne Comédie. Several American students, Bostonians and Philadelphians, myself among the number, used to breakfast at this café every morning. I have no doubt that I met various celebrities there, but I recall only one name which is likely to be known to most or many of my readers. A delicate-looking man, seated at one of the tables, was pointed out to me as Jouffroy. If I had known

as much about him as I learned afterwards, I
should have looked at him with more interest.
He had one of those imaginative natures, tinged
by constitutional melancholy and saddened by
ill health, which belong to a certain class of
poets and sentimental writers, of which Pascal
is a good example, and Cowper another. The
world must have seemed very cruel to him. I
remember that when he was a candidate for the
Assembly, one of the popular cries, as reported
by the newspapers of the time, was *A bas le
poitrinaire!* His malady soon laid him low
enough, for he died in 1842, at the age of forty-
six. I must have been very much taken up with
my medical studies to have neglected my opportunity of seeing the great statesmen, authors,
artists, orators, and men of science outside of
the medical profession. Poisson, Arago, and
Jouffroy are all I can distinctly recall, among
the Frenchmen of eminence whom I had all
around me.

The Café Procope has been much altered and
improved, and bears an inscription telling the
date of its establishment, which was in the year
1689. I entered the café, which was nearly or

quite empty, the usual breakfast hour being past.

Garçon !   Une tasse de café.

If there is a river of *mnēmē* as a counterpart of the river *lēthē*, my cup of coffee must have got its water from that stream of memory.   If I could borrow that eloquence of Jouffroy which made his hearers turn pale, I might bring up before my readers a long array of pallid ghosts, whom these walls knew well in their earthly habiliments.   Only a single one of those I met here still survives.   The rest are mostly well-nigh forgotten by all but a few friends, or remembered chiefly in their children and grandchildren.

"How much?" I said to the garçon in his native tongue, or what I supposed to be that language.   "*Cinq sous,*" was his answer.   By the laws of sentiment, I ought to have made the ignoble sum five francs, at least.   But if I had done so, the waiter would undoubtedly have thought that I had just come from Charenton. Besides, why should I violate the simple habits and traditions of the place, where generation after generation of poor students and threadbare

Bohemians had taken their morning coffee and pocketed their two lumps of sugar? It was with a feeling of virile sanity and Roman self-conquest that I paid my five sous, with the small additional fraction which I supposed the waiter to expect, and no more.

So I passed for the last time over the threshold of the Café Procope, where Voltaire had matured his plays and Piron sharpened his epigrams; where Jouffroy had battled with his doubts and fears; where, since their time, — since my days of Parisian life, — the terrible storming youth, afterwards renowned as Léon Michel Gambetta, had startled the quiet guests with his noisy eloquence, till the old *habitués* spilled their coffee, and the red-capped students said to each other, " *Il ira loin, ce gaillard-là !* "

But what to me were these shadowy figures by the side of the group of my early friends and companions, that came up before me in all the freshness of their young manhood? The memory of them recalls my own youthful days, and I need not go to Florida to bathe in the fountain of Ponce de Leon.

I have sometimes thought that I love so well the accidents of this temporary terrestrial residence, its endeared localities, its precious affections, its pleasing variety of occupation, its alternations of excited and gratified curiosity, and whatever else comes nearest to the longings of the natural man, that I might be wickedly homesick in a far-off spiritual realm where such toys are done with. But there is a pretty lesson which I have often meditated, taught, not this time by the lilies of the field, but by the fruits of the garden. When, in the June honeymoon of the seasons, the strawberry shows itself among the bridal gifts, many of us exclaim for the hundredth time with Dr. Boteler, " Doubtless God could have made a better berry, but doubtless God never did." Nature, who is God's handmaid, does not attempt a rival berry. But by and by a little woolly knob, which looked and saw with wonder the strawberry reddening, and perceived the fragrance it diffused all around, begins to fill out, and grow soft and pulpy and sweet; and at last a glow comes to its cheek, and we say the peach is ripening. When Nature has done with it, and delivers it to us in its perfection, we forget all the lesser fruits which have gone before it. If the flavor of the peach and the fragrance of the rose are not found in some fruit and flower which grow by the side of the river of life, an earth-born spirit might be forgiven for missing them. The strawberry and the pink are very delightful, but we could be happy without them.

So, too, we may hope that when the fruits of our brief early season of three or four score years have given us all they can impart for our happiness; when " the love of little maids and berries," and all other earthly prettinesses, shall " soar and sing," as Mr. Emerson sweetly reminds us that they all must, we may hope that the abiding felicities of our later life-season may far more than compensate us for all that have taken their flight.

I looked forward with the greatest interest to revisiting the Gallery of the Louvre, accompanied by my long-treasured recollections. I retained a vivid remembrance of many pictures, which had been kept bright by seeing great numbers of reproductions of them in photographs and engravings.

The first thing which struck me was that the pictures had been rearranged in such a way that I could find nothing in the place where I looked for it. But when I found them, they greeted me, so I fancied, like old acquaintances. The meek-looking "Belle Jardinière" was as lamb-like as ever; the pearly nymph of Correggio invited the stranger's eye as frankly as of old; Titian's young man with the glove was the calm, self-contained gentleman I used to admire; the splashy Rubenses, the pallid Guidos, the sunlit Claudes, the shadowy Poussins, the moonlit Girardets, Géricault's terrible shipwreck of the Medusa, the exquisite home pictures of Gerard Douw and Terburg, — all these and many more have always been on exhibition in my ideal gallery, and I only mention them as the first that happen to suggest themselves.

The Museum of the Hôtel Cluny is a curious receptacle of antiquities, many of which I looked at with interest; but they made no lasting impression, and have gone into the lumber-room of memory, from which accident may, from time to time, drag out some few of them.

After the poor unsatisfactory towers of Westminster Abbey, the two massive, noble, truly majestic towers of Notre Dame strike the traveller as a crushing contrast. It is not hard to see that one of these grand towers is somewhat larger than the other, but the difference does not interfere with the effect of the imposing front of the cathedral.

I was much pleased to find that I could have entrance to the Sainte Chapelle, which was used, at the time of my earlier visit, as a storehouse of judicial archives, of which there was a vast accumulation.

With the exception of my call at the office of the American Legation, I made but a single visit to any person in Paris. That person was M. Pasteur. I might have carried a letter to him, for my friend Mrs. Priestley is well acquainted with him, but I had not thought of asking for one. So I presented myself at his headquarters, and was admitted into a courtyard, where a multitude of his patients were gathered. They were of various ages and of many different nationalities, every one of them with the vague terror hanging over him or her. Yet the young people seemed to be cheerful enough, and very much like scholars out of school. I sent my card in to M. Pasteur, who was busily engaged in writing, with his clerks or students about him, and presently he came out and greeted me. I told him I was an American physician, who wished to look in his face and take his hand, — nothing more. I looked in his face, which was that of a thoughtful, hard-worked student, a little past the grand climacteric, — he was born in 1822. I took his hand, which has performed some of the most delicate and daring experiments ever ventured upon, with results of almost incalculable benefit to human industries, and the promise of triumph in the treatment of human disease which prophecy would not have dared to anticipate. I will not say that I have a full belief that hydrophobia, — in some respects the most terrible of all diseases, — is to be extirpated or rendered tractable by his method of treatment. But of his inventive originality, his unconquerable perseverance, his devotion to the good of mankind, there can be no question. I look upon him as one of the greatest experimenters that ever lived, one of the truest benefactors of his race ; and if I made my due obei-

sance before princes, I felt far more humble in
the presence of this great explorer, to whom
the God of Nature has entrusted some of her
most precious secrets.

There used to be, — I can hardly think it still
exists, — a class of persons who prided themselves
on their disbelief in the reality of any such distinct disease as hydrophobia. I never thought
it worth while to argue with them, for I have
noticed that this disbelief is only a special mani-
festation of a particular habit of mind. Its ad-
vocates will be found, I think, most frequently
among "the long-haired men and the short-
haired women." Many of them dispute the ef-
ficacy of vaccination. Some are disciples of
Hahnemann, some have full faith in the mind-
cure, some attend the *séances* where flowers
(bought from the nearest florist) are material-
ized, and some invest their money in Mrs. Howe's
Bank of Benevolence. Their tendency is to reject the truth which is generally accepted, and to
accept the improbable; if the impossible offers
itself, they deny the existence of the impossible.
Argument with this class of minds is a lever
without a fulcrum.

I was glad to leave that company of patients, still uncertain of their fate, — hoping, yet pursued by their terror: peasants bitten by mad wolves in Siberia; women snapped at by their sulking lap-dogs in London; children from over the water who had been turned upon by the irritable Skye terrier; innocent victims torn by ill-conditioned curs at the doors of the friends they were meaning to visit, — all haunted by the same ghastly fear, all starting from sleep in the same nightmare.

If canine rabies is a fearful subject to contemplate, there is a sadder and deeper significance in *rabies humana;* in that awful madness of the human race which is marked by a thirst for blood and a rage for destruction. The remembrance of such a distemper which has attacked mankind, especially mankind of the Parisian sub-species, came over me very strongly when I first revisited the Place Vendôme. I should have supposed that the last object upon which Parisians would, in their wildest frenzy, have laid violent hands would have been the column with the figure of Napoleon at its summit. We all know what happened in 1871. An artist, we should have thought, would be the last person to lead the iconoclasts in such an outrage. But M. Courbet has attained an immortality like that of Erostratus by the part he took in pulling down the column. It was restored in 1874. I do not question that the work of restoration was well done, but my eyes insisted on finding a fault in some of its lines which was probably in their own refracting media. Fifty years before an artist helped to overthrow the monument to the Emperor, a poet had apostrophized him in the bitterest satire since the days of Juvenal: —

" Encor Napoléon ! encor sa grande image !
  Ah ! que ce rude et dur guerrier
  Nous a coûté de sang et de pleurs et d'outrage
   Pour quelques rameaux de laurier !

  .   .   .   .

" Eh bien ! dans tous ces jours d'abaissement, de peine,
  Pour tous ces outrages sans nom,
  Je n'ai jamais chargé qu'un être de ma haine, . . .
   Sois maudit, O Napoléon ! "

After looking at the column of the Place Vendôme and recalling these lines of Barbier, I was ready for a visit to the tomb of Napoleon. The poet's curse had helped me to explain the painter's frenzy against the bronze record of his

achievements and the image at its summit. But
I forgot them both as I stood under the dome
of the Invalides, and looked upon the massive
receptacle which holds the dust of the imperial
exile. Two things, at least, Napoleon accomplished : he opened the way for ability of all
kinds, and he dealt the death-blow to the divine
right of kings and all the abuses which clung to
that superstition. If I brought nothing else
away from my visit to his mausoleum, I left it
impressed with what a man can be when fully
equipped by nature, and placed in circumstances
where his forces can have full play. "How infinite in faculty ! . . . in apprehension how like
a god ! " Such were my reflections ; very much,
I suppose, like those of the average visitor, and
too obviously having nothing to require contra-
diction or comment.

Paris as seen by the morning sun of three or
four and twenty and Paris in the twilight of the
superfluous decade cannot be expected to look
exactly alike. I well remember my first breakfast at a Parisian café in the spring of 1833.
It was in the Place de la Bourse, on a beautiful
sunshiny morning. The coffee was nectar, the

flute was ambrosia, the *brioche* was more than
good enough for the Olympians. Such an experience could not repeat itself fifty years later.
The first restaurant at which we dined was in
the Palais Royal. The place was hot enough to
cook an egg. Nothing was very excellent nor
very bad ; the wine was not so good as they gave
us at our hotel in London; the enchanter had
not waved his wand over our repast, as he did
over my earlier one in the Place de la Bourse,
and I had not the slightest desire to pay the
garçon thrice his fee on the score of cherished
associations. We dined at our hotel on some
days, at different restaurants on others. One
day we dined, and dined well, at the old Café
Anglais, famous in my earlier times for its
turbot. Another day we took our dinner at a
very celebrated restaurant on the boulevard.
One sauce which was served us was a gastronomic symphony, the harmonies of which were
new to me and pleasing. But I remember little
else of superior excellence. The garçon pocketed the franc I gave him with the air of having expected a napoleon.

Into the mysteries of a lady's shopping in

Paris I would not venture to inquire. But A—— and I strolled together through the Palais Royal in the evening, and amused ourselves by staring at the glittering windows without being severely tempted. Bond Street had exhausted our susceptibility to the shop-window seduction, and the napoleons did not burn in the pockets where the sovereigns had had time to cool.

Nothing looked more nearly the same as of old than the bridges. The Pont Neuf did not seem to me altered, though we had read in the papers that it was in ruins or seriously injured in consequence of a great flood. The statues had been removed from the Pont Royal, one or two new bridges had been built, but all was natural enough, and I was tempted to look for the old woman, at the end of the Pont des Arts, who used to sell me a bunch of violets, for two or three sous, — such as would cost me a quarter of a dollar in Boston. I did not see the three objects which a popular saying alleges are always to be met on the Pont Neuf: a priest, a soldier, and a white horse.

The weather was hot; we were tired, and did not care to go to the theatres, if any of

them were open. The pleasantest hours were
those of our afternoon drive in the Champs
Elysées and the Bois de Boulogne, — or " the
Boulogne Woods," as our American tailor's wife
of the old time called the favorite place for
driving. In passing the Place de la Concorde,
two objects in especial attracted my attention, —
the obelisk, which was lying, when I left it, in
the great boat which brought it from the Nile,
and the statue of Strasbourg, all covered with
wreaths and flags. How like children these
Parisians do act ; crying " A Berlin, à Berlin ! "
and when Berlin comes to Paris, and Strasbourg goes back to her old proprietors, instead
of taking it quietly, making all this parade of
patriotic symbols, the display of which belongs
to victory rather than to defeat !

I was surprised to find the trees in the Bois
de Boulogne so well grown : I had an idea that
they had been largely sacrificed in the time of
the siege. Among the objects which deserve
special mention are the shrieking parrots and
other birds and the yelping dogs in the grounds
of the Society of Acclimatization, — out of the
range of which the visitor will be glad to get as

soon as possible. A fountain visited by newly married couples and their friends, with a restaurant near by, where the bridal party drink the health of the newly married pair, was an object of curiosity. An unsteadiness of gait was obvious in some of the feasters. At one point in the middle of the road a mænad was flinging her arms about and shrieking as if she were just escaped from a madhouse. But the drive in the Bois was what made Paris tolerable. There were few fine equipages, and few distinguished-looking people in the carriages, but there were quiet groups by the wayside, seeming happy enough; and now and then a pretty face or a wonderful bonnet gave variety to the somewhat *bourgeois* character of the procession of fiacres.

I suppose I ought to form no opinion at all about the aspect of Paris, any more than I should of an oyster in a month without an *r* in it. We were neither of us in the best mood for sight-seeing, and Paris was not sitting up for company; in fact, she was " not at home." Remembering all this, I must say that the whole appearance of the city was dull and dreary. London out of season seemed still full of life;

Paris out of season looked vacuous and torpid. The recollection of the sorrow, the humiliation, the shame, and the agony she had passed through since I left her picking her way on the arm of the Citizen King, with his old *riflard* over her, rose before me sadly, ominously, as I looked upon the high board fence which surrounded the ruins of the Tuileries. I can understand the impulse which led the red caps to make a wreck of this grand old historical building. "Pull down the nest," they said, "and the birds will not come back." But I shudder when I think what "the red fool-fury of the Seine" has done and is believed capable of doing. I think nothing has so profoundly impressed me as the story of the precautions taken to preserve the Venus of Milo from the brutal hands of the mob. A little more violent access of fury, a little more fiery declamation, a few more bottles of *vin bleu*, and the Gallery of the Louvre, with all its treasures of art, compared with which the crown jewels just sold are but pretty pebbles, the market price of which fairly enough expresses their value, — much more, rather, than their true value, — that noble gallery, with all its masterpieces from the hands of Greek sculptors and Italian painters, would have been changed in a single night into a heap of blackened stones and a pile of smoking cinders.

I love to think that now that the people have, or at least think they have, the power in their own hands, they will outgrow this form of madness, which is almost entitled to the name of a Parisian endemic. Everything looked peaceable and stupid enough during the week I passed in Paris. But among all the fossils which Cuvier found in the Parisian basin, nothing was more monstrous than the *poissardes* of the old Revolution, or the *pétroleuses* of the recent Commune, and I fear that the breed is not extinct. An American comes to like Paris as warmly as he comes to love England, after living in it long enough to become accustomed to its ways, and I, like the rest of my countrymen who remember that France was our friend in the hour of need, who remember all the privileges and enjoyments she has freely offered us, who feel that as a sister republic her destinies are of the deepest interest to us, can have no other wish than for her continued safety, order, and prosperity.

We returned to London on the 13th of August by the same route we had followed in going from London to Paris. Our passage was rough, as compared to the former one, and some of the passengers were seasick. We were both fortunate enough to escape that trial of comfort and self-respect.

I can hardly separate the story of the following week from that of the one before we went to Paris. We did a little more shopping and saw a few more sights. I hope that no reader of mine would suppose that I would leave London without seeing Madame Tussaud's exhibition. Our afternoon drives made us familiar with many objects which I always looked upon with pleasure. There was the obelisk, brought from Egypt at the expense of a distinguished and successful medical practitioner, Sir Erasmus Wilson, the eminent dermatologist and author of a manual of anatomy which for many years was my favorite text-book. There was "The Monument," which characterizes itself by having no prefix to its generic name. I enjoyed looking at and driving round it, and thinking over Pepys's lively account of the Great Fire, and speculating as to where Pudding Lane and Pie Corner stood, and recalling Pope's lines which I used to read at school, wondering what was the meaning of the second one : —

> " Where London's column, pointing to the skies
> Like a tall bully, lifts its head and lies."

The week passed away rapidly enough, and we made ready for our departure. It was no easy matter to get a passage home, but we had at last settled it that we would return in the same vessel in which we had at first engaged our passage to Liverpool, the Catalonia. But we were fortunate enough to have found an active and efficient friend in our townsman, Mr. Montgomery Sears, who procured staterooms for us in a much swifter vessel, to sail on the 21st for New York, the Aurania.

Our last visitor in London was the faithful friend who had been the first to welcome us, Lady Harcourt, in whose kind attentions I felt the warmth of my old friendship with her admired and honored father and her greatly beloved mother. I had recently visited their place of rest in the Kensal Green Cemetery, recalling with tenderest emotions the many years in which I had enjoyed their companionship.

On the 19th of August we left London for Liverpool, and on our arrival took lodgings at the Adelphi Hotel.

The kindness with which I had been welcomed, when I first arrived at Liverpool, had left a deep impression upon my mind. It seemed very ungrateful to leave that noble city, which had met me in some of its most esteemed representatives with a warm grasp of the hand even before my foot had touched English soil, without staying to thank my new friends, who would have it that they were old friends. But I was entirely unfit for enjoying any company when I landed. I took care, therefore, to allow sufficient time in Liverpool, before sailing for home, to meet such friends, old and recent, as cared to make or renew acquaintance with me. In the afternoon of the 20th we held a reception, at which a hundred visitors, more or less, presented themselves, and we had a very sociable hour or two together. The Vice-Consul, Mr. Sewall, in the enforced absence of his principal, Mr. Russell, paid us every attention, and was very agreeable. In the evening I was entertained at a great banquet given by the Philomathean Society. This flourishing institution enrolls among its members a large proportion of the most cultivated and intelligent gentlemen of Liverpool. I enjoyed the meeting very highly, listened to pleasant things which were said about myself, and answered in the unpremeditated words which came to my lips and were cordially received. I could have wished to see more of Liverpool, but I found time only to visit the great exhibition, then open. The one class of objects which captivated my attention was the magnificent series of models of steamboats and other vessels. I did not look upon them with the eye of an expert, but the great number and variety of these beautiful miniature ships and boats excited my admiration.

On the 21st of August we went on board the Aurania. Everything was done to make us comfortable. Many old acquaintances, friends, and family connections were our fellow-passengers. As for myself, I passed through the same trying experiences as those which I have recorded as characterizing my outward passage. Our greatest trouble during the passage was from fog. The frequency of collisions, of late

years, tends to make everybody nervous when
they hear the fog-whistle shrieking. This sound
and the sight of the boats are not good for
timid people. Fortunately, no one was particularly excitable, or if so, no one betrayed any
special uneasiness.

On the evening of the 27th we had an entertainment, in which Miss Kellogg sang and I
read several poems. A very pretty sum was
realized for some charity, — I forget what, —
and the affair was voted highly successful. The
next day, the 28th, we were creeping towards
our harbor through one of those dense fogs
which are more dangerous than the old rocks of
the sirens, or Scylla and Charybdis, or the much-
lied-about maelstrom.

On Sunday, the 29th of August, my birthday,
we arrived in New York. In these days of
birthday-books our chronology is not a matter
of secret history, in case we have been much
before the public. I found a great cake had
been made ready for me, in which the number
of my summers was represented by a ring of
raisins which made me feel like Methuselah. A
beautiful bouquet which had been miraculously

preserved for the occasion was for the first time displayed. It came from Dr. Beach, of Boston, *via* London. Such is the story, and I can only suppose that the sweet little cherub who sits up aloft had taken special charge of it, or it would have long ago withered.

We slept at the Fifth Avenue Hotel, which we found fresh, sweet, bright, — it must have been recently rejuvenated, I thought. The next day we took the train for New Haven, Springfield, and Boston, and that night slept in our own beds, thankful to find ourselves safe at home after our summer excursion, which had brought us so many experiences delightful to remember, so many friendships which have made life better worth living.

In the following section I shall give some of the general impressions which this excursion has left in my memory, and a few suggestions derived from them.

VIII.

MY reader was fairly forewarned that this narrative was to be more like a chapter of autobiography than the record of a tourist. In the language of philosophy, it is written from a subjective, not an objective, point of view. It is not exactly a " Sentimental Journey," though there are warm passages here and there which end with notes of admiration. I remind myself now and then of certain other travellers: of Benjamin of Tudela, going from the hospitalities of one son of Abraham to another; of John Buncle, finding the loveliest of women under every roof that sheltered him; sometimes, perhaps, of that tipsy rhymester whose record of his good and bad fortunes at the hands of landlords and landladies is enlivened by an occasional touch of humor, which makes it palatable to coarse literary feeders. But in truth these papers have many of the characteristics of private letters written home to friends. They *are* written for friends, rather than for a public which cares nothing about the writer. I knew that there were many such whom it would please to know where the writer went, whom he saw and what he saw, and how he was impressed by persons and things.

If I were planning to make a tour of the United Kingdom, and could command the service of all the wise men I count or have counted among my friends, I would go with such a retinue summoned from the ranks of the living and the dead as no prince ever carried with him. I would ask Mr. Lowell to go with me among scholars, where I could be a listener; Mr. Norton to visit the cathedrals with me; Professor Gray to be my botanical oracle; Professor Agassiz to be always ready to answer questions about the geological strata and their fossils; Dr. Jeffries Wyman to point out and interpret the common objects which present themselves to a sharp-eyed observer; and Mr. Boyd Dawkins to pilot me among the caves and cairns. Then I should want a better pair of eyes and a better pair of ears, and, while I was reorganizing, perhaps a quicker apprehension and a more retentive memory; in short, a new outfit, bodily and mental. But Nature does not care to mend old shoes; she prefers a new pair, and a young person to stand in them.

What a great book one could make, with such aids, and how many would fling it down, and take up anything in preference, provided only that it were short enough; even this slight record, for want of something shorter!

Not only did I feel sure that many friends would like to read our itinerary, but another motive prompted me to tell the simple story of our travels. I could not receive such kindness, so great evidences of friendly regard, without a strong desire, amounting to a positive necessity, for the expression of my grateful sense of all that had been done for us. Individually, I felt it, of course, as a most pleasing experience. But I believed it to have a more important significance as an illustration of the cordial feeling existing between England and America. I know that many of my countrymen felt the attentions paid to me as if they themselves shared them with me. I have lived through many strata of feeling in America towards England.

My parents, full-blooded Americans, were both born subjects of King George III. Both learned in their early years to look upon Britons as the enemies of their country. A good deal of the old hostility lingered through my boyhood, and this was largely intensified by the war of 1812. After nearly half a century this feeling had in great measure subsided, when the War of Secession called forth expressions of sympathy with the slaveholding States which surprised, shocked, and deeply wounded the lovers of liberty and of England in the Northern States. A new generation is outgrowing that alienation. More and more the older and younger nations are getting to be proud and really fond of each other. There is no shorter road to a mother's heart than to speak pleasantly to her child, and caress it, and call it pretty names. No matter whether the child is something remarkable or not, it is *her* child, and that is enough. It may be made too much of, but that is not its mother's fault. If I could believe that every attention paid me was due simply to my being an American, I should feel honored and happy in being one of the humbler media through which the good - will of a great and generous country reached the heart of a far off people not always in friendly relations with her.

I have named many of the friends who did everything to make our stay in England and Scotland agreeable. The unforeseen shortening of my visit must account for many disappointments to myself, and some, it may be, to others.

First in the list of lost opportunities was that of making my bow to the Queen. I had the honor of receiving a card with the invitation to meet Her Majesty at a garden-party, but we were travelling when it was sent, and it arrived too late.

I was very sorry not to meet Mr. Ruskin, to whom Mr. Norton had given me a note of introduction. At the time when we were hoping to see him it was thought that he was too ill to receive visitors, but he has since written me that he regretted we did not carry out our intention. I lamented my being too late to see once more two gentlemen from whom I should have been sure of a kind welcome, — Lord Houghton and Dean Stanley, both of whom I had met in Boston. Even if I had stayed out the whole time I had intended to remain abroad, I should undoubtedly have failed to see many persons and many places that I must always feel sorry for having missed. But as it is, I will not try to count all that I lost; let me rather be thankful that I met so many friends whom it was a pleasure to know personally, and saw so much that it is a pleasure to remember.

I find that many of the places I most wish to see are those associated with the memory of some individual, generally one of the generations more or less in advance of my own. One of the first places I should go to, in a leisurely tour, would be Selborne. Gilbert White was not a poet, neither was he a great systematic naturalist. But he used his eyes on the world about him; he found occupation and happiness in his daily walks, and won as large a measure of immortality within the confines of his little village as he could have gained in exploring the sources of the Nile. I should make a solemn pilgrimage to the little town of Eyam, in Derbyshire, where the Reverend Mr. Mompesson, the hero of the plague of 1665, and his wife, its heroine and its victim, lie buried. I should like to follow the traces of Cowper at Olney and of Bunyan at Elstow. I found an intense interest in the Reverend Mr. Alger's account of his visit to the Vale of Llangollen, where Lady Eleanor Butler and Miss Ponsonby passed their peaceful days in long, uninterrupted friendship. Of course the haunts of Burns, the home of Scott, the whole region made sacred by Wordsworth and the group to which he belongs would be so many shrines to which I should make pilgrimages.

I own, also, to having something of the melodramatic taste so notable in Victor Hugo. I admired the noble façade of Wells cathedral and the grand old episcopal palace, but I begged the bishop to show me the place where his predecessor, Bishop Kidder and his wife, were killed by the falling chimney in the "Great Storm." — I wanted to go to Devizes, and see the monument in the market-place, where Ruth Pierce was struck dead with a lie in her mouth, — about all which I had read in early boyhood. I contented myself with a photograph of it which my friend, Mr. Willett, went to Devizes and bought for me.

There are twenty different Englands, every one of which it would be a delight to visit, and I should hardly know with which of them to begin.

The few remarks I have to make on what I saw and heard have nothing beyond the value of first impressions; but as I have already said, if these are simply given, without pretending to be anything more, they are not worthless. At least they can do little harm, and may sometimes amuse a reader whom they fail to instruct. But we must all beware of hasty conclusions. If a foreigner of limited intelligence were whirled through England on the railways, he would naturally come to the conclusion that the chief product of that country is *mustard*, and that its most celebrated people are Mr. Keen and Mr. Colman, whose great advertising boards, yellow letters on a black ground, and black letters on a yellow ground, stare the traveller in the face at every station.

Of the climate, as I knew it in May and the summer months, I will only say that if I had any illusions about May and June in England, my fireplace would have been ample evidence that I was entirely disenchanted. The Derby day, the 26th of May, was most chilly and uncomfortable; at the garden-party at Kensington Palace, on the 4th of June, it was cold enough to make hot drinks and warm wraps a comfort, if not a necessity. I was thankful to have passed through these two ordeals without ill consequences. Drizzly, or damp, or cold, cloudy days were the rule rather than the exception, while we were in London. We had some few hot days, especially at Stratford, in the early part of July. In London an umbrella is as often carried as a cane; in Paris "*un homme a parapluie*" is, or used to be, supposed to carry that useful article because he does not keep and cannot hire a carriage of some sort. He may therefore be safely considered a person, and not a personage.

The soil of England does not seem to be worn out, to judge by the wonderful verdure and the luxuriance of vegetation. It contains a great museum of geological specimens, and a series of historical strata which are among the most instructive of human records. I do not pretend to much knowledge of geology. The most interest-

ing geological objects in our New England that
I can think of are the great boulders and the
scratched and smoothed surface of the rocks;
the fossil footprints in the valley of the Connecticut; the trilobites found at Quincy. But the
readers of Hugh Miller remember what a variety of fossils he found in the stratified rocks
of his little island, and the museums are full
of just such objects. When it comes to underground historical relics, the poverty of New
England as compared with the wealth of Old
England is very striking. Stratum after stratum
carries the explorer through the relics of successive invaders. After passing through the characteristic traces of different peoples, he comes
upon a Roman pavement, and below this the
weapons and ornaments of a tribe of ancient
Britons. One cannot strike a spade into the
earth, in Great Britain, without a fair chance of
some surprise in the form of a Saxon coin, or a
Celtic implement, or a Roman fibula. Nobody
expects any such pleasing surprise in a New
England field. One must be content with an Indian arrowhead or two, now and then a pestle
and mortar, or a stone pipe. A top dressing of

antiquity is all he can look for. The soil is not humanized enough to be interesting; whereas in England so much of it has been trodden by human feet, built on in the form of human habitations, nay, has been itself a part of preceding generations of human beings, that it is in a kind of dumb sympathy with those who tread its turf. Perhaps it is not literally true that

> One half her soil has walked the rest
> In poets, heroes, martyrs, sages;

but so many of all these lie within it that the whole mother island is a *campo santo* to all who can claim the same blood as that which runs in the veins of her unweaned children.

The flora and fauna of a country, as seen from railroad trains and carriages, are not likely to be very accurately or exhaustively studied. I spoke of the trees I noticed between Chester and London somewhat slightingly. But I did not form any hasty opinions from what happened to catch my eye. Afterwards, in the oaks and elms of Windsor Park, in the elms of Cambridge and Oxford and Salisbury, in the lindens of Stratford, in the various noble trees, including the cedar of Lebanon, in which Tennyson very justly felt a pride as their owner, I saw enough to make me glad that I had not uttered any rash generalizations on the strength of my first glance. The most interesting comparison I made was between the New England and the Old England elms. It is not necessary to cross the ocean to do this, as we have both varieties growing side by side in our parks, — on Boston Common, for instance. It is wonderful to note how people will lie about big trees. There must be as many as a dozen trees, each of which calls itself the " largest elm in New England." In my younger days, when I never travelled without a measuring-tape in my pocket, it amused me to see how meek one of the great swaggering elms would look when it saw the fatal measure begin to unreel itself. It seemed to me that the leaves actually trembled as the inexorable band encircled the trunk in *the small- est place it could find*, which is the only safe rule. The English elm (*Ulmus campestris*) as we see it in Boston comes out a little earlier perhaps, than our own, but the difference is slight. It holds its leaves long after our elms are bare. It grows upward, with abundant dark foliage, while ours spreads, sometimes a hundred and twenty feet, and often droops like a weeping willow. The English elm looks like a much more robust tree than ours, yet they tell me it is very fragile, and that its limbs are constantly breaking off in high winds, just as happens with our native elms. Ours is not a very long-lived tree; between two and three hundred years is, I think, the longest life that can be hoped for it. Since I have heard of the fragility of the English elm, which is the fatal fault of our own, I have questioned whether it can claim a greater longevity than ours. There is a hint of a typical difference in the American and the Englishman which I have long recognized in the two elms as compared to each other. It may be fanciful, but I have thought that the compactness and robustness about the English elm, which are replaced by the long, tapering limbs and willowy grace and far-spreading reach of our own, might find a certain parallelism in the people, especially the females of the two countries.

I saw no horse-chestnut trees equal to those I

remember in Salem, and especially to one in Rockport, which is the largest and finest I have ever seen; no willows like those I pass in my daily drives.

On the other hand, I think I never looked upon a Lombardy poplar equal to one I saw in Cambridge, England. This tree seems to flourish in England much more than with us.

I do not remember any remarkable beeches, though there are some very famous ones, especially the Burnham beeches.

No apple-trees I saw in England compare with one next my own door, and there are many others as fine in the neighborhood.

I have spoken of the pleasure I had in seeing by the roadside primroses, cowslips, and daisies. Dandelions, buttercups, hawkweed, looked much as ours do at home. Wild roses also grew at the roadside, — smaller and paler, I thought, than ours.

I cannot make a chapter like the famous one on Iceland, from my own limited observation: *There are no snakes in England.* I *can* say that I found two small caterpillars on my overcoat, in coming from Lord Tennyson's grounds.

If they had stayed on his premises, they might perhaps have developed into "purple emperors," or spread "the tiger moth's deep damasked wings" before the enraptured eyes of the noble poet. These two caterpillars and a few house-flies are all I saw, heard, or felt, by day or night, of the native fauna of England, except a few birds, — rooks, starlings, a blackbird, and the larks of Salisbury Plain just as they rose; for I lost sight of them almost immediately. I neither heard nor saw the nightingales, to my great regret. They had been singing at Oxford a short time before my visit to that place. The only song I heard was that which I have mentioned, the double note of the cuckoo.

England is the paradise of horses. They are bred, fed, trained, groomed, housed, cared for, in a way to remind one of the Houyhnhnms, and strikingly contrasting with the conditions of life among the wretched classes whose existence is hardly more tolerable than that of those *quasi*-human beings under whose name it pleased the fierce satirist to degrade humanity. The horses that are driven in the hansoms of London are the best I have seen in any public conveyance.

I cannot say as much of those in the four-wheelers.

Broad streets, sometimes, as in Bond Street, with narrow sidewalks; *islands* for refuge in the middle of many of them; deep areas; lofty houses; high walls; plants in the windows; frequent open spaces; policemen at near intervals, always polite in my experience, — such are my recollections of the quarter I most frequented.

Are the English taller, stouter, lustier, ruddier, healthier, than our New England people? If I gave my impression, I should say that they are. Among the wealthier class, tall, athletic-looking men and stately, well-developed women are more common, I am compelled to think, than with us. I met in company at different times five gentlemen, each of whom would be conspicuous in any crowd for his stature and proportions. We could match their proportions, however, in the persons of well-known Bostonians. To see how it was with other classes, I walked in the Strand one Sunday, and noted carefully the men and women I met. I was surprised to see how many of both sexes were of low stature. I counted in the course of a few minutes' walk no less than twenty of these little people. I set this experience against the other. Neither is convincing. The anthropologists will settle the question of man in the Old and in the New World before many decades have passed.

In walking the fashionable streets of London one can hardly fail to be struck with the well-dressed look of gentlemen of all ages. The special point in which the Londoner excels all other citizens I am conversant with is the hat. I have not forgotten Béranger's

" Quoique leurs chapeaux soient bien laids
*** ***! moi, j'aime les Anglais ; "

but in spite of it I believe in the English hat as the best thing of its ugly kind. As for the Englishman's feeling with reference to it, a foreigner might be pardoned for thinking it was his fetich, a North American Indian for looking at it as taking the place of his own medicine-bag. It is a common thing for the Englishman to say his prayers into it, as he sits down in his pew. Can it be that this imparts a religious character to the article? However this may be,

the true Londoner's hat is cared for as reveren-
tially as a High-Church altar. Far off its coming shines. I was always impressed by the fact
that even with us a well-bred gentleman in re-
duced circumstances never forgets to keep his
beaver well brushed, and I remember that long
ago I spoke of the hat as the *ultimum moriens*
of what we used to call gentility, — the last
thing to perish in the decay of a gentleman's
outfit. His hat is as sacred to an Englishman
as his beard to a Mussulman.

In looking at the churches and the monuments
which I saw in London and elsewhere in England, certain resemblances, comparisons, paral-
lels, contrasts, and suggestions obtruded themselves upon my consciousness. We have one
steeple in Boston which to my eyes seems absolutely perfect: that of the Central Church, at
the corner of Newbury and Berkeley streets.
Its resemblance to the spire of Salisbury had always struck me. On mentioning this to the late
Mr. Richardson, the very distinguished architect, he said to me that he thought it more
nearly like that of the Cathedral of Chartres.

One of our best living architects agreed with me
as to its similarity to that of Salisbury. It does
not copy either exactly, but, if it had twice its
actual dimensions, would compare well with the
best of the two, if one is better than the other.
Saint-Martin's-in-the-Fields made me feel as if I
were in Boston. Our Arlington Street Church
copies it pretty closely, but Mr. Gilman left out
the columns. I could not admire the Nelson
Column, nor that which lends monumental distinction to the Duke of York. After Trajan's
and that of the Place Vendôme, each of which
is a permanent and precious historical record,
accounting sufficiently for its existence, there
is something very unsatisfactory in these nude
cylinders. That to the Duke of York might
well have the confession of the needy knife
grinder as an inscription on its base. I confess
in all honesty that I vastly prefer the monument
commemorating the fire to either of them.
That *has* a story to tell and tells it, — with a lie
or two added, according to Pope, but it tells it
in language and symbol.

As for the kind of monument such as I see
from my library window standing on the sum-

mit of Bunker Hill, and have recently seen for the first time at Washington, on a larger scale, I own that I think a built-up obelisk a poor affair as compared with an Egyptian monolith of the same form. It was a triumph of skill to quarry, to shape, to transport, to cover with expressive symbols, to erect, such a stone as that which has been transferred to the Thames Embankment, or that which now stands in Central Park, New York. Each of its four sides is a page of history, written so as to endure through scores of centuries. A built-up obelisk requires very little more than brute labor. A child can shape its model from a carrot or a parsnip, and set it up in miniature with blocks of loaf sugar. It teaches nothing, and the stranger must go to his guide-book to know what it is there for. I was led into many reflections by a sight of the Washington Monument. I found that it was almost the same thing at a mile's distance as the Bunker Hill Monument at half a mile's distance; and unless the eye had some means of measuring the space between itself and the stone shaft, one was about as good as the other. A mound like that of Marathon or that at Waterloo, a cairn, even a shaft of the most durable form and material, are fit memorials of the place where a great battle was fought. They seem less appropriate as monuments to individuals. I doubt the durability of these piecemeal obelisks, and when I think of that vast inverted pendulum vibrating in an earthquake, I am glad that I do not live in its shadow. The Washington Monument is more than a hundred feet higher than Salisbury steeple, but it does not look to me so high as that, because the mind has nothing to climb by. But the forming taste of the country revels in superlatives, and if we could only have the deepest artesian well in the world sunk by the side of the tallest column in all creation, the admiring, not overcritical patriot would be happier than ever was the Athenian when he looked up at the newly erected Parthenon.

I made a few miscellaneous observations which may be worth recording. One of these was the fact of the repetition of the types of men and women with which I was familiar at home. Every now and then I met a new acquaintance whom I felt that I had seen before. Presently

I identified him with his double on the other side. I had found long ago that even among Frenchmen I often fell in with persons whose counterparts I had known in America. I began to feel as if Nature turned out a batch of human beings for every locality of any importance, very much as a workman makes a set of chessmen. If I had lived a little longer in London, I am confident that I should have met myself, as I did actually meet so many others who were duplicates of those long known to me.

I met Mr. Galton for a few moments, but I had no long conversation with him. If he should ask me to say how many faces I can visually recall, I should have to own that there are very few such. The two pictures which I have already referred to, those of Erasmus and of Dr. Johnson, come up more distinctly before my mind's eye than almost any faces of the living. My mental retina has, I fear, lost much of its sensitiveness. Long and repeated exposure of an object of any kind, in a strong light, is necessary to fix its image.

Among the gratifications that awaited me in

England and Scotland was that of meeting many before unseen friends with whom I had been in correspondence. I have spoken of Mr. John Bellows. I should have been glad to meet Mr. William Smith, the Yorkshire antiquary, who has sent me many of his antiquarian and biographical writings and publications. I do not think I saw Mr. David Gilmour, of Paisley, whose "Paisley Folk" and other writings have given me great pleasure. But I did have the satisfaction of meeting Professor Gairdner, of Glasgow, to whose writings my attention was first called by my revered instructor, the late Dr. James Jackson, and with whom I had occasionally corresponded. I ought to have met Dr. Martineau. I should have visited the Reverend Stopford Brooke, who could have told me much that I should have liked to hear of dear friends of mine, of whom he saw a great deal in their hours of trial. The Reverend Mr. Voysey, whose fearless rationalism can hardly give him popularity among the conservative people I saw most of, paid me the compliment of calling, as he had often done of sending me his published papers. Now and then some less known correspondent

would reveal himself or herself in bodily presence. Let most authors beware of showing
themselves to those who have idealized them,
and let readers not be too anxious to see in the
flesh those whom they have idealized. When I
was a boy, I read Miss Edgeworth's "L'Amie
Inconnue." I have learned to appreciate its
meaning in later years by abundant experiences,
and I have often felt unwilling to substitute my
real for my imaginary presence. I will add
here that I must have met a considerable number of persons, in the crowd at our reception and
elsewhere, whose names I failed to hear, and
whom I consequently did not recognize as the
authors of books I had read, or of letters I had
received. The story of my experience with the
lark accounts for a good deal of what seemed
like negligence or forgetfulness, and which must
be, not pardoned, but sighed over.

I visited several of the well-known clubs,
either by special invitation, or accompanied by
a member. The Athenæum was particularly attentive, but I was unable to avail myself of the
privileges it laid freely open before me during
my stay in London. Other clubs I looked in

upon were: the Reform Club, where I had the pleasure of dining at a large party given by the very distinguished Dr. Morell Mackenzie; the Rabelais, of which, as I before related, I have been long a member, and which was one of the first places where I dined; the Saville; the Savage; the St. George's. I saw next to nothing of the proper club-life of London, but it seemed to me that the Athenæum must be a very desirable place of resort to the educated Londoner, and no doubt each of the many institutions of this kind with which London abounds has its special attractions.

My obligations to my brethren of the medical profession are too numerous to be mentioned in detail. Almost the first visit I paid was one to my old friend and fellow-student in Paris, Dr. Walter Hayle Walshe. After more than half a century's separation, two young friends, now old friends, must not expect to find each other just the same as when they parted. Dr. Walshe thought he should have known me; my eyes are not so good as his, and I would not answer for them and for my memory. That he should have dedicated his recent original and ingenious work to me, before I had thought of visiting England, was a most gratifying circumstance. I have mentioned the hospitalities extended to me by various distinguished members of the medical profession, but I have not before referred to the readiness with which, on all occasions, when professional advice was needed, it was always given with more than willingness, rather as if it were a pleasure to give it. I could not have accepted such favors as I received had I not remembered that I, in my time, had given my services freely for the benefit of those of my own calling. If I refer to two names among many, it is for special reasons. Dr. Wilson Fox, the distinguished and widely known practitioner, who showed us great kindness, has since died, and this passing tribute is due to his memory. I have before spoken of the exceptional favor we owed to Dr. and Mrs. Priestley. It enabled us to leave London feeling that we had tried, at least, to show our grateful sense of all the attentions bestowed upon us. If there were any whom we overlooked, among the guests we wished to honor, all such accidental omissions will be pardoned, I feel sure, by those who know how great and bewildering is the pressure of social life in London.

I was, no doubt, often more or less confused, in my perceptions, by the large number of persons whom I met in society. I found the dinner-parties, as Mr. Lowell told me I should, very much like the same entertainments among my home acquaintances. I have not the gift of silence, and I am not a bad listener, yet I brought away next to nothing from dinner-parties where I had said and heard enough to fill out a magazine article. After I was introduced to a lady, the conversation frequently began somewhat in this way : —

"It is a long time since you have been in this country, I believe?"

"It is a *very* long time: fifty years and more."

"You find great changes in London, of course, I suppose?"

"Not so great as you might think. The Tower is where I left it. The Abbey is much as I remember it. Northumberland House with its lion is gone, but Charing Cross is in the same old place. My attention is drawn especially to the things which have *not* changed, — those which I remember."

That stream was quickly dried up. Conversation soon found other springs. I never knew the talk to get heated or noisy. Religion and politics rarely came up, and never in any controversial way. The bitterest politician I met at table was a quadruped, — a lady's dog, — who refused a desirable morsel offered him in the name of Mr. Gladstone, but snapped up another instantly on being told that it came from Queen Victoria. I recall many pleasant and some delightful talks at the dinner-table; one in particular, with the most charming woman in England. I wonder if she remembers how very lovely and agreeable she was? Possibly she may be able to identify herself.

People, — the right kind of people, — meet at a dinner-party as two ships meet and pass each other at sea. They exchange a few signals; ask each other's reckoning, where from, where bound; perhaps one supplies the other with a little food or a few dainties; then they part, to see each other no more. But one or both may remember the hour passed together all their days, just as I recollect our brief parley with the brig Economist, of Leith, from Sierra Leone, in mid ocean, in the spring of 1833.

I am very far from despising the science of gastronomy, but if I wished to institute a comparison between the tables of England and America, I could not do it without eating my way through the four seasons. I will say that I did not think the bread from the bakers' shops was so good as our own. It was very generally tough and hard, and even the muffins were not always so tender and delicate as they ought to be. I got impatient one day, and sent out for some biscuits. They brought some very excellent ones, which we much preferred to the tough bread. They proved to be the so-called "sea-foam" biscuit from New York. The potatoes never came on the table looking like new-fallen snow, as we have them at home. We were surprised to find both mutton and beef overdone, according to our American taste. The French talk about the Briton's "*bifteck saignant*," but we never saw anything cooked so as to be, as we should say, "rare." The tart is national with the English, as the pie is national with us. I

never saw on an English table that excellent
substitute for both, called the Washington pie,
in memory of him whom we honor as first in
pies, as well as in war and in the hearts of his
countrymen.

The truth is that I gave very little thought to
the things set before me, in the excitement of
constantly changing agreeable companionship.
I understand perfectly the feeling of the good
liver in Punch, who suggests to the lady next
him that their host has one of the best cooks in
London, and that it might therefore be well to
defer all conversation until they adjourned to the
drawing-room. I preferred the conversation,
and adjourned, indefinitely, the careful apprecia-
tion of the *menu*. I think if I could devote a
year to it, I might be able to make out a graduated scale of articles of food, taking a well-
boiled fresh egg as the unit of gastronomic
value, but I leave this scientific task to some
future observer.

The most remarkable piece of European
handiwork I remember was the steel chair at
Longford Castle. The most startling and
frightful work of man I ever saw or expect to

see was another specimen of work in steel, said to have been taken from one of the infernal chambers of the Spanish Inquisition. It was a complex mechanism, which grasped the body and the head of the heretic or other victim, and by means of many ingeniously arranged screws and levers was capable of pressing, stretching, piercing, rending, crushing, all the most sensitive portions of the human body, one at a time or many at once. The famous Virgin, whose embrace drove a hundred knives into the body of the poor wretch she took in her arms, was an angel of mercy compared to this masterpiece of devilish enginery.

Ingenuity is much better shown in contrivances for making our daily life more comfortable. I was on the lookout for everything that promised to be a convenience. I carried out two things which seemed to be new to the Londoners : the Star Razor, which I have praised so freely, and still find equal to all my commendations ; and the mucilage pencil, which is a very handy implement to keep on the writer's desk or table. I found a contrivance for protecting the hand in drawing corks, which all who are their own butlers will appreciate, and luminous match-boxes which really shine brightly in the dark, and that after a year's usage; whereas one professing to shine by night, which I bought in Boston, is only visible by borrowed light. I wanted a very fine-grained hone, and inquired for it at a hardware store, where they kept everything in their line of the best quality. I brought away a very pretty but very small stone, for which I paid a large price. The stone was from Arkansas, and I need not have bought in London what would have been easily obtained at a dozen or more stores in Boston. It was a renewal of my experience with the sea-foam biscuit. "Know thyself" and the things about thee, and "Take the good the gods provide thee," if thou wilt only keep thine eyes open, are two safe precepts.

Who is there of English descent among us that does not feel with Cowper,

"England, with all thy faults, I love thee still" ?

Our recently naturalized fellow-citizens, of a different blood and different religion, must not suppose that we are going to forget our inborn love for the mother to whom we owe our being.

Protestant England and Protestant America are coming nearer and nearer to each other every year. The interchange of the two peoples is more and more frequent, and there are many reasons why it is likely to continue increasing.

Hawthorne says in a letter to Longfellow, " Why don't you come over, being now a man of leisure and with nothing to keep you in America? If I were in your position, I think I should make my home on this side of the water, — though always with an indefinite and never-to-be-executed intention to go back and die in my native land. America is a good land for young people, but not for those who are past their prime. . . . A man of individuality and refinement can certainly live far more comfortably here — provided he has the means to live at all — than in New England. Be it owned, however, that I sometimes feel a tug at my very heart-strings when I think of my old home and friends." This was written from Liverpool in 1854.

We must not forget that our fathers were exiles from their dearly loved native land, driven by causes which no longer exist. " Freedom to worship God " is found in England as fully as in America, in our day. In placing the Atlantic between themselves and the Old World civilizations they made an enormous sacrifice. It is true that the wonderful advance of our people in all the arts and accomplishments which make life agreeable has transformed the wilderness into a home where men and women can live comfortably, elegantly, happily, if they are of contented disposition; and without that they can be happy nowhere. What better provision can be made for a mortal man than such as our own Boston can afford its wealthy children? A palace on Commonwealth Avenue or on Beacon Street; a country-place at Framingham or Lenox; a seaside residence at Nahant, Beverly Farms, Newport, or Bar Harbor; a pew at Trinity or King's Chapel; a tomb at Mount Auburn or Forest Hills; with the prospect of a memorial stained window after his lamented demise, — is not this a pretty programme to offer a candidate for human existence?

Give him all these advantages, and he will still be longing to cross the water, to get back to that old home of his fathers, so delightful in

itself, so infinitely desirable on account of its
nearness to Paris, to Geneva, to Rome, to all
that is most interesting in Europe. The less
wealthy, less cultivated, less fastidious class of
Americans are not so much haunted by these
longings. But the convenience of living in the
Old World is so great, and it is such a trial and
such a risk to keep crossing the ocean, that it
seems altogether likely that a considerable cur-
rent of re-migration will gradually develop itself among our people.

Some find the climate of the other side of the
Atlantic suits them better than their own. As
the New England characteristics are gradually
superseded by those of other races, other forms
of belief, and other associations, the time may
come when a New Englander will feel more as
if he were among his own people in London
than in one of our seaboard cities. The vast
majority of our people love their country too
well and are too proud of it to be willing to ex-
patriate themselves. But going back to our old
home, to find ourselves among the relatives from
whom we have been separated for a few generations, is not like transferring ourselves to a land

where another language is spoken, and where there are no ties of blood and no common religious or political traditions. I, for one, being myself as inveterately rooted an American of the Bostonian variety as ever saw himself mirrored in the Frog Pond, hope that the exchanges of emigrants and re-migrants will be much more evenly balanced by and by than at present. I hope that more Englishmen like James Smithson will help to build up our scientific and literary institutions. I hope that more Americans like George Peabody will call down the blessings of the English people by noble benefactions to the cause of charity. It was with deep feelings of pride and gratitude that I looked upon the bust of Longfellow, holding its place among the monuments of England's greatest and best children. I see with equal pleasure and pride that one of our own large-hearted countrymen has honored the memory of three English poets, Milton, and Herbert, and Cowper, by the gift of two beautiful stained windows, and with still ampler munificence is erecting a stately fountain in the birthplace of Shakespeare. Such acts as these make us feel more and more the truth of the generous sentiment which closes the ode of Washington Allston, "America to Great Britain:" "We are one!"

I have told our story with the help of my daughter's diary, and often aided by her recollections. Having enjoyed so much, I am desirous that my countrymen and countrywomen should share my good fortune with me. I hesitated at first about printing names in full, but when I remembered that we received nothing but the most overflowing hospitality and the most considerate kindness from all we met, I felt sure that I could not offend by telling my readers who the friends were that made England a second home to us. If any one of them is disturbed by such reference as I have made to him or to her, I most sincerely apologize for the liberty I have taken. I am far more afraid that through sheer forgetfulness I have left unmentioned many to whom I was and still remain under obligations.

If I were asked what I think of people's travelling after the commonly accepted natural term of life is completed, I should say that everything depends on constitution and habit. The old soldier says, in speaking of crossing the Beresina, where the men had to work in the freezing stream constructing the bridges, "Faut du tempérament pour cela!" I often thought of this expression, in the damp and chilly weather which not rarely makes English people wish they were in Italy. I escaped unharmed from the windy gusts at Epsom and the nipping chill of the Kensington garden-party; but if a score of my contemporaries had been there with me, there would not improbably have been a funeral or two within a week. If, however, the super-septuagenarian is used to exposures, if he is an old sportsman or an old officer not retired from active service, he may expect to elude the pneumonia which follows his footsteps whenever he wanders far from his fireside. But to a person of well-advanced years coming from a counting-room, a library, or a studio, the risk is considerable, unless he is of hardy natural constitution; any other will do well to remember, "Faut du tempérament pour cela!"

Suppose there to be a reasonable chance that he will come home alive, what is the use of one's

going to Europe after his senses have lost their
acuteness, and his mind no longer retains its full
measure of sensibilities and vigor? I should
say that the visit to Europe under those circumstances was much the same thing as the *petit
verre*, — the little glass of Chartreuse, or Ma-
raschino, or Curaçoa, or, if you will, of plain
Cognac, at the end of a long banquet. One has
gone through many courses, which repose in the
safe recesses of his economy. He has swallowed
his coffee, and still there is a little corner left
with its craving unappeased. Then comes the
drop of liqueur, *chasse-café*, which is the last
thing the stomach has a right to expect. It
warms, it comforts, it exhales its benediction on
all that has gone before. So the trip to Europe
may not do much in the way of instructing the
wearied and overloaded intelligence, but it gives
it a fillip which makes it feel young again for a
little while.

Let not the too mature traveller think it will
change any of his habits. It will interrupt his
routine for a while, and then he will settle down
into his former self, and be just what he was
before. I brought home a pair of shoes I had

made in London; they do not fit like those I had before I left, and I rarely wear them. It is just so with the new habits I formed and the old ones I left behind me.

But am I not glad, for my own sake, that I went? Certainly I have every reason to be, and I feel that the visit is likely to be a great source of happiness for my remaining days. But there is a higher source of satisfaction. If the kindness shown me strengthens the slenderest link that binds us in affection to that ancestral country which is, and I trust will always be to her descendants, "dear Mother England," that alone justifies my record of it, and to think it is so is more than reward enough. If, in addition, this account of our summer experiences is a source of pleasure to many friends, and of pain to no one, as I trust will prove to be the fact, I hope I need never regret giving to the public the pages which are meant more especially for readers who have a personal interest in the writer.

INDEX.

NOTE TO THE INDEX.

THERE are various ways of reading a book. A few diligent persons read, mark, learn, and inwardly digest every page, sentence, word, and syllable. Quick-witted students glance through a volume, and find in a few moments what it has which is likely to be of interest for them. Some run their eyes rapidly over the Index, when there is one, which is no more than every book worth printing is entitled to. Some are satisfied with the Table of Contents. Others find the Title-page as much as they want, and there are many books, the wallflowers of book-shops and libraries, which we are content to read by the lettering on their backs, without calling them out from their places.

The following Index, made for me under the direction of my Publishers, frightened me, when I first locked at it, by its exhaustiveness and its extent. I struck out a few headings, altered a few others, and concluded to let it stand as a monument of industry and fidelity. But I must say that so long a tail to so small a kite is almost without a precedent in my literary experience.

The class of readers, however, who depend upon the Index for all they wish to know about the contents of a volume will not complain of its length and minuteness of detail. I myself have nothing but gratitude to the literary laborer who undertook the tedious task of making it.

INDEX.

Standard and Popular Library Books

SELECTED FROM THE CATALOGUE OF

HOUGHTON, MIFFLIN AND COMPANY.

A Club of One. An Anonymous Volume, $1.25.

Brooks Adams. The Emancipation of Massachusetts, crown 8vo, $1.50.

John Adams and Abigail Adams. Familiar Letters of, during the Revolution, 12mo, $2.00.

Oscar Fay Adams. Handbook of English Authors, 16mo, 75 cents ; Handbook of American Authors, 16mo, 75 cents.

Louis Agassiz. Methods of Study in Natural History,·Illustrated, 12mo, $1.50; Geological Sketches, Series I. and II., 12mo, each, $1.50; A Journey in Brazil, Illustrated, 12mo, $2.50; Life and Letters, edited by his wife, 2 vols. 12mo, $4.00; Life and Works, 6 vols. $10.00.

Anne A. Agge and Mary M. Brooks. Marblehead Sketches. 4to, $3.00.

Elizabeth Akers. The Silver Bridge and other Poems, 16mo, $1.25.

Thomas Bailey Aldrich. Story of a Bad Boy, Illustrated, 12mo, $1.50; Marjorie Daw and Other People, 12mo, $1.5c ; Prudence Palfrey, 12mo, $1.50; The Queen of Sheba, 12mo, $1.50; The Stillwater Tragedy, 12mo, $1.50; Poems, *Household Edition*, Illustrated, 12mo, $1.75 ; full gilt, $2.25; The above six vols. 12mo, uniform, $9.00; From Ponkapog to Pesth, 16mo, $1.25 ; Poems, Complete, Illustrated, 8vo, $3.50 ; Mercedes, and Later Lyrics, cr. 8vo, $1.25.

Rev. A. V. G. Allen. Continuity of Christian Thought, 12mo, $2.00.

American Commonwealths. Per volume, 16mo, $1.25.

Virginia. By John Esten Cooke.
Oregon. By William Barrows.
Maryland. By Wm. Hand Browne.
Kentucky. By N. S. Shaler.
Michigan. By Hon. T. M. Cooley.

Kansas. By Leverett W. Spring.
California. By Josiah Royce.
New York. By Ellis H. Roberts. 2 vols.
Connecticut. By Alexander Johnston.

(In Preparation.)

Tennessee. By James Phelan.
Pennsylvania. By Hon. Wayne MacVeagh.
Missouri. By Lucien Carr.
Ohio. By Rufus King.
New Jersey. By Austin Scott.

American Men of Letters. Per vol., with Portrait, 16mo, $1.25.

Washington Irving. By Charles Dudley Warner.
Noah Webster. By Horace E. Scudder.
Henry D. Thoreau. By Frank B. Sanborn.
George Ripley. By O. B. Frothingham.
J. Fenimore Cooper. By Prof. T. R. Lounsbury.
Margaret Fuller Ossoli. By T. W. Higginson.
Ralph Waldo Emerson. By Oliver Wendell Holmes.
Edgar Allan Poe. By George E. Woodberry.
Nathaniel Parker Willis. By H. A. Beers.

(In Preparation.)

Benjamin Franklin. By John Bach McMaster.
Nathaniel Hawthorne. By James Russell Lowell.
William Cullen Bryant. By John Bigelow.
Bayard Taylor. By J. R. G. Hassard.
William Gilmore Simms. By George W. Cable.

American Statesmen. Per vol., 16mo, $1.25.

John Quincy Adams. By John T. Morse, Jr.
Alexander Hamilton. By Henry Cabot Lodge.
John C. Calhoun. By Dr. H. von Holst.
Andrew Jackson. By Prof. W. G. Sumner.
John Randolph. By Henry Adams.
James Monroe. By Pres. D. C. Gilman.
Thomas Jefferson. By John T. Morse, Jr.
Daniel Webster. By Henry Cabot Lodge.
Albert Gallatin. By John Austin Stevens.
James Madison. By Sydney Howard Gay.
John Adams. By John T. Morse, Jr.

John Marshall.   By Allan B. Magruder.
Samuel Adams.   By J. K. Hosmer.
Thomas H. Benton.   By Theodore Roosevelt.
Henry Clay.   By Hon. Carl Schurz.   2 vols.
(*In Preparation.*)
Martin Van Buren.   By Edward M. Shepard.
George Washington.   By Henry Cabot Lodge.   2 vols.
Patrick Henry.   By Moses Coit Tyler.

Martha Babcock Amory.   Life of Copley, 8vo, $3.00.

Hans Christian Andersen.   Complete Works, 10 vols. 12mo, each $1.00.   New Edition, 10 vols. 12mo, $10.00.

Francis, Lord Bacon.   Works, 15 vols. cr. 8vo, $33.75; *Popular Edition*, with Portraits, 2 vols. cr. 8vo, $5.00; Promus of Formularies and Elegancies, 8vo, $5.00; Life and Times of Bacon, 2 vols. cr. 8vo, $5.00.

L. H. Bailey, Jr.   Talks Afield, Illustrated, 16mo, $1.00.

M. M. Ballou.   Due West, cr. 8vo, $1.50; Due South, $1.50.

Henry A. Beers.   The Thankless Muse.   Poems.   16mo, $1.25.

E. D. R. Bianciardi.   At Home in Italy, 16mo, $1.25.

William Henry Bishop.   The House of a Merchant Prince, a Novel, 12mo, $1.50; Detmold, a Novel, 18mo, $1.25; Choy Susan and other Stories, 16mo, $1.25; The Golden Justice, 16mo, $1.25.

Bjornstjerne Bjornson.   Complete Works.   New Edition, 3 vols. 12mo, the set, $4.50; Synnove Solbakken, Bridal March, Captain Mansana, Magnhild, 16mo, each $1.00.

Anne C. Lynch Botta.   Handbook of Universal Literature, New Edition, 12mo, $2.00.

British Poets.   *Riverside Edition*, cr. 8vo, each $1.50; the set, 68 vols. $100.00.

John Brown, A. B.   John Bunyan.   Illustrated.   8vo, $4.50.

John Brown, M. D.   Spare Hours, 3 vols. 16mo, each $1.50.

Robert Browning.   Poems and Dramas, etc., 15 vols. 16mo, $22.00; Works, 8 vols. cr. 8vo, $13.00; Ferishtah's Fancies, cr. 8vo, $1.00; Jocoseria, 16mo, $1.00; cr. 8vo, $1.00; Parleyings with Certain People of Importance in their Day, 16mo or cr. 8vo, $1.25.   Works, *New Edition*, 6 vols. cr. 8vo. $10.00.

William Cullen Bryant.   Translation of Homer, The Iliad cr. 8vo, $2.50; 2 vols. royal 8vo, $9.00; cr. 8vo, $4.00. The Odyssey, cr. 8vo, $2.50; 2 vols. royal 8vo, $9.00; cr. 8vo, $4.00.

Sara C. Bull. Life of Ole Bull. *Popular Edition.* 12mo, $1.50.

John Burroughs. Works, 7 vols. 16mo, each $1.50.

Thomas Carlyle. Essays, with Portrait and Index, 4 vols. 12mo, $7.50; *Popular Edition*, 2 vols. 12mo, $3.50.

Alice and Phœbe Cary. Poems, *Household Edition*, Illustrated, 12mo, $1.75; cr. 8vo, full gilt, $2.25; *Library Edition*, including Memorial by Mary Clemmer, Portraits and 24 Illustrations, 8vo, $3.50.

Wm. Ellery Channing. Selections from His Note-Books, $1.00.

Francis J. Child (Editor). English and Scottish Popular Ballads. Eight Parts. (Parts I.–IV. now ready). 4to, each $5.00. Poems of Religious Sorrow, Comfort, Counsel, and Aspiration. 16mo, $1.25.

Lydia Maria Child. Looking Toward Sunset, 12mo, $2.50; Letters, with Biography by Whittier, 16mo, $1.50.

James Freeman Clarke. Ten Great Religions, Parts I. and II., 12mo, each $2.00; Common Sense in Religion, 12mo, $2.00; Memorial and Biographical Sketches, 12mo, $2.00.

John Esten Cooke. My Lady Pokahontas, 16mo, $1.25.

James Fenimore Cooper. Works, new *Household Edition*, Illustrated, 32 vols. 16mo, each $1.00; the set, $32.00; *Fireside Edition*, Illustrated, 16 vols. 12mo, $20.00.

Susan Fenimore Cooper. Rural Hours. 16mo, $1.25.

Charles Egbert Craddock. In the Tennessee Mountains, 16mo, $1.25; Down the Ravine, Illustrated, $1.00; The Prophet of the Great Smoky Mountains, 16mo, $1.25; In The Clouds, 16mo, $1.25.

C. P. Cranch. Ariel and Caliban. 16mo, $1.25; The Æneid of Virgil. Translated by Cranch. 8vo, $2.50.

T. F. Crane. Italian Popular Tales, 8vo, $2.50.

F. Marion Crawford. To Leeward, 16mo, $1.25; A Roman Singer, 16mo, $1.25; An American Politician, 16mo, $1.25.

M. Creighton. The Papacy during the Reformation, 4 vols. 8vo, $17.50.

Richard H. Dana. To Cuba and Back, 16mo, $1.25; **Two Years** Before the Mast, 12mo, $1.00.

G. W. and Emma De Long. Voyage of the Jeannette. 2 vols. 8vo, $7.50; New One-Volume Edition, 8vo, $4.50.

Thomas De Quincey. Works, 12 vols. 12mo, each $1.50; the set, $18.00.

Madame De Stael. Germany, 12mo, $2.50.

Charles Dickens. Works, *Illustrated Library Edition*, with Dickens Dictionary, 30 vols. 12mo, each $1.50; the set, $45.00.

J. Lewis Diman. The Theistic Argument, etc., cr. 8vo, $2.00; Orations and Essays, cr. 8vo, $2.50.

Theodore A. Dodge. Patroclus and Penelope, Illustrated, 8vo, $3.00. The Same. Outline Illustrations. Cr. 8vo, $1.25.

E. P. Dole. Talks about Law. Cr. 8vo, $2.00; sheep, $2.50.

Eight Studies of the Lord's Day. 12mo, $1.50.

George Eliot. The Spanish Gypsy, a Poem, 16mo, $1.00.

Ralph Waldo Emerson. Works, *Riverside Edition*, 11 vols. each $1.75; the set, $19.25; *"Little Classic"* Edition, 11 vols. 18mo, each, $1.50; Parnassus, *Household Edition*, 12mo, $1.75; *Library Edition*, 8vo, $4.00; Poems, *Household Edition*, Portrait, 12mo, $1.75; Memoir, by J. Elliot Cabot, 2 vols. $3.50.

English Dramatists. Vols. 1–3, Marlowe's Works; Vols. 4–11, Middleton's Works; Vols. 12–14, Marston's Works; each vol. $3.00; *Large-Paper Edition*, each vol. $4.00.

Edgar Fawcett. A Hopeless Case, 18mo, $1.25; A Gentleman of Leisure, 18mo, $1.00; An Ambitious Woman, 12mo, $1.50.

Fénelon. Adventures of Telemachus, 12mo, $2.25.

James T. Fields. Yesterdays with Authors, 12mo, $2.00; 8vo, Illustrated, $3.00; Underbrush, 18mo, $1.25; Ballads and other Verses, 16mo, $1.00; The Family Library of British Poetry, royal 8vo, $5.00; Memoirs and Correspondence, cr. 8vo, $2.00.

John Fiske. Myths and Mythmakers, 12mo, $2.00; Outlines of Cosmic Philosophy, 2 vols. 8vo, $6.00; The Unseen World, and other Essays, 12mo, $2.00; Excursions of an Evolutionist, 12mo, $2.00; The Destiny of Man, 16mo, $1.00; The Idea of God, 16mo, $1.00; Darwinism, and Other Essays, New Edition, enlarged, 12mo, $2.00.

Edward Fitzgerald. Works. 2 vols. 8vo, $10.00.

O. B. Frothingham. Life of W. H. Channing. Cr. 8vo, $2.00.

William H. Furness. Verses, 16mo, vellum, $1.25.

Gentleman's Magazine Library. 14 vols. 8vo, each $2.50; Roxburgh, $3.50; *Large-Paper Edition*, $6.00. I. Manners and Customs. II. Dialect, Proverbs, and Word-Lore. III. Popular Superstitions and Traditions. IV. English Traditions and Foreign Customs. V., VI. Archæology. VII. Romano-British Remains: Part I. (*Last two styles sold only in sets.*)

John F. Genung. Tennyson's In Memoriam, cr. 8vo, $1.25.

Johann Wolfgang von Goethe. Faust, Part First, Translated by C. T. Brooks, 16mo, $1.25; Faust, Translated by Bayard Taylor, cr. 8vo, $2.50; 2 vols. royal 8vo, $9.00; 2 vols. 12mo, $4.00; Correspondence with a Child, 12mo, $1.50; Wilhelm Meister, Translated by Carlyle, 2 vols. 12mo, $3.00. Life, by Lewes, together with the above five 12mo vols., the set, $9.00.

Oliver Goldsmith. The Vicar of Wakefield, 32mo, $1.00.

Charles George Gordon. Diaries and Letters, 8vo, $2.00.

George H. Gordon. Brook Farm to Cedar Mountain, 1861-2. 8vo, $3.00. Campaign of Army of Virginia, 1862. 8vo, $4.00. A War Diary, 1863-5. 8vo, $3.00.

George Zabriskie Gray. The Children's Crusade, 12mo, $1.50; Husband and Wife, 16mo, $1.00.

F. W. Gunsaulus. The Transfiguration of Christ. 16mo, $1.25.

Anna Davis Hallowell. James and Lucretia Mott, $2.00.

R. P. Hallowell. Quaker Invasion of Massachusetts, revised, $1.25. The Pioneer Quakers, 16mo, $1.00.

Arthur Sherburne Hardy. But Yet a Woman, 16mo, $1.25; The Wind of Destiny, 16mo, $1.25.

Bret Harte. Works, 6 vols. cr. 8vo, each $2.00; Poems, *Household Edition*, Illustrated, 12mo, $1.75; cr. 8vo, full gilt, $2.25; *Red-Line Edition*, small 4to, $2.50; *Cabinet Edition*, $1.00; In the Carquinez Woods, 18mo, $1.00; Flip, and Found at Blazing Star, 18mo, $1.00; On the Frontier, 18mo, $1.00; By Shore and Sedge, 18mo, $1.00; Maruja, 18mo, $1.00; Snow-Bound at Eagle's, 18mo, $1.00; The Queen of the Pirate Isle, Illustrated, small 4to, $1.50; A Millionaire, etc., 18mo, $1.00; The Crusade of the Excelsior, 16mo, $1.25.

Nathaniel Hawthorne. Works, "*Little Classic*" *Edition*, Illustrated, 25 vols. 18mo, each $1.00; the set $25.00; *New Riverside Edition*, Introductions by G. P. Lathrop, 11 Etchings and Portrait, 12 vols. cr. 8vo, each $2.00; *Wayside Edition*, with Introductions, Etchings, etc., 24 vols. 12mo, $36.00;

Fireside Edition, 6 vols. 12mo, $10.00; The Scarlet Letter, 12mo. $1.00.

John Hay. Pike County Ballads, 12mo, $1.50; Castilian Days, 16mo, $2.00.

Caroline Hazard. Memoir of J. L. Diman. Cr. 8vo, $2.00.

Franklin H. Head. Shakespeare's Insomnia. 16mo, parchment paper, 75 cents.

The Heart of the Weed. Anonymous Poems. 16mo, parchment paper, $1.00.

S. E. Herrick. Some Heretics of Yesterday. Cr. 8vo, $1.50.

George S. Hillard. Six Months in Italy. 12mo, $2.00.

Oliver Wendell Holmes. Poems, *Household Edition*, Illustrated, 12mo, $1.75; cr. 8vo, full gilt, $2.25; *Illustrated Library Edition*, 8vo, $3.50; *Handy-Volume Edition*, 2 vols. 32mo, $2.50; The Autocrat of the Breakfast-Table, cr. 8vo, $2.00; *Handy-Volume Edition*, 32mo, $1.25; The Professor at the Breakfast-Table, cr. 8vo, $2.00; The Poet at the Breakfast-Table, cr. 8vo, $2.00; Elsie Venner, cr. 8vo, $2.00; The Guardian Angel, cr. 8vo, $2.00; Medical Essays, cr. 8vo, $2.00; Pages from an Old Volume of Life, cr. 8vo, $2.00; John Lothrop Motley, A Memoir, 16mo, $1.50; Illustrated Poems, 8vo, $4.00; A Mortal Antipathy, cr. 8vo, $1.50; The Last Leaf, Illustrated, 4to, $10.00.

Nathaniel Holmes. The Authorship of Shakespeare. New Edition. 2 vols. $4.00.

Blanche Willis Howard. One Summer, Illustrated, 12mo, $1.25; One Year Abroad, 18mo, $1.25.

William D. Howells. Venetian Life, 12mo, $1.50; Italian Journeys, 12mo, $1.50; Their Wedding Journey, Illustrated, 12mo, $1.50; 18mo, $1.25; Suburban Sketches, Illustrated, 12mo, $1.50; A Chance Acquaintance, Illustrated, 12mo, $1.50; 18mo, $1.25; A Foregone Conclusion, 12mo, $1.50; The Lady of the Aroostook, 12mo, $1.50; The Undiscovered Country, 12mo, $1.50.

Thomas Hughes. Tom Brown's School-Days at Rugby, 16mo, $1.00; Tom Brown at Oxford, 16mo, $1.25; The Manliness of Christ, 16mo, $1.00; paper, 25 cents.

William Morris Hunt. Talks on Art, 2 Series, each $1.00.

Henry James. A Passionate Pilgrim and other Tales, 12mo, $2.00; Transatlantic Sketches, 12mo, $2.00; Roderick Hudson, 12mo, $2.00; The American, 12mo, $2.00; Watch and Ward, 18mo, $1.25; The Europeans, 12mo, $1.50; Confidence, 12mo, $1.50; The Portrait of a Lady, 12mo, $2.00.

Anna Jameson. Writings upon Art Subjects. New Edition, 10 vols. 16mo, the set, $12.50.

Sarah Orne Jewett. Deephaven, 18mo, $1.25; Old Friends and New, 18mo, $1.25; Country By-Ways, 18mo, $1.25; Play-Days, Stories for Children, square 16mo, $1.50; The Mate of the Daylight, 18mo, $1.25; A Country Doctor, 16mo, $1.25; A Marsh Island, 16mo, $1.25; A White Heron, 18mo, $1.25.

Rossiter Johnson. Little Classics, 18 vols. 18mo, each $1.00; the set, $18.00.

Samuel Johnson. Oriental Religions: India, 8vo, $5.00; China, 8vo, $5.00; Persia, 8vo, $5.00; Lectures, Essays, and Sermons, cr. 8vo, $1.75.

Charles C. Jones, Jr. History of Georgia, 2 vols. 8vo, $10.00.

Malcolm Kerr. The Far Interior. 2 vols. 8vo, $9.00.

Omar Khayyám. Rubáiyát, *Red-Line Edition*, square 16mo., $1.00; the same, with 56 Illustrations by Vedder, folio, $25.00; The Same, *Phototype Edition*, 4to, $12.50.

T. Starr King. Christianity and Humanity, with Portrait, 12mo, $1.50; Substance and Show, 16mo, $2.00.

Charles and Mary Lamb. Tales from Shakespeare. *Handy-Volume Edition*. 32mo, $1.00.

Henry Lansdell. Russian Central Asia. 2 vols. $10.00.

Lucy Larcom. Poems, 16mo, $1.25; An Idyl of Work, 16mo, $1.25; Wild Roses of Cape Ann and other Poems, 16mo, $1.25; Breathings of the Better Life, 18mo, $1.25; Poems, *Household Edition*, Illustrated, 12mo, $1.75; full gilt, $2.25; Beckonings for Every Day, 16mo, $1.00.

George Parsons Lathrop. A Study of Hawthorne. 18mo, $1.25.

Henry C. Lea. Sacerdotal Celibacy, 8vo, $4.50.

Sophia and Harriet Lee. Canterbury Tales. New Edition. 3 vols. 12mo, $3.75.

Charles G. Leland. The Gypsies, cr. 8vo, $2.00; Algonquin Legends of New England, cr. 8vo, $2.00.

George Henry Lewes. The Story of Goethe's Life, Portrait, 12mo, $1.50; Problems of Life and Mind, 5 vols. 8vo, $14.00.

A. Parlett Lloyd. The Law of Divorce, cloth, $2.00; sheep, $2.50.

J. G. Lockhart. Life of Sir W. Scott, 3 vols. 12mo, $4.50.

Henry Cabot Lodge. Studies in History, cr. 8vo, $1.50.

Henry Wadsworth Longfellow. Complete Poetical and Prose Works, *Riverside Edition*, 11 vols. cr. 8vo, $16.50; Poetical Works, *Riverside Edition*, 6 vols. cr. 8vo, $9.00; *Cambridge Edition*, 4 vols. 12mo, $7.00; Poems, *Octavo Edition*, Portrait and 300 Illustrations, $7.50; *Household Edition*, Illustrated, 12mo, $1.75; cr. 8vo, full gilt, $2.25; *Red-Line Edition*, Portrait and 12 Illustrations, small 4to, $2.50; *Cabinet Edition*, $1.00; *Library Edition*, Portrait and 32 Illustrations, 8vo, $3.50; Christus, *Household Edition*, $1.75; cr. 8vo, full gilt, $2.25; *Cabinet Edition*, $1.00; Prose Works, *Riverside Edition*, 2 vols. cr. 8vo, $3.00; Hyperion, 16mo, $1.50; Kavanagh, 16mo, $1.50; Outre-Mer, 16mo, $1.50; In the Harbor, 16mo, $1.00; Michael Angelo: a Drama, Illustrated, folio, $5.00; Twenty Poems, Illustrated, small 4to, $2.50; Translation of the Divina Commedia of Dante, *Riverside Edition*, 3 vols. cr. 8vo, $4.50; 1 vol. cr. 8vo, $2.50; 3 vols. royal 8vo, $13.50; cr. 8vo, $4.50; Poets and Poetry of Europe, royal 8vo, $5.00; Poems of Places, 31 vols. each $1.00; the set, $25.00.

James Russell Lowell. Poems, *Red-Line Edition*, Portrait, Illustrated, small 4to, $2.50; *Household Edition*, Illustrated, 12mo, $1.75; cr. 8vo, full gilt, $2.25; *Library Edition*, Portrait and 32 Illustrations, 8vo, $3.50; *Cabinet Edition*, $1.00; Fireside Travels, 12mo, $1.50; Among my Books, Series I. and II. 12mo, each $2.00; My Study Windows, 12mo, $2.00; Democracy and other Addresses, 16mo, $1.25; Uncollected Poems.

Thomas Babington Macaulay. Works, 5 vols. 12mo, $20.00.

Mrs. Madison. Memoirs and Letters of Dolly Madison, 16mo, $1.25.

Harriet Martineau. Autobiography, New Edition, 2 vols. 12mo, $4.00; Household Education, 18mo, $1.25.

H. B. McClellan. The Life and Campaigns of Maj.-Gen. J. E. B. Stuart. With Portrait and Maps, 8vo, $3.00.

G. W. Melville. In the Lena Delta, Maps and Illustrations, 8vo, $2.50.

small 4to, $2.50; *Cabinet Edition*, $1.00; *Household Edition*, Illustrated, 12mo, $1.75; full gilt, cr. 8vo, $2.25.

Sir Walter Scott. Waverley Novels, *Illustrated Library Edition*, 25 vols. 12mo, each $1.00; the set, $25.00; Tales of a Grandfather, 3 vols. 12mo, $4.50; Poems, *Red-Line Edition* Illustrated, small 4to, $2.50; *Cabinet Edition*, $1.00.

W. H. Seward. Works, 5 vols. 8vo, $15.00; Diplomatic History of the War, 8vo, $3.00.

John Campbell Shairp. Culture and Religion, 16mo, $1.25; Poetic Interpretation of Nature, 16mo, $1.25; Studies in Poetry and Philosophy, 16mo, $1.50; Aspects of Poetry, 16mo, $1.50.

William Shakespeare. Works, edited by R. G. White, *Riverside Edition*, 3 vols. cr. 8vo, $7.50; The Same, 6 vols., cr. 8vo, uncut, $10.00; The Blackfriars Shakespeare, per vol. $2.50, *net.* (*In Press.*)

A. P. Sinnett. Esoteric Buddhism, 16mo, $1.25; The Occult World, 16mo, $1.25.

M. C. D. Silsbee. A Half Century in Salem. 16mo, $1.00.

Dr. William Smith. Bible Dictionary, *American Edition*, 4 vols. 8vo, $20.00.

Edmund Clarence Stedman. Poems, *Farringford Edition*, Portrait, 16mo, $2.00; *Household Edition*, Illustrated, 12mo, $1.75; full gilt, cr. 8vo, $2.25; Victorian Poets, 12mo, $2.00; Poets of America, 12mo, $2.25. The set, 3 vols., uniform, 12mo, $6.00; Edgar Allan Poe, an Essay, vellum, 18mo, $1.00.

W. W. Story. Poems, 2 vols. 16mo, $2.50; Fiammetta: A Novel, 16mo, $1.25. Roba di Roma, 2 vols. 16mo, $2.50.

Harriet Beecher Stowe. Novels and Stories, 10 vols. 12mo, uniform, each $1.50; A Dog's Mission, Little Pussy Willow, Queer Little People, Illustrated, small 4to, each $1.25; Uncle Tom's Cabin, 100 Illustrations, 8vo, $3.00; *Library Edition*, Illustrated, 12mo, $2.00; *Popular Edition*, 12mo, $1.00.

Jonathan Swift. Works, *Edition de Luxe*, 19 vols. 8vo, the set, $76.00.

T. P. Taswell-Langmead. English Constitutional History. New Edition, revised, 8vo, $7.50.

Bayard Taylor. Poetical Works, *Household Edition*, 12mo, $1.75; cr. 8vo. full gilt, $2.25; Melodies of Verse, 18mo, vellum, $1.00; Life and Letters, 2 vols. 12mo, $4.00; Dramatic Poems, 12mo, $2.25; *Household Edition*, 12mo, $1.75; Life and Poetical Works, 6 vols. uniform. Including Life, 2 vols.; Faust, 2 vols.; Poems, 1 vol.; Dramatic Poems, 1 vol. The set, cr. 8vo, $12.00.

Alfred Tennyson. Poems, *Household Edition*, Portrait and Illustrations, 12mo, $1.75; full gilt, cr. 8vo, $2.25; *Illustrated Crown Edition*, 2 vols. 8vo, $5.00; *Library Edition*, Portrait and 60 Illustrations, 8vo, $3.50; *Red-Line Edition*, Portrait and Illustrations, small 4to, $2.50; *Cabinet Edition*, $1.00; Complete Works, *Riverside Edition*, 6 vols. cr. 8vo, $6.00.

Celia Thaxter. Among the Isles of Shoals, 18mo, $1.25; Poems, small 4to, $1.50; Drift-Weed, 18mo, $1.50; Poems for Children, Illustrated, small 4to, $1.50; Cruise of the Mystery, Poems, 16mo, $1.00.

Edith M. Thomas. A New Year's Masque and other Poems, 16mo, $1.50; The Round Year, 16mo, $1.25.

Joseph P. Thompson. American Comments on European Questions, 8vo, $3.00.

Henry D. Thoreau. Works, 9 vols. 12mo, each $1.50; the set, $13.50.

George Ticknor. History of Spanish Literature, 3 vols. 8vo, $10.00; Life, Letters, and Journals, Portraits, 2 vols. 12mo, $4.00.

Bradford Torrey. Birds in the Bush, 16mo, $1.25.

Sophus Tromholt. Under the Rays of the Aurora Borealis, Illustrated, 2 vols. $7.50.

Mrs. Schuyler Van Rensselaer. H. H. Richardson and his Works.

Jones Very. Essays and Poems, cr. 8vo, $2.00.

Annie Wall. Story of Sordello, told in Prose, 16mo, $1.00.

Charles Dudley Warner. My Summer in a Garden, *Riverside Aldine Edition*, 16mo, $1.00; *Illustrated Edition*, square 16mo, $1.50; Saunterings, 18mo, $1.25; Backlog Studies, Illustrated, square 16mo, $1.50; *Riverside Aldine Edition*, 16mo, $1.00; Baddeck, and that Sort of Thing, 18mo, $1.00; My Winter on the Nile, cr. 8vo, $2.00; In the Levant, cr. 8vo, $2.00; Being a Boy, Illustrated, square 16mo, $1.50; In the

Wilderness, 18mo, 75 cents; A Roundabout Journey, 12mo,
$1.50.

William F. Warren, LL. D.   Paradise Found, cr. 8vo, $2.00.

William A. Wheeler.   Dictionary of Noted Names of Fiction, 12mo, $2.00.

Edwin P. Whipple.   Essays, 6 vols. cr. 8vo, each $1.50.

Richard Grant White.   Every-Day English, 12mo, $2.00;
Words and their Uses, 12mo, $2.00; England Without and
Within, 12mo, $2.00; The Fate of Mansfield Humphreys,
16mo, $1.25; Studies in Shakespeare, 12mo, $1.75.

Mrs. A. D. T. Whitney.   Stories, 12 vols. 12mo, each $1.50;
Mother Goose for Grown Folks, 12mo, $1.50; Pansies, 16mo,
$1.25; Daffodils, 16mo, $1.25; Just How, 16mo, $1.00; Bonnyborough, 12mo, $1.50; Holy Tides, 16mo, 75 cents; Homespun Yarns, 12mo, $1.50.

John Greenleaf Whittier.   Poems, *Household Edition*, Illustrated, 12mo, $1.75; full gilt, cr. 8vo, $2.25; *Cambridge Edition*, Portrait, 3 vols. 12mo, $5.25; *Red-Line Edition*, Portrait, Illustrated, small 4to, $2.50; *Cabinet Edition*, $1.00;
Library Edition, Portrait, 32 Illustrations, 8vo, $3.50; Prose
Works, *Cambridge Edition*, 2 vols. 12mo, $3.50; The Bay of
Seven Islands, Portrait, 16mo, $1.00; John Woolman's Journal, Introduction by Whittier, $1.50; Child Life in Poetry,
selected by Whittier, Illustrated, 12mo, $2.00; Child Life in
Prose, 12mo, $2.00; Songs of Three Centuries, selected by
Whittier: *Household Edition*, Illustrated, 12mo, $1.75; full
gilt, cr. 8vo, $2.25; *Library Edition*, 32 Illustrations, 8vo,
$3.50; Text and Verse, 18mo, 75 cents; Poems of Nature, 4to,
Illustrated, $6.00; St. Gregory's Guest, etc., 16mo, vellum,
$1.00.

Woodrow Wilson.   Congressional Government, 16mo, $1.25.

J. A. Wilstach.   Translation of Virgil's Works, 2 vols. cr. 8vo,
$5.00.

Justin Winsor.   Reader's Handbook of American Revolution, 16mo, $1.25.

W. B. Wright.   Ancient Cities from the Dawn to the Daylight, 16mo, $1.25.